LIKE YOU HATE ME

BETHANY WINTERS

CONTENT WARNING

Certain aspects of this story may be disturbing and/or triggering for some readers, such as: graphic language, explicit sex, addiction, (underage) alcohol and substance abuse, depression, ideation of suicide, overdose, death of a sibling and best friend, violence (between the main characters), stalking, obsession, mentions of sexual assault, blackmail, and homophobic slurs.

PLAYLIST

"mars"
YUNGBLUD

"FUCKED UP"
jxdn

"Move Along"
The All-American Rejects

"lonely"
Machine Gun Kelly

"sTrAnGeRs"
Bring Me The Horizon

"Animals"
Maroon 5

"Mind Games"
Sickick

"forget me too"
Machine Gun Kelly & Halsey

"idfc"
blackbear

"I'm a Mess"
Bebe Rexha

"Drown"
Bring Me The Horizon

"I Hate Everything About You"
Three Days Grace

"Good For You"
Selena Gomez & A$AP Rocky

"Come & Get It"
Selena Gomez

"Houndin"
Layto

"Take What You Want"
Post Malone, Ozzy Osbourne & Travis Scott

"Church"
Chase Atlantic

"the 1"
blackbear

"Scars to Your Beautiful"

Alessia Cara

"Ghost"
Justin Bieber

"Bones"
MOD SUN

"@ my worst"
blackbear

"What I've Done"
Linkin Park

"WANNA BE"
jxdn & Machine Gun Kelly

"Power Over Me"
Dermot Kennedy

"Beautiful Way"
You Me At Six

"Poison"
Rita Ora

Listen on Spotify & Amazon Music

"I hate him. I hate what he makes me feel.
If only it didn't feel so damn good."

-Andi Jaxon

For Becca

PROLOGUE
3 MONTHS AGO

Xavi

I shouldn't be here.

I made a promise to the only friend I've ever had, a promise that's getting harder and harder to keep. I've thought about breaking it hundreds of times—at least once a day since the day she left me—but I've never actually had the balls to go through with it.

Tonight, though…it feels different. *I* feel different. I'm in too deep this time and I just want it to stop. No more pain. No more guilt. No more misery.

With any luck, it'll just feel like…nothing. Blackness. *The end.*

Clutching the blindfold I've kept on me for almost two years, I'm straddling my motorbike on the edge of the bend in the road my brother died on, facing the steep cliff overlooking the forest below.

Ride a motorcycle.

Jump off a cliff.

"That's two birds with one stone right here, babe." I laugh

through the pain in my chest. Then, I lean over to get a better look. "I'm gonna do it."

But I'm not finished yet.

And this probably isn't what she meant when she wrote that list.

She didn't want to die. She *promised*, just like I did.

Lightning strikes above me, and I wrap my arms around myself. There's a storm coming. The rain hasn't started yet, but it's so windy and cold, I can barely feel my hands as I reach into my hoodie pocket. The bottle of whiskey I stole from my dad's office tonight is long gone, so I swallow a couple pills instead, then light the joint I rolled earlier and take a hit.

My filthy, unwashed hair blows into my eyes, blocking my vision, but it doesn't matter. I don't need to see anything. I just need to drive. Just a few more meters.

Come on, you pussy.

Come on, come on, come on...

My phone buzzes between the handlebars, and I almost ignore it this time.

Almost.

I squint at the text message on the screen, the paralyzing fear coiling around my lungs and squeezing as I read the words. And then I look at the pictures...

I think I'm gonna puke.

I don't stop to think before I've got the phone pressed to my ear. He takes forever to answer, but when he does, he sounds wide awake and highly amused, the sounds of the party he's at echoing in the background. "What do you want?" he teases.

"I need your help."

"Again?" I think he laughs, but I can barely hear him over the ringing in my ears. "You can't be serious."

"Please," I rasp, flinching at the next flash of lightning in the sky. "He—It's Nate."

He pauses, then asks, "Where are you right now?"

I shake my heavy head, feeling dizzy as I look around at my surroundings. "I..."

"Never mind. Fuckin' drama queen. I'll be there soon."

After he hangs up, I pocket the phone and wait, but I don't hold my breath. *Soon* could mean five minutes or five hours. He won't rush because he doesn't really give a shit about me. I don't blame him. I don't give a shit about me either.

The rain starts, pours, then pours some more. I'm soaked from head to toe within seconds. I don't know how much more time passes while I smoke my joint, shielding it inside my hoodie to try to keep it dry. Once it's gone, I toss the roach and tip my head back, taking one last look at the dark sky before I pull the blindfold into place.

Another text comes through, and I squeeze my eyes shut behind the fabric. Lifting it up an inch, I quickly delete all the messages he's sent me and block his number. My phone will probably break when it hits the bottom, but I can't risk anyone finding it down there and seeing what's on it.

I can't risk Nate finding out what I've done.

Shoving the blindfold back over my eyes, I hold on to the handlebars and creep a little closer toward the edge. "Sorry, Katy," I whisper.

But then I hesitate, swallowing as I flex my fingers.

Just twist it, Xavi.

Just fucking do it already.

Just fucking—

CHAPTER ONE
2 YEARS AGO

Xavi

I'm at the hospital, high, stumbling through the never-ending halls as I make my way to the waiting room on the third floor. The walls feel like they're closing in on me, and I can barely see where I'm going, but I don't stop to catch my breath. It won't work anyway. I won't breathe right again until I know Katy's okay.

Please be okay.

When I finally get to where I need to be, I stop just inside the room, holding onto the vending machine on my left to keep myself steady. There are a lot of people in here, low voices and soft cries coming from...I don't know where. My eyes refuse to focus on anyone but him. Like magnets, they won't let him go. He's sitting by himself in the middle of the room, elbows resting on his knees as he runs his thumb over the black ring he's holding—*my* ring. It's chunky and black with the number *13* written on the face. I let Katy borrow it a few weeks ago when she was having a bad day. The doctors must have taken it off her finger when they brought her in here and given it to him. That's the only reason he has it. That *has* to be the reason. Because if he was the one who took it from her...If he was the one who found her like that...

Like he senses my presence here, he lifts his head to look at me.

Fuck.

He looks furious, his usually light brown eyes now red and bloodshot, his short, dark hair sticking up at the top as if he's been yanking on it repeatedly. His knuckles look busted too, like he's punched a few walls. I think he's been crying, but when he looks at me, there are no tears left. There's only hate and rage.

"Nate," I say and take a slow, cautious step closer to him. "What happened?"

He just stares up at me, which is weird because it's usually me looking up at him. He's only nineteen, two years older than me and his little sister, but he's a tall motherfucker with a huge body built for basketball. He and I both know he could snap my skinny ass in half if he wanted to.

"Who called you?" he asks, ignoring my question.

"My dad," I whisper. "He's on his way."

He nods slowly, his hands shaking slightly as he continues to play with the ring. "Get out."

I swallow and look over at his parents for the first time. His mom is sobbing into her hands in the corner, his dad on the chair next to her, gently rubbing his wife's back as he stares off into space.

"Nate..." I try again. "Please, just tell me wh—"

He's up and coming for me before I can finish, pulling on my jacket and then slamming me back into the vending machine, causing a few people to look this way. I wince and wrap my hands around his, holding my breath as he moves in closer, erasing the small amount of distance between us.

"Nathaniel, let him go," his mother says quietly, her voice raw from crying. "It's not his fault."

"Fuck that. He's fucking high right now, Mom," he growls, still looking at me, lowering his voice so she can't hear the next part. "You wanna know what happened, party boy?" he taunts, cruel and menacing. "You killed her. My sister's dead because of you."

"No," I choke out, shaking my head. "You're lying."

She's not dead.

She *can't* be dead.

But he's not lying.

A broken noise escapes my throat, the tears bursting from my eyes, and I can feel him watching them fall as if he's fascinated by them. He's staring at me again, his fingers clutching my shirt as if he knows I'll fall apart if he doesn't hold me up.

I wish he'd let me fall.

"It should have been you," he says after a minute, granting my unspoken wish and letting me go.

I slide down to the floor, struggling not to throw up as I scoot away from him.

I didn't think it was possible to feel this much pain again, but there it is, eating me up and swallowing me from the inside out.

This feels worse than it did when I lost my older brother three years ago. At least when he died, there was nothing I could have done. I was just a kid, and he was killed in a car accident.

But Katy...I could have been there for her tonight. I could have stopped her from taking those pills. I could have saved her.

Pulling myself back up to my feet, I stumble my way toward the door I walked through a minute ago. I don't want to leave my best friend here without saying goodbye, without telling her how sorry I am and how much I love her, but he's not letting me stay. And even if I had the energy to fight him right now, I'd lose anyway.

"Xavi?" he calls, waiting until I turn my head to look him in the eye. "You're dead to me, you understand? If I ever have to look at your face again, I'll break it."

"MARS" by YUNGBLUD plays on repeat through my car stereo—the last song I remember Katy listening to before I dropped her off at home last night. I'm torturing myself, but I can't stop.

"Xavi!" she sings my name, her goofy laugh hitting my ears for the hundredth time in the last two hours. "You know I hate it when you ghost me like this. Where are you? I wanna go out. Call me right now or I'm going without you!"

I hit the play button again, tipping my head back against the headrest.

Katy's blind—*was* blind—and even though she could text if she wanted to, she preferred using voice notes.

I stare at the roof and listen to her voice, tears soaking my face and neck as I sip the bottle of vodka I found under her seat.

"Xavi!" she sings my name...

CHAPTER TWO
PRESENT

Nate

"I 'm just saying, guys are usually so much easier to fuck around with than girls," Frankie says, holding on to my shoulder as I all but carry her out of my car. "They don't ask for much. They hardly ever want anything serious. They just wanna get their dicks wet, right? I thought Myles was like that. But then he catches some freshman guy doing a body shot off my chest and he just loses it. Says I'm out here making a fool out of him or some shit. How was I supposed to know that'd make him jealous? I'm not his girlfriend or his mother. You know what I mean?"

I don't have a clue what she's talking about, but I still nod, helping her along toward the huge, six-bedroom house that my best friend Carter and I rented for college. I like it because it's far away enough from campus that I don't have to deal with anyone, but close enough that it only takes me ten minutes to get to class and practice.

It was only supposed to be the two of us at first, but then our teammate Easton got thrown out of his apartment by his girl-friend last year, so Carter thought it'd be fun to let him move in with us. Frankie moved in just a few months ago. She was in a bit of a tough spot when I met her, so I told her she could stay a couple nights until she figured something else out. I'm still waiting for her to leave.

She stumbles *again* and then angrily rips her heels off her feet. "Stupid shoes."

"I don't think it's the shoes, Frank."

"Eat my ass," she sasses, shoving the heels at my abs.

It's not even four in the afternoon yet, but this is what she gets for partying with the boys all night and then continuing on for half the day. The break between New Year and the start of next semester is basically one long party in this town, a way for us to get it all out of our systems before it's back to the grind next week.

My teammates love having her around because she's cool as shit, but then this thing went down with Myles today and Easton called me to pick her up before she cut the boy's dick off and made him suck it in front of everyone. Her words, not his, apparently.

"Come on," I urge, moving her tangled, white blonde hair out of her face so she can see where she's going. "Let's get you to bed."

"But you said we were gonna party at home."

"I lied to get you out of there."

She looks at me like I betrayed her, and I let out a laugh. Just then, someone makes a quiet, coughing sound. I was so focused on Frankie, I didn't even see the dark-haired guy leaning against the motorcycle parked beside Frankie's truck. I narrow my eyes to get a good look at him, then freeze. My blood runs cold as I take in his dark features, his shoulders hooked up to his ears with his hands tucked into his pockets. He looks nervous as he stares right back at me, but then something seems to dawn on him and he pales. "Fuck."

His low voice snaps me out of my momentary state of shock, and I drop Frankie's shoes to the ground as I move toward him. He curses again, stepping away from the bike to face me head-on.

He opens that big mouth of his to say something, but it's too late for that. I'm already shoving my fist into it, knocking his ass to the gravel with one hit.

"Nate!" Frankie shrieks behind me.

I ignore her, too busy looking down at Xavi Hart and wondering what the fuck he thinks he's doing on my driveway. He hasn't changed much since the last time I saw him. He's still just as short as he was when he was seventeen, his messy hair still the same shade of dark brown. He's wearing dark ripped jeans and a black hoodie. His eyes look a little bluer and brighter than they used to, but that doesn't mean shit. He might not be on anything right now, but this worthless little fuckup could never stay off it for long.

"Get up."

"Give me a second, will you?" He winces, squinting at the gray sky above us.

Pussy.

I didn't even hit him that hard. Definitely not as hard as I did when he had the nerve to show up to my sister's funeral. Or on her birthday a few weeks later when I found him passed out on the ground in front of her headstone.

"Who is he?" Frankie asks from behind me.

"Go upstairs. I'll be there in a minute," I tell her, then to Xavi, I repeat, "*Get up.*"

Sighing, he swipes the blood off his lip and pushes himself up. He's still got a piercing there—a little black ring on the corner of his mouth—and all I can think about is hitting it again. My face must show my intent before I can act on it because he quickly jumps back a step and lifts his hands up in surrender. "Nate..."

God, I hate the way he says my name.

Frankie still hasn't gone inside like I told her to, cursing me under her breath as she picks up her shoes. "These are Jimmy Choos, you know?"

"I'll buy you new ones."

"Nate."

"*Frankie*," I snap, turning to look at her again.

She hesitates as if she's unsure whether it's safe to leave me alone with him. Then, with an eye roll, she takes the keys I hand her and stumbles over to the front door.

"Fine. But if you kill him, you're digging the hole all by yourself. I'm passing out now."

"Drink some water first."

"Yeah, yeah," she calls, half waving at me over her head.

Once she's gone, I take a step closer to Xavi and study his bloody mouth, watching the way he keeps poking at that goddamn piercing with his tongue. I wanna rip it out of his face and choke him with it.

"Why are you here?"

"I..." He stops talking, his features twisting with anxiety as he rubs the back of his neck. "I thought you knew."

"Knew *what*?"

"I'm moving in for freshman year."

"The fuck you are."

"Nate—"

"I said *no*, you little prick."

No.

There's no way this is happening.

We stare at each other. I already know what he's thinking before he voices it. I can see the questions he has for me written all over his face. The need to know what the hell I've been doing for the last—

"Two years," he says softly, finishing my thought. "You haven't been home in *two years*, Nate. You don't call or want anyone to come to your games. Your family's worried sick—"

"Jesus, don't you get it?" I cut in, grabbing his jaw to shut him up. "I don't care, Xavi. I'm done with that town and everyone in it."

He frowns at that, looking up at me in confusion. "Since when?"

Since you, I think to myself, but I don't bother saying it out loud. Still, I think he knows the answer because he winces and tears his eyes away.

After Katy died, I fell off the rails and spent the better part of a month drowning myself in alcohol and fucking everyone in sight. My dad caught me with the pool boy while his golfing buddies were in the house and told me it was time I cut the shit. I wanted to quit the team—to quit college altogether—but he wasn't having it. His daughter was in the ground, but *life goes on* and all that shit.

I hated him.

I hated everyone.

He'd never hit me before, but I earned a back hand to the face for my attitude that day. Then he gave me a choice—be the star he raised me to be or check myself into rehab. I walked out without saying goodbye and haven't spoken to him since. He showed up to my first few games after that, but I wouldn't talk to him or even acknowledge his presence there, so he eventually gave up trying. Not because he was giving me the space I wanted, but because I embarrassed him by ignoring him.

I've spoken to my mom on the phone a few times, but I haven't seen her in person since the day I left home for good, and I don't plan on doing so any time soon. That might make me a heartless asshole, but it's better this way for all of us. I'm not a very good person when I'm around them—when I'm around *him.* I haven't been the same since Xavi took my little sister away from me and ruined my fucking life. Since my parents decided that even if Katy might be gone, keeping up appearances is always most important. Since I became so broken with grief and disgust that I couldn't even stand to look at them anymore.

It all comes back to *him* as far as I'm concerned.

Everything is his fault.

And I hate him for it.

Knowing what's coming, Xavi snatches his jaw out of my hand, trying his hardest to get away from me. Before he can move, I grab him by the collar of his hoodie and punch him again, knocking him back into the side of Frankie's truck. My knuckles are killing me, but I don't care. I like the burn, especially when it comes from him. It feels like a drug. My first hit in almost two years.

"Don't even bother walking into this house," I say, backing up toward the front door. "Get your ass back on that bike, choose another school, and get the fuck out of my life."

But I already know he's not about to do any of those things.

Something's changed in his eyes since I saw him last. I can see it now. Just for a second, he's the old Xavi again, the one he was before Katy died. The bratty, defiant little bitch who never did a damn thing he was told. The way he's looking at me...

The kid's got balls, I'll give him that.

CHAPTER THREE

Xavi

The front door closes behind him.

"Fuck," I whisper, cupping the back of my neck as I stare at the big iron gates I drove through a little while ago.

I thought I was ready for this, but after seeing him again, after getting my ass kicked *again* and finding out he had no idea I was coming...

I dig my fingers into my throbbing eye sockets.

This was a mistake. I should have just gone back to my hole where I belong.

Before I went to rehab three months ago, I was spending most of my time locked away in my bedroom at my mom's house, blinds and windows closed, lights off. My very own pity party pad for one.

I took a year off after I graduated high school because everything just felt so meaningless without Katy. It felt wrong at the time, and it still does, coming to the same college we were supposed to go to together. Hawthorne University—an elite campus for spoiled rich kids like ourselves, about an hour's drive from our hometown.

I'm not here by choice, but I'll admit it didn't take much to convince me. Because deep down, I know she'd want this for me. She'd want me to do this *for her*. I never wanted to go—I'm not really the college kid type—but she begged and assured me we'd have the time of our lives. She had it all planned out. We'd live with Nate and Carter in their badass house off campus, whether they liked it or not, and then once they graduated, it would be all ours for our final two years. I eventually agreed because I'd have done anything for her. I'd have followed her off a bridge if she asked me to. She was my best friend. My only fucking friend.

Dropping my ass down on the freezing cold ground, I lean back against the side of my bike and try calling the prick I already tried three times when I first pulled up. He was supposed to meet me here almost an hour ago.

He doesn't answer the phone, so I text him again.

XAVI

Where are you, man?

Sighing, I dig my wallet out of my pocket and pull out the folded-up strip of photos I keep inside. I told myself I wouldn't do this when I got here, but I can't help it. Looking at this calms me down just as much as it breaks my heart.

Careful not to crease it more than it already is, I run my fingers over Katy's beautiful face, remembering the day we took these pictures together. We were messing around at the mall. She really needed to pee, and I thought it'd be funny to drag her into one of those old school photo booths and trap her in there with me. She was laughing so hard she was screaming, and she almost pissed herself right there when I pinned her to the seat and tickled her until she throat-punched me.

She had a whole box of photos in her closet when she was alive, but I have no idea where they are now. I wasn't allowed in her house after she died. I don't know what her parents did to her room or what they kept and didn't keep. I have my own pictures, videos, and voice notes stored on my phone, but this strip of photos is one of the only two physical things I have left of her, one of the only things I have that actually belonged to her.

My phone rings, and I swipe my eyes before I pick it up, deflating when I see it's my dad.

"Hello?"

"I told you I expect you to call me," he says as his greeting, sounding like he's distracted at work, as usual. "Are you there yet?"

"Yeah," I answer, picking at the stones on the ground between my feet.

I told him I was driving up here today, but he doesn't know where I'm staying. I told him it was handled when he offered to help me out with housing, and he surprisingly left it alone. He probably thinks my mom hooked me up with an apartment, which is pretty laughable. I love her, but she can barely remember I exist most days, let alone rent me a place to live.

"How's the apartment?"

"Fine."

"You don't sound very excited about it."

"I'm thrilled, Dad. Really."

"Watch the attitude, Xavier," he warns, but I'm no longer listening.

I tune him out when he starts with his regular lecture. My thoughts drift back to Nate, and I turn my face to peek at the house behind me, wondering what he's doing with that drunk girl he brought home with him. She's stunning. Ash blonde hair, big blue eyes, curves for days and a body I'm sure most guys would kill for a piece of.

"...stay out of trouble and do not embarrass me."

I bet he worships every inch of her when he fucks her.

A sick thrill shoots through me, and I find myself picturing what he looks like when he's on top of her. He's probably taking his anger out on her right this second, bruising her thighs and fucking into her as hard as he can, thinking of me as he does it.

I hear a deep sigh in my ear and then, "Are you on drugs again, Xavier?"

"Fucking hell, Dad."

"That's not an answer."

"I told you I'm sober."

"Addicts are compulsive liars. Do you really expect me to believ—"

"You know what? You're right. I gotta go. My dealer's on the other line."

"*Xavier.*"

I roll my eyes and hang up the phone. I should probably stop being such a brat to him, considering he's the one paying my tuition, but fuck it. No point in trying to be better for a man who knows I never will be.

It's so much easier with Mom. She might not be the most loving parent in the world, but at least she's not riding my ass twenty-four seven. She's a retired model, living her best life with the rock singer she's dating who's closer to my age than he is hers.

After my parents divorced when I was seven, she was granted full custody of me and my older brother. I'm pretty sure she only fought our dad for us out of spite. She never cared enough to ask what we were doing or where we were doing it, but as we got older, we didn't mind that so much. We used it to our advantage and got away with murder.

My dad blames her for Blaine's death. Says the only reason he drove drunk that night was because she refused to try to control him like a proper parent would.

He treats me and her like dirt, like the *problems* he's forced to deal with, and then walks around with his nose in the air as if he's some kind of saint—the man who's never made a damn mistake in his life.

Are you on drugs again, Xavier?

I wish, Dad.

Needing to do something with my hands, I put the strip of photos away and pull out the half empty pack of cigarettes from my jeans. I take one out and stare at it between my fingers, slowly rolling it back and forth. It hasn't been that long. I can still remember the way it felt when the smoke would fill my mouth and travel down to my lungs. The way the nicotine would relax me. Maybe take some of the pain away, just for a minute or two.

My face hurts like a bitch, but I don't mind it. Everything always hurts on the inside anyway, so it's kind of nice to feel some pain on the outside again. Like maybe it'll override it if I concentrate on the throb in my nose hard enough.

It doesn't work.

I snap the cigarette at the roach and shove both pieces into my pocket, propping my elbows on my knees to drop my face into my hands.

And then I wait.

Again.

CHAPTER FOUR

Nate

S itting on the edge of my bed, I stare at the phone in my hand, rubbing small circles over Frankie's ankle with my thumb. I checked on her as soon as I came inside, took her dress off her body, changed her into one of my old shirts, then force-fed her some water.

She's passed out again now. In my bed, as usual. She likes sleeping in here with me when she's drunk. Says it's just in case she pukes, she doesn't want her own room to stink of it.

Covering her feet with the blanket, I look over at the window, listening for movement outside. I haven't heard his bike start, so I know he's still out there.

Defiant little bastard.

Again, I squeeze my palm around the phone I'm holding, still trying to figure out how this is happening.

Why is he here?

Xavi's dad and mine are best friends, but even if I was on speaking terms with either of them—which I'm not—there's no way they'd send him to live with me. They know how much I hate him. Everyone does. I've never tried to keep it a secret.

I quietly shut my bedroom door behind me and walk downstairs to the den at the front of the house. I can see him through this window without having to go right up to it. He's sitting on the ground next to his bike, elbows resting on his knees, using his forearms as a pillow, probably freezing his scrawny ass off. His face is turned away from me, so I can only see the back of his head, making it impossible for me to know what he's thinking about. I pretend I'm not wishing for him to turn this way so I can take a guess.

Calling the number I've been hovering over for the last thirty minutes, I cut him off before he can get a word in.

"You're a dead man."

"You got my gift," he says with a smile in his voice. I hear a car door open and close, followed by the roar of his engine starting. "Do you love it?"

This motherfucker.

I clench my teeth, not even bothering to act surprised. This is some typical Carter Westwood bullshit. I've known him my whole life, and this isn't the first time he's pulled something like this on me. He loves fucking with people's lives, plotting and scheming and stringing them along like puppets, all for his own twisted entertainment.

Making my way over to the bar, I grab a bottle of whiskey and uncap it, not bothering with a glass. I swallow a big mouthful, trying to calm my racing heart. The alcohol burns as it goes down, just like I wanted it to. Desperate to feel the pain, I drink some more.

"Aw, you're speechless," Carter continues. "It's okay. You don't have to thank me. Just throat my dick real good when I get home and we'll call it ev—"

"You think you're funny?" I growl, wiping my mouth with my sleeve. "What is wrong with you, Carter?"

"Will you stop being so ungrateful? I did you a favor."

"How's that?"

"Don't play with me," he teases. "I know what you want. He's yours now, Nate. You can beat him, fuck him, kill him and be done with it if it's gonna make you feel better. Just *feel better* so you can stop being such a moody prick and go back to being my best friend. You know, the one who knows how to have fun without acting like a mopey little bitch all the time."

"You fucking cunt."

"You wanna fuck my cunt?" he jokes. "I'll be home soon, baby."

"*Carter—*"

He hangs up on me, dismissing me. The whiskey leaves my hand before I'm thinking, the bottle hitting the wall next to the window with a satisfying smash, pieces of glass flying everywhere. Although it's only satisfying for about three seconds.

"Fuck."

Xavi's head swings around toward the window, and I quickly jerk back into the shadows, closing my eyes as I knock my head back against the wall.

I changed my mind. I don't want to see the look on his face.

CHAPTER FIVE

3 YEARS AGO

Nate

Carter moans into my mouth, holding my upper arms to steady himself as I push him into my bedroom. I squeeze his hip and pull his head back by his dirty blond hair, demanding better access. He gives it over willingly, stumbling when his foot gets caught beneath mine.

"Why are we doing this again?"

"Because I didn't want pussy tonight and you were the hottest guy at the party," I answer, playing his game and feeding his massive ego.

He grins and kisses me hungrily, wincing when I tighten my grip on his hair.

"Jesus, Nate, *easy*," he rasps. "You're being too rough."

"Fuck off." I laugh, knowing he's messing with me.

He chuckles darkly, and I turn us around to shove him back against my closed door. His hands go for my jeans, and I bite his lower lip, dragging it out between my teeth the way he likes it. He moans again, and I pull back to take my shirt off, tossing it down on the floor. I go for his shirt next, smacking his fumbling hands away from my zipper because he's taking too damn long.

We've done this a few times before, but we know it means nothing. It's just a way for us to let off a little steam from time to time.

Once I've got my dick in my hand, I grab the lube and use it to get myself slick, amused at the way he's grinding into me impatiently. I haven't even touched his cock yet, but I can feel how hard it is, poking into my hip beneath his jeans.

"You ever gonna let me top you?" he asks, grunting when I grab a fistful of his hair and twist his head to the side, pushing his cheek into the wood.

"Stop playing and turn around."

He smirks and does as he's told, both hands braced on the doorframe, watching me over his shoulder as I push his jeans and boxers down over his ass. I squirt some more lube into my hand and find his hole with my fingertips, rubbing and pushing on it to open him up for me. I slide my middle finger inside and twist it around. I kiss him because it makes him feel less used, and sometimes I'll let him suck my dick for a while before I fuck him, but other than that, I always make sure it's quick and to the point. In and out. No strings, no drama.

Just as I'm about to line myself up, I hear a distant thud followed by a shriek. Carter's eyes hit mine, probably thinking the same thing I am, and then we're moving. He yanks his jeans back up and I quickly tuck myself away, wiping my lube covered hands on my thighs before I swing the door open. He's hot on my heels as I all but run to her bedroom at the end of the hall, following the sounds coming from her en-suite bathroom. As soon as I step inside, I skid to a halt at the scene in front of me, frowning at the puddles of soapy water all over the floor.

What the fuck?

She and Xavi Hart are standing in the huge, clawfoot bathtub in the middle of the room, fully clothed and covered in bubbles.

"Move Along" by The All-American Rejects is blaring from the
waterproof sound system I got her for Christmas last year. She's
singing the words at the top of her lungs, using the open bottle of
wine she's holding as a microphone, laughing as he holds her
arm up over head and spins her around like they're on a fucking
dance floor. I see red then, realizing that must be why she
screamed just now. He let her fall. She looks unharmed and free
of any cuts and bruises, but still. He let my blind little sister slip
and fall in the bathtub.

God, I hate him.

The thick layer of black eyeliner she's wearing is smeared all
over her face, and I can't tell whether that's because she's been
crying or because they've decided to turn the bathroom into a
water park. Her dark hair is soaked, sticking to her skin, and it's
only then I spot the faint outline of her nipples through the
drenched white shirt she's wearing. I immediately cut my eyes to
Carter, finding him already looking up at the corner of the ceiling, but I don't miss the amusement on his face like he knows I'm
about to lose my shit.

"Katy!" I bite out, but of course she can't see or hear me over
the music.

My nostrils flare as I walk over to the sound system in the
shower, angrily jabbing the touch screen with my thumb until I
find the stop button. Silence cuts through the bathroom, and
Katy jumps with a gasp, both her and Xavi spinning in my direction, her back to his chest. His eyes widen when he sees me
standing here, and judging by the look on his face, he already
knows exactly what I'm thinking.

I'm going to kill you.

"Xav?" my sister asks, her voice shaking with fear.

He blinks and leans down to speak in her ear, gently taking
her forearms and crossing them over her chest. Whatever he
whispers to her makes her face go pale and then she blushes,
tightening her arms over her body to hide her breasts. She looks

guilty as fuck, as she should. Our parents are out of town this weekend for their nineteenth wedding anniversary. Katy told me she was staying at a friend's house tonight, which I had no problem with. I dropped her off at the chick's front door a few hours ago, meaning she played me and lied to my face, left her imaginary sleepover, met up with this little punk instead, and brought him home with her. *Alone.*

"Nate..." she says carefully, attempting to placate me with that doe-eyed look she's been hitting me with since we were kids. "I—"

"Don't even try it." I shake my head, walking over to the bath to snatch the bottle of wine from her hand. "Get out of there and go to bed. You're grounded."

"You can't ground me, you asshole," she hisses. "I'm sixteen."

"Exactly!" I yell at her. "You're *sixteen* and you're getting wasted on Mom's stash and doing fuck knows what with this loser." I swing the bottle in Xavi's direction with a sneer, more for his benefit than hers. "What are you even doing with this guy, Katy?"

"He's my *friend*," she stresses. "He makes me laugh and he's one of the only people who actually gives a shit. He gets it," she adds, muttering, "unlike some people."

"What?"

She wipes the sudden tears from her cheeks with the back of her hand. I should feel like a piece of shit for making her cry, and usually I would, but I'm too livid to care right now.

With one arm still covering her chest, she takes Xavi's hand and allows him to help guide her out of the tub, stunning me because she never accepts help from anyone anymore.

He links their soapy fingers together as he carefully walks her over the wet tiles, side-stepping around Carter to get her to her bedroom door.

"You good?" he asks quietly, and I can tell he's not asking if she can make it to her room without help. He knows she can do it. He's asking if she's good mentally, not physically.

She nods, giving him a small smile. "Night, Xav."

"Night, babe."

I glare at him when he calls her that, but he doesn't look fazed. The cocky little shit saunters back over to the bath and grabs his hoodie off the floor, throwing it on over his soaking wet body. "You should watch the way you speak to her," he says, brave enough to look me dead in the eye.

"Get out before I throw you out the fucking window."

He scoffs out a laugh and shakes his head at me, shoving his feet into his sneakers without bothering to dry them first. His devil-may-care attitude pisses me off—*everything* about him pisses me off. I take a step closer to him, grinding my teeth when Carter grabs my shoulder to stop me.

"He's sixteen," he reminds me, kneading his fingertips into my flesh, probably trying to soothe the tension in my muscles.

Knowing he's right—I can't beat the shit out of a *child*—I grab Carter's hand and pull him into me, his bare chest and abs pressed flush against mine. I'd forgotten we were still shirtless until he touched me, but now I use it to my advantage. I don't miss the way Xavi's tongue slips out to lick his lip ring as he bounces his eyes between us. Smirking, I pull Carter's mouth to mine but keep my eyes on Xavi, using the only way I know I can get to him. I lick around Carter's tongue and snake my hand around to his back, sliding it down into his jeans to finger his already wet, open hole, picking up where we left off. I ignore the way my dick gets harder at the flash of heat in Xavi's eyes. Or maybe it's jealousy. Probably a little of both.

Most people think he's only friends with my sister because he wants to fuck her, but I know better. I know what he really wants, and it *kills* him that he can't have it.

"What are you still doing here?" I ask him, purposely

crooking my finger inside Carter to make him moan, licking a long line up the side of his neck.

Xavi's eyes narrow on me, but then he slides that easy grin of his back into place, making a point to lift his middle finger up before slamming the door on his way out.

Brat.

"Baby boy got his feelings hurt," Carter jokes, a knowing laugh escaping him when I push his head back by his jaw and dig my fingers into his face.

"Shut up."

CHAPTER SIX
PRESENT

Xavi

"He really left you out here in the cold?" Carter laughs, grinning down at me as he takes in the bruises on my face and the blood on my chin.

"What did you expect, Carter?" I glare at him as I move to stand, ignoring his hand when he holds it out for me. "You told me you wouldn't blindside him."

"And you believed me?"

Not really.

But what choice did I have? Carter did me a favor. He saved my ass in more ways than one. And anyone who knows Carter Westwood knows he doesn't do shit for anyone for free. This is the price I'm paying. Move in with them for my first year of college—or for what's left of it, at least. I wasn't in the best shape back in September, which is why I'm starting my freshman year in January.

"Come on." He walks for the house and tosses me a key. "Your room's upstairs, third door on the right." He smirks over his shoulder. "Nate's is the second."

Of course it is.

I grab my bag and sling it over my shoulder. He opens the front door, and I hesitate at the threshold, running my thumb over the jagged edge of the key at my side. "He hates me, Carter."

He stops and turns to face me. Slowly running his eyes over my body from head to toe, he nods as he takes in my appearance. "I think you'll live."

I doubt it, but okay.

I follow him inside the vast entryway and through to the massive kitchen on our left, taking in the bright white walls and the dark wooden countertops, the sink free of dishes and the appliances all lined up just so. This place is spotless, but that doesn't surprise me. Nate's a clean freak. I bet he inspects every inch of this place every time the cleaners leave, obsessively scrubbing any spots they missed.

"What are you smiling at?" Carter asks.

"Nothing." I shake my head. "Where's your room?"

"Right opposite Nate's."

"What about the girl?" I ask, trying to act unfazed as I set my bag down on the floor next to the island. "Frankie. Does she have her own room?"

"Yeah, but she sleeps in Nate's most of the time."

I nod and look away, annoyed at the stab of jealousy twisting my insides. "Right."

Carter smirks again and opens the freezer door, grabbing an ice pack and wrapping it up in a hand towel. "Here," he says, tipping his chin at my face as he passes it over.

I take it and hold it up to my cheek, watching as he wets another towel at the sink and walks over to me. Moving my ass back against the counter, he pushes his hips into mine, gently taking my jaw in his hand to wipe the blood off. I fight a cringe and turn my face away from his, taking the towel from him to do it myself. He grins wickedly as he steps back, hands raised in mock surrender. I narrow my eyes, still unsure what the hell he thinks he's playing at. He's always loved messing with people, but this is fucked up, even for him.

"Why am I here, Carter?" I whisper, not wanting anyone else in this house to hear me. "Why are you doing this?"

"Because it's fun."

He leaves me alone then, disappearing through the door without a backward glance.

Once I've finished cleaning myself up, I rinse the blood from the towel and ring it out in the sink. I'd rather not get my ass handed to me for making a mess, so I wipe up the water, then find the laundry room off the kitchen and toss the towels into the hamper. Grabbing my bag, I don't dare check out any of the other rooms down here on my way back to the entryway. I walk up the staircase and along the hall, stopping outside the third door on the right.

He better not be fucking with me.

Carefully, as if I'm handling a ticking bomb, I twist the handle and peek inside the room, relieved when I find it empty. I wouldn't put it past Carter to set me up and make me walk into Nate's room unannounced.

Stepping inside, I quietly close the door behind me and set my bag down on the floor. The room is huge, just like Katy said it would be. The walls are white up here too, the floors a light, dusty gray color. The queen-sized bed is made up with white sheets, topped with a fluffy gray throw blanket and matching pillows. There's a TV on the wall opposite, a ridiculously big walk-in closet Katy would have had no problem filling, and an equally big en-suite bathroom in the corner of the room.

Leaving my clothes on, I crawl onto the bed and lie on top of the covers, folding my arm beneath my head. Then I take out my wallet and stare at the big-ass smile on my best friend's face.

"I told you I'd come, babe," I whisper. "I'm here."

And I'm miserable without you.

CHAPTER SEVEN

Nate

"It stinks of whiskey in here."

My jaw ticks, but I don't open my eyes, my head tipped back on the couch in the den.

Frankie's right. It does. I picked up all the broken glass and cleaned up as much as I could, but I couldn't get it all out of the carpet. The wall is ruined as well. Now I have to wait until Monday for the cleaning crew and the painters to come over and cover up the mess I made.

"What happened, Nate?"

I ignore her again, cracking one eye open when I realize she's not gonna take a hint.

It's only been a few hours since she passed out in my room, but she's already freshly showered and dressed up for yet another night of partying. Her blonde hair is dead straight, the ends grazing the curve of her waist every time she moves, and she's wearing a little black skirt with some type of bra for a top. The black, spiky choker around her throat looks like a dog collar, but I don't dare point that out to her.

A memory comes back to me then, one of Xavi wearing something like that once while he was hanging out at my house. I remember thinking what a punk he looked like at the time, but now I'm imagining him wearing one again. Me hooking my fingers beneath the silk and dragging him closer, making him my little plaything, my *gift*—

"You gonna share that?" Frankie asks, tipping her chin at the new bottle of whiskey I've got wedged between my legs.

I pass it up to her. She grabs a couple tumblers from the bar and pours two fingers into each one, topping them off with some Coke from the fridge. She hands me mine, and I take it, eyeing her form over the top as I take a sip. "You goin' out?"

"*We're* going out," she corrects me. "Go shower and get changed. You look like shit."

"I'm too hot to look like shit," I try to joke.

She breathes out a sigh, her white, lethally sharp fingernails tapping the edge of her glass. "Who's the new boy?"

"Don't."

"Is he yours?" she asks. "Because if not, I—"

"I said *don't*," I bite out, harsher than I intended to. "Stay away from him, Frank. Please," I add, softer this time.

She stares at me, searching my eyes. She must see something there because after a quick glance at my red, swollen knuckles, she nods once and says, "All right."

All right.

If only it was that simple for my baby sister. If only she'd said *all right*, maybe I wouldn't have lost her to him. Maybe she'd still be here. Maybe...

"Can I have another one?" I ask, holding my empty glass up.

"Nope." She shakes her head, snatching it from my hand. "Shower. Now."

I glare at her, and she grins, shaking her bossy little ass as she walks over to the mirror above the bar. I could tell her to go fuck herself, but I don't do that. She'll only stay in here and annoy me until I cave, which is why I decide to save myself the headache. Forcing myself to stand, I make my way upstairs. Checking to make sure no one's around, I bypass my room and stop at the next one over, listening for movement inside. Hearing nothing, I silently open the door and peek through the gap. I expected him to be awake, but he's not. He's lying on top of the sheets in the middle of the bed, curled up into a little ball with his hands tucked beneath his chin, sound asleep like he hasn't got a fucking care in the world. My hand tightens on the door frame, and it takes some serious willpower not to walk in there, climb on top of him, and suffocate him with a pillow.

Too easy.

If I was gonna kill him, I'd make it hurt.

I'd make him scream.

My heart beats a little faster, and I back up before I do something stupid. I close the door with a soft click and make my way to the bathroom inside my room, peeling my shirt off before I turn the shower on. My fingers find the chain around my neck, and I reach up to undo the clasp, my eyes glued to the ring I've been wearing on my chest every day since the day I took it. I cried into my sister's shoulder that night and stole it from her limp, lifeless body, lying on the floor of that filthy, strange house I found her in.

I shouldn't have done it, but I couldn't let her go with that piece of him on her finger.

Now I wear it as a punishment. As a reminder and a promise.

I'll never forget what he did to her.

CHAPTER EIGHT

Xavi

It's dark outside when I wake up. I didn't mean to fall asleep, but a quick glance at my phone tells me it's almost nine, meaning I've been out for almost three hours.

Groaning, I roll out of bed. In the bathroom, I avoid looking at the mirror and rub the grit from my eyes, hissing at the throbbing pain that follows.

I feel like shit. I probably look like shit too, and I definitely didn't ice my face for long enough.

I brush my teeth, take a two-minute shower, and get dressed. Running my fingers through my damp hair, I make my way downstairs. I haven't eaten since yesterday and I'm starving. It feels weird to have food delivered here, so I take my phone out and search for the closest pizza place I can drive to, stopping in the entryway when I hear movement in the kitchen.

Just keep walking.

Ignoring my instincts, I veer right, keeping my steps light as I peek through the open door. I don't know whether I'm disappointed or relieved when I see it's not Nate like I thought it was.

It's Easton Miller, one of the guys I recognize from Nate and Carter's team. He's got light brown hair and an easy-going smile on his face. Busy on his phone, he sets his duffel bag on the floor by the laundry room. I try not to make a face as I take in his gym clothes and the basketball he's spinning on his forefinger.

Of course there's another ball boy here.

I've gotten into countless fights with guys like this. Mostly back in high school, with the asshole jocks who used to think it was funny to put hands on Katy. They teased her, pushed her around and gave her hell every chance they got, so I gave it right back to them. Got my ass kicked more times than I can count, but I didn't let that stop me. Every time, I got right back up and kept on swinging until one of the teachers came along to break it up.

After it became clear they had to go through me to get to her, everyone at school thought we were dating. Even our parents thought there was something more going on between us. Probably because I've never bothered to tell them pussy doesn't make my dick hard. Not that I give a shit what they think. I'd just rather save myself the headache. Luckily for me, everyone I meet usually takes one look at me and just assumes I'm straight.

Almost everyone...

I clear my throat when I realize Easton's caught me standing here, his eyebrows pulled down as he studies the dark bruises around my eyes, then the black hoodie I'm wearing and the too big, holey jeans hanging off my narrow hips.

"Hey," he says nicely enough. "You're Xavi, right?"

I frown, unsure how he knows that. If Carter didn't even bother telling Nate I was coming, why would he tell this guy?

"Frankie texted me and told me you were here," he explains. "I'm Easton."

I nod, awkwardly tucking my hands into my pockets. I don't really know what to make of him or what Nate's told these people about me, so I just watch him for a minute, slowly backing up the way I came. "Okay, well, I'll just...uh, go—"

"You hungry?" he asks, holding up a bag of Chinese food before setting it down on the island. "I was starving so I got one of everything."

"Um..."

He begins taking containers out and opening them up, raising a brow at me as he leans over and taps the counter with a pair of chopsticks. "Sit down, Xavi. I don't bite."

Okay then.

I take the seat opposite him, and he opens the fridge, pulling out two beers. "Want one?"

My heart starts pounding faster. "No thanks."

There.

Easy.

Fucking breathe, man.

Easton shrugs as he puts one back and grabs me a soda instead, holding it up in offering. I take it and pop the cap off the top, watching as he dishes out enough food to feed a small village. He keeps looking at my face as we eat, and I can tell he's curious about the black eye, but he doesn't ask me about it. Instead, he tells me about his classes and games and his spot on the team, talking my ears off about everything and anything. He's kind of sweet, and I find myself more relaxed around him than I thought I would.

"There's a party tonight," he says as we begin cleaning up. "You wanna come?"

I automatically open my mouth to say no, but then I think about Katy, imagining her grabbing me by my hair and shoving my antisocial ass toward him.

I still hesitate, wanting to ask if he knows if Nate will be there, but of course I don't do that.

"Yeah," I tell him, forcing the words out around the lump in my throat. "I'll come."

"WHAT HAPPENED to the girl you lived with?" I ask Easton, looking up at the house he brought me to as we climb the wide steps leading up to it.

The whole place is made out of glass and pearly white marble.

"She burned all my shit and kicked my ass to the curb," he answers, laughing lightly at the look on my face. "Don't feel bad for me." He shakes his head, pushing the front door open and allowing me to step in first. "I deserved it."

"Why? What did you do?"

"I fucked her sister."

I raise a brow at that, turning to face him as I back up into the house. "You tell everybody you just met that you're a cheating asshole?"

"Only the ones I *really* like," he jokes, slinging his big arm over my shoulder and spinning me to walk me forward into the crowd.

I tense against his side, unsure what I'm supposed to do with my hands. His fingers squeeze my collarbone through my hoodie, and I fight to keep my dick in check, telling myself not to read too much into it. Not to think about the way his hot body feels against mine, or how that easy smile of his comes out to play when he looks at me.

For the love of God, don't.

Don't start crushing on the straight basketball player who also happens to be one of Nate's best friends, you idiot.

He steers me toward the kitchen, bumping a few fists and grinning at a few girls as we pass them. I stay wedged against his side and let him move me, nodding along as he points out the guys on the team and tells me which positions they play. He tells me their names, and I don't bother telling him I already know them. I'll keep that little secret to myself.

He starts talking to Bryson West—the guy whose parents own this house. I look over at the pool through the window behind us, chewing my lip as I search for any exit points out there. There must be something. A side gate or—

"Xavi." Easton shakes my shoulder, pulling my attention back to him and Bryson.

"Hm?"

"I said you obviously don't like beer, so what's your drink?"

I shift from foot to foot and eye the several bottles of alcohol lined up on the island. "Water."

His brows pinch, but he sobers faster than I thought he would. "Okay. Water it is."

He moves around me and grabs a bottle from the fridge, his back to all the people in here as he uncaps it and pours it into a solo cup. I could drink it from the bottle, but I think he's doing that so I can blend in with every other drunk college kid here. He knows something's up, and he's trying to help me avoid drawing any unwanted attention to myself. Or maybe I'm just desperate for someone to give a shit and I'm reading too much into things again.

He hands me my drink, and I lean back against the counter as I lift it to my lips, moving my eyes over all the people bumping and grinding on each other throughout the house. It's been a little while since I've been to a party like this, but it's not all that different from the ones I used to go to back in high school as far as I can tell. Alcohol. Drugs. Sex. Bad decisions... Nothing ever changes.

I spot at least a dozen couples tongue-fucking each other, some making their way to the glass staircase in the corner. There's a half-naked girl lying on the dining room table on her back, a few guys around her snorting lines of coke off her bare flesh. I clear my throat and tear my eyes away from the scene, already regretting my decision to come here. I rub my chest with my knuckles as the panic rises, stealing my breath and blurring my vision.

Damn it, I shouldn't be here.

I can't be here.

I can't, I can't, I can't—

"Hey." Someone touches me. It's Easton, his hand clutching my shoulder again as he bends to level with me. "Dude, are you good?"

"Yeah," I breathe out, nodding too fast, but then I'm shaking my head and backing away from him. "I need some air. I'm gonna go outside for a sec."

He says something else, but I don't hear him as I turn around and all but stumble out the back door. As soon as I'm out of there, I pull in a breath and let it out slowly. That helps, so I do it again, three more times until the mess inside my head starts to clear. I drink some water and carry on walking, the loud music fading the further away I get from the source. There are just as many people out here, if not more, but the groups are more spread out than they are inside, so it doesn't feel as crowded. Nobody pays me any attention as I lean back against the side of the house and scrub a hand over my face. Taking out my cigarettes, I thumb the pack open and slide one out with my teeth, my head lowered as I search my pocket for my lighter.

Fuck it.

Just one won't hurt.

I just need one fucking—

I feel more than see the glare on me the second I flick the lighter on, the flame hovering just a couple inches from the tip. Cutting my eyes up, I snatch the cigarette from my mouth and let my arms fall to my sides.

Nate's sitting on the other side of the yard, the neon blue lights from the pool shadowing his face and making his features look even darker. Frankie and the group of people with him are laughing and having a good time, but his stare doesn't leave mine. Even when he knows I've caught him, he doesn't react or look away. He looks furious, and he has every right to be. I'm not proud of the person he sees when he looks at me—the cocky, stupid little shit I was two years ago. That guy was reckless and selfish and all he cared about was chasing the next high. I hate him just as much as Nate does. For corrupting Katy. For turning the town's good girl into the horror story they all whisper about. For encouraging her, enabling her because it hurt less not to hurt alone.

It's all his fault.

My fault.

Swallowing, I duck my head like the coward I am and go back inside. Easton's still standing in the same place, surrounded by double the amount of people who were here a few minutes ago. He takes the empty solo cup I'm holding and replaces it with a full one. "Don't worry," he says, leaning over sideways to shout over the music. "I made sure no one spiked it."

"Thanks," I mumble into the cup, not missing the eyes burning a hole into the back of my head.

Just then, Carter appears at my side with a drink in hand, shamelessly eye-fucking the good-looking guy standing a few feet away from us. The guy eye-fucks him right back, and I shake my head with a barely there smile. Carter makes it look so easy, being out. He might be an asshole, but I can't deny I respect the way he's happy to just be who he is. Nate's never really advertised the fact that he likes to hook up with guys as well as girls—his dad wouldn't allow it—but Carter genuinely couldn't care less what his parents, his coach, or anyone else has to say about him. He's always been that way.

"Having fun, Xav?"

"What do you want, Carter?"

"Nate's avoiding me." He feigns a pout, and I roll my eyes at his stupidity.

"That's probably because as soon as he comes near you, he's gonna kick your ass."

He laughs at that, glancing at something over my head as he moves toward his entertainment for tonight. "Funny, 'cause it looks to me like he wants *your* ass a hell of a lot more than he wants mine."

I ignore the way that fills me with both dread and heat all at once. He didn't mean it like that. He's just trying to mess with me. Trying to fuck with my head and make me hope for something I have no business hoping for.

The hairs on the back of my neck stand up when I realize Nate's right behind me. His hand comes into view as he rests it on the island next to my hip. "Why are you here?"

"I already told you—"

"I mean *here*, at this party," he grits out, his mouth near my ear as he uncaps a bottle of something and pours himself a drink.

"Easton brought me."

"Did he?" he asks casually enough, but I'm not stupid. He's pissed and he wants me to know about it. "And why would he do that after we told him to ignore you and leave your ass at the house?"

"Maybe he likes me better than you," I mutter. I know it's not wise to provoke him, but I guess old habits really do die hard. "Katy always did."

As soon as her name leaves my lips, he makes me regret it. He doesn't seem to care who might be watching as he grabs a fistful of my hair and drags me outside, throwing me around like a rag doll. My back hits the marble wall I was leaning against before, the cup of water slipping from my hand and soaking us both. He doesn't seem to care about that either, his huge body crowding mine as he forces me to meet his eyes.

He's so close.

Too close.

What the fuck is he doing?

"Don't act surprised, party boy," he taunts. "You just asked me for this. Plain and fucking simple."

Maybe he's right.

I've earned his wrath, after all. It's only fair he gives it to me.

I don't even try to fight him when he digs his fingers into my throat, making it hard to breathe. He doesn't let me look away from his eyes, and now that the initial shock of seeing him again has worn off, I...

Fuck, I forgot how much it hurts to look at him.

His thumb grazes the edge of my jaw beneath my ear, and I try not to make a sound as he finds the small scar I got the day he found me sleeping next to Katy's grave on her birthday a couple years ago. I don't remember much about that fight. I was too out of it, but I do know that was the last time he saw me in person before today.

"Did I give you this?" he asks, still thumbing that same spot on my jaw.

I nod once, and a hint of a smirk touches his lips.

He likes that.

He's still holding me in place, but he's not hurting me anymore. Somehow this is worse, especially when I see the flash of amusement in his eyes, like he knows exactly what I'm thinking right now.

It's never mattered how hard I try to hide it. He's always been able to see me for what I am.

Broken. Pathetic. *Gay.*

My dick is hard for him, and I know he can feel it through our clothes. My breath quickens when he pushes his thigh between my legs, his mouth lowering until it's just an inch away from mine, giving me a taste of something I'll never have.

"You want more?" he whispers.

More scars or more...him?

Whatever it is, I'll take it.

When I nod, he keeps hold of my face and slowly wedges his free hand down between us, boldly palming my cock through my jeans. He strokes me through the material, and a shocked sound leaves my throat before I can stop it, my hips automatically bucking into his.

"Fuck," I breathe against his lips. "*Fuck—*"

Something happens then, and he turns to stone against me. His head pulls back and he stares at my mouth, down at the fallen cup next to my feet, then back up to my face, his jaw locked as he studies every inch of me. I blink at him in confusion, my brows lowering at the sudden return of his anger. Not that it ever left, but this feels different. He looks like he's in pain, his light brown eyes glassing up as he searches mine.

"What..." he trails off.

My eyes start to water too, the realization of what he's thinking carving off yet another piece of my broken heart.

"What was in that drink?"

"Nate."

"Fuck you, Xavi," he spits out, his nostrils flaring as he backs away from me. "Fuck you."

"Yeah," I whisper to myself, closing my eyes so I don't have to watch him walk away. "Fuck me."

"I THINK I'M DRUNK."

"You think?" I laugh, following behind Easton as he walks upstairs, bumping into the railing as he goes.

"Are *you* drunk?" he asks.

"Nah, man, I'm good."

He hums and wraps his arm around my neck, pulling me into

him and smushing his cheek against mine. Not for the first time tonight, I find myself wondering whether he's just super friendly or if he's into guys. I know he had a girlfriend, but he could be bi.

Maybe he's hooked up with Nate before...

"How old are you?"

"Nineteen," I answer.

"Shit. I'm a bad influence, aren't I?"

I smile and shake my head. I don't tell him he's nothing compared to the real bad influences I'm used to. The shitty people who got me hooked on drugs when I was barely fourteen.

"You're underage," he teases, his lips against my temple, and I swear I'm not imagining it this time.

I think he might actually be into me.

"How old are you?" I ask.

"Twenty-one."

Same as Nate, I think to myself. Every thought I have tonight seems to roll right back around to him. I can't stop thinking about the way he was watching my every move at the party. The way it felt to be trapped between his body and the wall.

The way he looked at me when he realized I was sober...

Just as I think it, I round the corner to find the devil himself leaning back against my door frame. He looks tired, his eyes unfocused as he lifts a bottle of whiskey to his mouth. I haven't seen him since he left me outside earlier. Carter and Easton were still in the kitchen when I went back inside, but Nate was nowhere to be found. I didn't know where he went or who he was with, but now I'm guessing he came back here to get trashed all by himself.

Easton trips over his feet and laughs, his arm still locked around my neck, his lips on my face. I try to hold him up with my arm around his waist, but I don't think I'm helping much, considering he's almost twice my size. He opens his mouth to say something to me, shutting it just as quick when his eyes find Nate's. The two of them seem to have some kind of wordless conversation for a second, and then Easton sighs and lets me go.

"I don't think he likes me very much tonight," he whispers in my ear, grinning as he walks backward into his bedroom. "Night, boys."

I don't mean to, but I find myself grinning as well, awkwardly dipping my head down to hide it. My face feels hot all of a sudden, and I hope Nate's too drunk to notice.

He's not.

He cocks his head at me and gestures to Easton's closed door with the whiskey bottle. "Really?"

"What?" I ask, risking a glance at him. "I like him."

"You're pathetic."

My shoulders drop, and I avert my eyes, folding my arms over my chest as I stare at the floor next to his feet.

Ouch.

"Don't think you're something special. He's like that with everyone. At first," he adds cryptically. "I'd lock your door at night if I were you."

I laugh lightly at that, forcing myself to look up at him. "You make jokes now?"

"I'm not kidding."

We stare at each other for a moment, neither of us moving or saying anything as we listen to Easton banging into something inside his room.

"What are you doing out here, Nate?" I ask softly, watching him take another drink.

My body inches forward like it wants to go to him, like it wants to try to comfort him or some shit, but I stay put, leaving a safe distance between us. His brows dip, and he looks around as if he's only just realized where he is.

Blocking my door.

Waiting for me...

He says nothing, so I push a little harder. "What do you want from me?"

"I want you to leave."

But I'm already shaking my head. "I can't."

"Why not?"

I hesitate, unsure how to answer that.

"Xavi, I swear to god. Move out or—"

"Or what, Nate?" I sigh. "You'll throw me out? Kick my ass again? I've heard it all before, man."

"I mean it this time."

"No," I tell him, lifting my chin up in defiance. "You don't."

I'm not sure why I'm so confident about that. I just am.

His brown eyes darken, and I swear I can see the thrill in there as he steps closer, invading my space and smearing the tip of the bottle over my bottom lip. "You sure you wanna play this game with me, party boy?"

I flinch and turn my head away, holding my breath as he uses the bottle to bring my face right back to his.

There can't be more than a drop of whiskey on my mouth, but still...

It's too much.

I quickly wipe it away with my sleeve, and he shakes his head at me in anger.

That was a test, and I'm pretty sure I failed.

"Lock your door," he reminds me.

And then he's gone.

CHAPTER NINE

Xavi

I creep through the empty backyard and look at the house over my shoulder, chewing the inside of my cheek when I see Bryson West's parents standing in their kitchen. I was only here a few nights ago, but it looks like a completely different house than it did then, freshly cleaned and free of all the mess, the makeshift bar, and the bodies dry-fucking each other on those very surfaces they're leaning on.

It would be easier to do this when they're not home, but Katy wouldn't have done this half-assed. She'd have loved the thrill and the fear of being caught.

Stripping all my clothes off, I set them down on the table Nate was sitting on the other night, shaking my head when I start to think about him again.

Stop it, Xavi.

This isn't about him.

Pulling the blindfold over my eyes, I cover my dick and balls with my hand and jump headfirst into the heated pool. Coming up for air, I manage to swim two lengths before I hear the shouts coming from somewhere beside me. It's Bryson's parents, probably pissed as hell to find some naked stranger making himself at home in their fancy pool.

"Hey!" Mr. West barks on my left. "What the hell are you doing?!"

I swing my head the other way and dive toward the edge, hauling myself out before I make a run for it. I don't get very far before I crash into a chair, bust my knees and fall on my ass, scrambling to get away from the hands trying to grab at my ankles.

"You little prick."

I kick him away and stand up. Feeling around for the table, I find my clothes and ball them up against my chest, hiding myself as much as possible as I sprint across the yard. I crash into something else and let out a grunt, laughing to myself as I clutch my aching ribs.

Jesus, how did she make this look so easy?

I'm running blind with my heart in my damn throat. By some miracle, I manage to find the wall I climbed to get in here and toss my clothes over the top, pulling myself up and quickly hopping down on the other side. I can still hear them both yelling at me as I snatch my stuff off the ground, rip the blindfold off, and run back to my bike parked on the side of the road down the street. I'm freezing and my teeth are chattering like crazy, but the adrenaline keeps me going as I shove my clothes back on and swing my leg over the seat, still laughing to myself as I speed away. I drive for a couple minutes with no destination in mind, just far enough from the house that I'm sure Bryson's dad won't catch up and beat the shit out of me. Once I've pulled over, I dry my hands and pull out the list I brought with me, uncapping my black marker pen with my teeth as I find task number five.

Go skinny dipping in a stranger's pool.

Crossing it out, I refold the paper and put it away, my chest heaving as I swipe the wet hair from my forehead. Shoving my helmet on, I can almost hear Katy's hysterical laughter in my ears as I start the engine and drive back to her brother's house.

BEING BLIND MUST SUCK. My knees and elbows hurt, my ass and ribs feel bruised, and the inside of my thigh is dripping with blood. I didn't notice it at the time, but I must have cut myself on something when I climbed back over the wall.

Limping into the kitchen, I grab an ice pack and head back to the stairs, jumping out of my skin when Nate walks in through the front door.

"Jesus, you scared me."

He stops in his tracks when he sees me, his eyes narrowing as he takes in my disheveled form.

He hasn't said a word to me since that first night in the hall. I don't even think he's looked at me once in the last three days. But he's looking now.

I'm not sure whether I should love or hate it.

"What are you doing?"

"Nothing," I answer, probably a little too quickly.

He cocks his head and grabs the strap of the gym bag on his shoulder, eyes never leaving mine as he drops it on the floor. He's wearing a black pair of shorts and one of those tight, long sleeved gym shirts that clings to his skin, showing off every hard dip and curve of his upper body.

Don't look at his abs.

Don't look.

Don't—

I look, and he stalks toward me, lifting my chin up with his finger and making a point to close my open mouth.

Asshole.

"Why are you wet?"

My cheeks heat, and I fight a shiver as his warm fingers make their way across my ice-cold face.

"I went in the pool."

Even though I'm not technically lying—I did go in *a* pool, just not *his* pool—I think he knows I'm hiding something. He doesn't call me out on it though.

"Did you hurt yourself?" he asks, his eyebrows pulled in as he dips his head down to my leg.

I blink at him, confused at his concern for me. "Do you care?"

"Not even a little bit." He shoves my face away and leans over to grab his bag. He shoulder-checks me on his way to the stairs, almost knocking me over with the force of it. "Clean the blood off my floor."

I catch myself on the railing, waiting for the sound of his bedroom door closing before I grab a rag from the kitchen and get to work.

CHAPTER TEN

Nate

He doesn't lock his door.

Every night since he got here, I've tried the handle and found it unlocked, sneaking into his bedroom to watch him sleep. Right now, I'm standing by the open window, smoking the cigarette I stole from the pack on his nightstand.

He doesn't even smoke.

I've seen him ripping up cigarettes and tossing them into the trash when he thinks no one's looking, but I haven't seen him actually light one up and take a hit.

I turn my head to blow my smoke outside, remembering the first time I caught him and my sister behind the garage when they were fifteen, the little punks, laughing and whispering to each other as they passed a cigarette back and forth. I lost my shit and kicked him out of the house, but all he did was laugh.

I wish I'd killed him.

I wish I'd have known back then so I could have done more to stop him.

I wish he was dead instead of her.

Flicking the roach outside, I close the window and move over to sit on his bed next to him, carefully pulling the blanket down to reveal his body. Lying on his side with his leg hooked up, his lean arms are wrapped around his pillow, his dark hair hiding his face from me. He's wearing a tiny pair of shorts and a black, short-sleeved crop top, the hem resting just below his sternum. I've caught him wearing skimpy little outfits like this a couple times before, but only ever when it was just him and Katy. He'd never wear something like this in public. God forbid his father finds out he's got a queer little fairy boy for a son.

I graze my fingers over his stomach and up to his chest, stopping at the barbell I feel on his nipple. He's got both pierced, I realize, and I hate it.

I hate how hot he is.

I hate how hot he makes *me* as I swirl my finger around the metal.

He doesn't flinch. I move my hand a little lower, not caring if he wakes up and catches me touching him. He sleeps like a corpse, so it's not likely.

Grabbing his knee, I carefully spread his legs and squint into the darkness, studying the small bruises all over him, glaring at the fresh cut I find on his inner thigh.

I don't know what happened to him tonight, but I want to.

I want to know everything.

Lowering my head, I look up at his face as I run my lips over the soft flesh next to the wound, a low noise escaping my throat as I rub my hard dick beneath my sweats.

I don't know what's gotten into me.

This hate inside me feels like a living, breathing thing, and it wants Xavi Hart. Now that he's within reach, it wants to take him and own him, to pin him down and punish him for what he's done, to make him cry and beg for me to make it stop.

He hisses through his teeth, and I look down, releasing him

when I realize I was digging my fingers into the cut, hard enough to make it bleed again.

Still fast asleep, he groans and rolls over onto his other side, knocking his knee into my head before he curls up with his back to me. I lean over him and chuck the blanket on the floor out of his reach, hoping he freezes to death.

I should leave now, but I don't.

I want to *know*, damn it.

Grabbing his phone off the charger on the nightstand, I unlock it with the passcode I guess on the first try. Katy's birthday. Same as mine.

Opening his recent call list, I scroll through and try to figure out if he was with anyone tonight. The only people he's talked to in the last week are his dad, Carter, and a single call from Easton. He doesn't have any of his own friends, the fucking loser.

I go to his messages next, but there's nothing exciting there. The only one of interest to me is from his dad. He texted him this afternoon but Xavi never replied.

DAD

> Don't forget you have an appointment with your
> therapist tomorrow at nine a.m. Do not be late.

I scoff and open his alarm app, turning off the one set for eight in the morning. I put his phone back but don't put it on charge, then pick up his wallet and snoop through that as a last resort. There's nothing in here either. Just a little cash and...

I blink and drop my elbows on my knees, my head lowered as I look at the pictures of him and my baby sister. My happy, grinning, *laughing* baby sister. Tears fill my eyes before I can stop it, and I lock my jaw, turning my face toward the boy sleeping next to me.

"I hate you."

CHAPTER ELEVEN

Nate

"**G**od fucking damn it."

My lips twitch at the panic in Xavi's voice, my hands wrapped around my coffee cup as I sit next to Frankie at the kitchen island. Carter's sitting opposite us, shirtless and hungover, his head lowered as he inhales the breakfast I made this morning.

I couldn't sleep last night. When I can't sleep, I clean. And when there's nothing left to clean, I cook as much food as I can so I can clean all over again.

My friends aren't usually up before noon when we don't have classes to get to, but every time I cook, it's like they sense the food and come running for it.

Xavi finally appears at the bottom of the stairs, and I watch through the doorway as he paces and rips his hands through his hair. It's after nine already, meaning he's late for his appointment. His phone keeps ringing in his pocket, but he's ignoring it. He looks a little crazed, barely sparing the three of us a glance as he walks into the kitchen and crouches to look beneath the freezer.

"What's wrong with you?" Carter asks him around a mouthful of bacon.

"I—" Xavi stops and does a double take at me, his face falling as he slowly rises back up to his feet. "Nate..."

"Party boy."

He curses and bangs the freezer door with the edge of his fist, making a sleepy Frankie jump beside me. With her fork halfway to her mouth, she lifts her eyes and looks between me and Xavi, not moving a muscle. Carter's mouth stretches into a slow grin, but I don't look away from the pissy little bitch behind him, dropping back in my seat as I watch the emotions flick across his face. I can almost hear the thoughts running through his head as he tries to fit the pieces together, his teeth grinding when he figures out what I've done.

That right there, I suddenly realize.

That's what I want.

I've barely gotten a reaction out of him before now. Every time I knock him down, it's like he's content to just lie there and take it.

Not this time though.

This time, he looks *pissed*, and I like it.

I want more of it.

Leaning back a little more, I twist in my seat and widen my legs.

Come here.

I don't say it out loud, but his feet still move toward me like he heard the command. Slowly, he walks over until he's standing between my open thighs, fingers twitching restlessly at his sides. We stare at each other for a few beats, and then he snaps, his small hands grabbing for my sweats to search my pockets. I snatch his wrists and twist, making him cry out as I pin them behind his back. With my other hand, I grab the hem of his shirt and pull until his chest bumps mine, my knuckles brushing the soft, warm skin just above his waistband. Instead of fighting me back, he lets out a sigh and melts against me. A single, defeated tear slips over his cheek as his body goes limp in my arms.

Fucking pathetic.

"I know you have it," he breathes out.

"Have *what*?" I ask, daring him with my eyes to say it.

He doesn't—not in front of Frankie and Carter—which is the only reason I don't shove my fist into that black eye of his and make him cry for real.

"Please," he whispers just for me. "I'll do anything you want, just...Please, Nate."

"Anything, huh?"

He nods.

"What if I told you to pack your shit and get out of my house?"

"I'll do it," he says without hesitation. "I'll leave."

My eyes narrow, and I tug on his body again, bringing him in until his face is right next to mine. Reaching into my sweats, I pull out the strip of photos I stole from his wallet last night, discreetly sliding it into the front pocket of his jeans. He sighs again, relieved, and I run my nose over the scar on his jaw line, enjoying the way he shivers against me.

I don't tell him to leave.

"Lock your door," I whisper slowly, ensuring he understands me this time.

He pulls back a bit and blinks at me, nodding mutely as he removes himself from my grip. I let him go, watching his back as he walks out of the kitchen and lifts his phone up to his ear, almost barreling into Easton as he goes. Easton grabs his sides to steady him, and Xavi mutters an embarrassed apology, dipping his head to hide his warm face as he walks out the front door.

Easton comes in and grabs himself a plate, still half asleep and smiling like a dumbass, his steps faltering when he catches the glare I throw his way.

"You're *still* mad at me about the party the other night?" he grumbles, snatching a piece of bacon and tearing off a bite with his teeth. "I said I was sorry."

"I told you not to bring him."

"Carter told me you were kidding."

"Carter's a lying motherfucker."

Carter snorts, and I stand up to place my empty mug in the dishwasher, grabbing the back of his neck and shoving his face into his plate on my way out. He just laughs, shaking his head at me with that stupid, knowing grin on his lips.

LATER THAT NIGHT, I stare up at the ceiling and will myself to fall asleep, to forget about him and his crop tops and the piercings on his body, that damn cut on his inner thigh that I can't stop thinking about...

Just go to sleep, Nate.

But I can't.

I have to know.

Climbing out of bed, I throw on some sweats and walk out into the hallway. Grabbing the handle on the door next to mine, I push down, my jaw ticking when it doesn't budge.

He locked it.

He actually locked it.

I don't know why I'm pissed all of a sudden.

This is what I wanted, isn't it?

So why does it feel like I just lost something?

CHAPTER TWELVE

Xavi

Collegesucks.

Classes started today, and I'm already regretting my decision to come here and try to get back to my life—or what's left of the mess I made of it, at least.

Not only am I a freshman, I'm also the new kid on campus because I was too much of a fuckup to start in September with everybody else.

It's harder than I thought it would be, having no friends and no desire to make new ones.

I'm studying business, just like my dad wanted me to. I wish I was good at something else—*anything* else just to spite him—but I'm not, so business it is.

I hate it.

I'm finally done for the day, but I'm not going back to the house yet. It feels wrong, being there alone. Partly because it's not mine, but also because the place is huge and kind of creepy. It freaks me out, feeling like I'm being watched all the time. Like there's something waiting around every corner, ready to jump out on me and scratch my eyes out.

I wrap my arms around my middle, keeping my gaze down as I make my way through the crowd and down the stairs.

My chest aches when I spot a group of girls walking out of the music building with their instruments. If things were different, Katy could have been right there with them.

All her life, all she wanted to do was sing. She was amazing. She had this raspy, powerful voice that sent chills down my spine every time I heard it. I told her every chance I got that she'd make it someday, that I would be right there with her, always.

God, I miss her.

I was planning on going to the library to study for a while, but I'm not feeling it anymore. I haven't eaten since yesterday—again —so I turn around and head toward the coffee shop on the other side of the courtyard. I push the door open and step inside. It's busy, but the line moves quickly enough. It doesn't take long before I'm holding a steaming hot cup of coffee and a chocolate chip muffin. I thank the barista and turn around, freezing when I find Frankie sitting at a table in the corner with a guy and a girl I haven't seen before. Of course the only empty table in here is the one right next to hers. I consider bailing, but she's already caught me, one of those perfect little eyebrows of hers raised in a silent challenge. I'll look like an idiot *and* a pussy if I run out of here now.

Walking over, I drop down into one of the seats and take the lid off my coffee, blowing on it to cool it while I scroll through my phone. I try to mind my own business, but it's kind of hard when I can hear everything they're saying.

"Do you know him?" the girl asks, talking to Frankie, I'm guessing, but I don't hear her say anything back. "Damn, he's fine. Does he have a girlfriend?"

"He can hear you, big mouth," the guy mock-whispers, and a small smile touches my lips as I bite off a piece of my muffin.

"Hey, emo boy," the girl calls, and I turn my head to look her way, trying not to laugh when she smirks and wiggles her brows at me. "Hi."

I wave and lick the chocolate from my lips before I say, "Hi."

"Oh my God, he's adorable." She feigns a groan, grabbing her wallet before she moves to stand behind me, leaning over with her hands on the back of my chair. "I'm Taylor."

"I'm Xavi."

"Can I have your number, Xavi?"

"Um..."

Shit.

I'm not about to tell her I'm gay, but I don't want to lead her on either. Even if she's fucking with me, which she probably is, I have no idea what to do or say right now.

I peek at Frankie, who's simply watching us as she sips her coffee, one leg crossed over the other, wearing these black tights and heeled boots that remind me of Katy. She didn't dress like that often, especially not in front of her family because they would have had a fit, but I know she would have eventually if she'd lived long enough to tell them to fuck off. We both would have. Me in my crop tops and chokers and her in her fishnets and chunky boots. Two little fuckups against the world.

Taylor clicks her tongue behind me, and it's only now I realize I'm still staring at Frankie's legs.

"No fair." Taylor pouts, misreading the situation completely. "You always get them first."

Frankie shrugs noncommittally, still saying nothing. Taylor laughs goodheartedly before she and the guy walk over to the counter to get more coffees. Ears burning, I go back to my own coffee and continue eating my muffin, not missing Frankie's stare on the side of my face. I can tell she's got questions, but she doesn't push.

"I was told to stay away from you," she says, breaking the awkward silence between us.

I frown at that, turning my head just enough to meet her gaze. "Maybe you should listen."

"Maybe," she echoes, running a long, pointed fingernail over the edge of her cup.

"What did he tell you?" I ask, unable to help myself, but she just cocks her head at me.

Right.

Whether he told her nothing or everything, there's no way she's about to sit there and repeat any of it to me. I barely know this girl, but I can tell she's loyal.

I still can't figure out what's going on between her and Nate, whether they're just friends, fuck buddies, or something more, and I hate it.

I hate how jealous I am of her.

Because whatever they are, she gets to have him in a way that I don't. She *knows* him in a way I never will. I met him first, but he and I might as well be strangers.

Frankie and her friends leave soon after that, and I make a point not to watch them go. I put my headphones in and pick a random playlist on Spotify, shutting out everyone around me and hoping they leave me alone.

Alone.

Just like always.

CHAPTER THIRTEEN

Nate

"Since when do you venture all the way over here?" Frankie asks, grinning at me over her shoulder as I follow her into the coffee shop.

"Shut up."

She chuckles and moves up to the counter to place her order. Looking around, I find Xavi sitting at his usual table by the window, wearing a dark gray hoodie with the hood pulled up over his head. I force my face to remain cold and impassive as I watch him be, enjoying the way he shifts in his seat and pulls his sleeves down over his knuckles. His eyes crinkle at the corners when they find me, like he's trying not to wince.

My face is a punishment for him. And if he insists on sticking around, I've got no problem going out of my way to make him look at it every chance I get.

"Nate," Frankie says, probably not for the first time.

"Yeah?"

"What do you want?"

"Whatever you're having is fine."

She raises a brow at that. "A pumpkin spice latte?" she asks, and I scrunch my nose in disgust. "That's what I thought." She laughs, turning back to the barista. "He'll have a cappuccino."

Once we've got our drinks, we sit side by side at one of the empty tables in the corner, both of us people watching for a while as we warm our hands with our cups. We don't say anything, but it's not awkward. It's easy with Frankie. Comfortable.

A group of people rush inside the shop, relieved to be out of the cold, and I don't miss the way the guy at the back of the group turns his head to look at Xavi, chewing his lip as he takes in his form.

"Does that happen everywhere he goes?" Frankie asks, subtly tipping her chin at Xavi. "Girls and guys?"

I nod, my hands clenching into fists on the table.

"He has no idea, does he?"

"Not a fucking clue."

He's always been this way. Even back in high school, the kid was oblivious to all the attention he got. He's oblivious now too, his head lowered as he tries to pretend he's not peeking up at me every five seconds to check what I'm doing. I like that I'm his sole focus, that he's clearly jealous of me and Frankie, but at the same time, that sad, broken look in his eyes makes me want to throttle him. All I can think about is forcing him to his knees, digging my thumbs into his jugular, and shoving my cock down his throat so hard he chokes on it. Taking him as hard and as roughly as I can and giving him something to really be sad about.

"Jesus, the way you look at him..." Frankie mutters. "I wish someone would look at me like that."

"Like what?"

"Like they wanna fight me and fuck me at the same time." She smirks, and I smirk right back, leaning into her space and taking her chin between my thumb and forefinger. "You hate it, don't you?" she whispers against my lips, playing along like the good friend she is. "The way you want him. It pisses you off."

"Right now, the only thing pissing me off is you," I tell her, digging my fingertips into her skin, but not hard enough to hurt. Never as hard as I'd do it to Xavi.

"That's not very nice."

"I'm not a very nice person, Frank."

"I know," she says. "That's why you're my favorite."

Fighting a grin, I tilt my head to the side, kissing the corner of her mouth. "Is he gone?"

"Mhm."

My grin slips free, and I kiss her cheek this time. She playfully pushes my face away, and I drop back in my seat, resting my arm on the back of her chair. Lifting my coffee to take a sip, I laugh under my breath as I watch Xavi storm off through the courtyard.

CHAPTER FOURTEEN

Xavi

It's the first basketball game of the new year tonight. As usual, the stands are filled with people, the excitement rolling off the crowd as the Hawthorne boys move around the court. They're undefeated this season, well on their way to winning the championship for the fourth year in a row.

Nate Grayson might be a bad-tempered, miserable asshole, but he's fucking good at what he does. Really fucking good.

My eyes follow the number 13 on his back, his black and blue jersey clinging to his body like glue as he bounces the ball and wipes the sweat from his forehead. I stick to the shadows like I always do, my hood pulled low over my head as I sit in the back row with my elbows on my thighs, my hands linked together between my knees.

I know it's practically a sure win—they're up by thirteen points with less than four minutes left on the clock—but I'm still nervous, my eyes constantly cutting between Nate and the scoreboard as I dig my fingers into my knuckles.

He doesn't know I still come to his games. Katy started dragging me along with her back in high school so I could tell her what was happening, and I loved it. Even after she died and I was drowning myself in my own misery, I kept coming. He might not have seen me since that night at the cemetery, but I've been seeing him. Every game for the last two years—except for the twelve weeks I was in rehab—I've been right here, watching his heart sink with every shot, the light in his eyes fading more and more as time went on. It wasn't long before the light went out completely and never came back.

He used to love it down there, but he doesn't get excited about it anymore. He doesn't celebrate on the court after a win, or off the court, as far as I know. It makes him look like a dick, but I get it. Why does he get to live his dream when Katy doesn't get to live hers? It's how I feel too. About everything. Getting sober and coming to college...Listening to her favorite songs...Life in general...

It's not fucking fair.

The final buzzer sounds just as Nate slams the ball through the hoop, and then the crowd around me are on their feet, popcorn and drinks flying everywhere as they shout his name over and over. Carter, Easton, and the rest of the team are all grinning, jumping around and slapping each other on the back, but not one of them tries to touch their captain. They know by now to leave him be and let him do his own thing.

Nate walks toward the edge of the court, and Coach grabs him, smiling proudly as he squeezes his shoulder and leans in to say something to him. Nate nods repeatedly, but his attention is elsewhere, only half listening, by the looks of it. Even from all the way up here, I can see the sharp lines of his jaw, the small tick there as if he's grinding his teeth together. He's been doing that a lot tonight, looking up at the stands...

Is he looking for me?

Not possible.

Shaking my head, I turn around and sneak out of the

stadium. Once I get to the parking lot, I get on my bike and make the hour drive to the cemetery in my hometown, sitting down at Katy's grave to give her a play-by-play of the game, just like I always do.

WHEN I GET BACK to the house later that night, the driveway is full of cars and there's a raging afterparty going on inside. I take my helmet off and walk through the open front door, stepping back when a blonde girl wearing a white bikini almost runs into me, squealing as Easton chases her.

"Hey," Easton calls to me, wrapping his arms around her from behind. "Don't even think about it."

"What?"

"All you do is mope around in your room. Go have some fun for once."

"I don't *mope.*"

He shakes his head at me with a smile, tipping his chin toward the den. "There's a girl in there who won't stop asking about you."

"What girl?"

"I don't know." He shrugs, burying his nose into the blonde girl's neck. "She's tight with Frankie. Brown hair, big mouth, no filter. Her name's Tia or something like that."

"Taylor," I correct him, remembering the girl from the coffee shop the other day.

"Yeah, her," he says, wiggling his brows. "Go get her, *emo boy.*"

My eyes widen slightly, and he laughs at the look on my face, guiding the girl he's holding back toward the pool with his hands on her ass and his lips on her chest.

I chew the inside of my cheek and glance between the den

and the kitchen, choosing the kitchen. Despite what Easton said about me having some fun, I don't plan on staying down here long. These aren't my friends, and this isn't my scene anymore. I just want to see Nate, to know what he's doing and where his head is at after the game.

I sidestep my way around a group of people standing by the island, recognizing a few of the boys from the team passing out tequila shots. I shake my head when they offer me one, grabbing myself a bottle of Coke from the fridge and twisting the cap off the top.

Nate's not in here with them, but as I make my way across the hall, it doesn't take me long to find him. He's sitting in the corner of the den, a far-away look in his eyes as he lifts a glass of amber liquid up to his lips. He looks...sad, tired, lonely even though he's surrounded by people who worship and adore him. He's so far gone from the person he used to be, and it breaks my heart.

I don't move from the doorway, not wanting him or that Taylor girl to know I'm here, but of course it doesn't work out that way. As if sensing my presence, Nate rolls his head on the back of the couch, watching me as he swallows his drink and pours himself another.

Always watching...

A gorgeous brunette girl—one of the cheerleaders, I think—leans over the back of the couch to say something to him, and he nods as he reaches back for her hand and guides her around, pulling her into his lap. My stupid heart sinks, and I break eye contact first, tensing up when two muscular arms come around me from behind.

"Did you have fun watching us tonight?" Carter asks, his breath tickling my ear. "I know you were there. You're always there, aren't you, Xav?"

"You don't know shit."

"Sure I don't."

I try to maneuver myself out of his grip, but he doesn't let me get far, his fingers wrapping around my arm as he drags me out of the room. I stumble as he pulls me toward the entryway, up the stairs and down the hall until we get to the bedrooms.

"What are you doing?" I ask, my stomach twisting with nerves.

Is he sending me to bed or *taking* me to bed?

Easton told me upstairs is off-limits when they throw parties, so there's no one up here, but still, anyone could wander up and see him with his hands all over me.

"Carter—"

"Relax. I'm helping you," he whispers, caging me in against the wall. "Trust me, baby boy. This won't take long."

"Carter, stop."

"That's not what you said last time," he teases, louder than before. "You begged me *not* to stop, remember?"

Embarrassment courses through me as I recall the night I've tried to forget about, the night I tried to kill myself on the edge of that cliff three months ago.

Carter's hands grab my waist, and I'm about to fucking punch him, but I don't get the chance before he's being yanked away from me by the back of his head, his ass hitting the floor with a crash as his best friend punches him instead. *Hard.*

"Jesus, Nate," I hiss, my eyes wide as the blood gushes from Carter's nose.

"You fucked him," Nate says as he walks right into me, his chest bumping mine.

"I..."

"When, Carter?" he bites out, and it's only now I realize he's not talking to me, even though his eyes haven't left mine yet.

"Dude, will you chill?" Carter laughs as he sits up, catching the blood in his palm. "I didn't touch him until after he was eighteen."

"*After* my sister died," he growls, turning away from me like he's about to go for him a second time. "I'm gonna kill you."

Without thinking, I reach out for him and fist the front of his shirt, pulling him back until he's against me again. His nostrils flare as he glares at me, his hands clenched into fists on the wall on either side of my head. It's probably not a good idea to touch him right now, but I don't care. I want his attention on me—only me. Fuck Carter and his stupid games.

"Just let him go," I say quietly. "Please."

His glare deepens, but he surprisingly does as I ask, neither of us moving as Carter stands and brushes the imaginary dirt off his chest. *You're welcome*, he mouths to me, winking before he disappears around the corner.

I sneer at him before looking up at Nate, staring into his bloodshot eyes as his hands move down to my waist. He grabs me there like Carter did just minutes ago, only harder. I try not to moan at the contact.

"I could have punched him myself, you know?"

He breathes out a laugh, but it's not a nice one. He's laughing *at* me, not with me. "Oh, yeah?" he asks. "And why would you have done that?"

"Because I don't want him."

His grip on my waist tightens as he stares at my mouth. "What *do* you want, party boy?"

"Don't act like you don't know."

His forehead touches mine, and I curl my fingers into his shirt, bracing myself for whatever comes next. Just when I think he's about to do something crazy, like kiss me—or hit me—a rough, broken sound leaves his throat, and he tears his face away from mine. "*Fuck.*" He looks disgusted. With himself or me, I don't know. Probably a little of both.

He snatches the Coke from my left hand and glares at it, launching it down the hallway as hard as he can. I jump when he faces me again, swaying on his feet as he grabs two handfuls of my hair and yanks my head back, making me wince.

Shit.

Shit, he looks mad.

"You're scared," he says.

"You're drunk."

But that's not the problem. The problem is I'm *not*. I'm sober and he hates it. He doesn't understand it and it's killing him.

"Tell me why," he says, his voice full of pain and torment as he flicks his eyes between mine. "Why do you get a second chance? Why do you get to live while she's buried in the ground? It's not fucking fair."

I swallow, remembering how I thought that exact same thing just a few hours ago.

"I know," I whisper, barely audible over the crack in my voice. "I'm s—"

"Just tell me why," he bites out, losing his temper. "Why do you get to be better?"

"It's not like that, I..." I shake my head, my lips trembling. "I hate myself for what I did to her, Nate. I know it's my fault she's gone. I didn't quit the drugs because I wanted to turn my life around after she died. I did it because they make me feel..."

"What?!" he shouts, making me jump again.

"Nothing," I choke out, sniffing as a stray tear falls over my cheek. "They make me feel nothing, okay? Not doing them makes me feel it all. All the pain and the guilt and the fucking misery. I'm sober because I deserve it. Because it hurts more."

He blinks at that, his gaze following the tear as it falls off my chin. "You wanna hurt?"

I nod, my vision blurring, and a slow smirk touches his full lips, right before he pulls my face up and crashes his mouth into mine.

CHAPTER FIFTEEN

Nate

I don't know what I'm doing, but I'm too drunk to think twice about it. I want him beneath me and I'm done pretending otherwise. At least for right now.

Without breaking the kiss, I shove him into my room and slam the door behind me. My teeth latch onto his bottom lip as I walk him over to the bed, sucking on his lip ring the way I've thought about doing since the first time I saw it on him.

That was years ago.

Years, I've wanted this.

He holds on to my neck for balance as I rip open the button on his jeans, pushing them down over the tight, round globes of his ass. His dick is as hard as mine is, our lower bodies rutting against each other.

"Nate," he rasps. "What are you doing?"

I still don't know, but I don't feel like telling him that.

Instead of answering, I pull the zipper of his hoodie down and shove it over his shoulders. "Take it off," I demand, my hands going back to his jeans.

He obeys me and strips his t-shirt off as well, tossing it on the floor before running his fingers through the hair at the back of my head. It tingles where he touches me, and I fight a shiver, licking into his mouth to get to his tongue. He gives it to me, tipping his head back with a moan when I rub his dick with my hand over his boxers.

"More," he pleads, and I shake my head at him, squeezing his ass with my free hand as I tease my thumb over the wet tip.

"Shut up and take what I give you."

He whimpers, grunting when I push him down on my bed. I remove his jeans and boxers and toss them onto the pile of clothes on the floor, pausing when I get a proper look at the piercings in his nipples and his leaking cock resting on his lower abdomen. He's bigger than I thought he'd be, longer than even me and just as thick. I raise a brow at him, and he grins like the cocky little demon he is, leaning up on one elbow as he gives himself a slow, teasing stroke. "You just gonna stand there eye-fucking me all night or you gonna do it for real?"

Grabbing his hair, I pull him up to sit on the edge of the mattress. He yelps out in pain, and I push his face into my hip so he can't see the small hint of a smile on my lips. "I thought I told you to shut up."

"Make me."

Unbuttoning my jeans, I pull my dick out and rub the tip over his soft, slightly flushed cheek. He starts to say something else, but I don't let him, tilting my hips to shove my cock into his big mouth. I don't give him a second to get ready. Using my grip on his hair, I pull his head back and forth and fuck myself into him, groaning at the feel of his wet, warm tongue sliding over the underside of my dick. He gags and chokes on it, digging his short nails into my waist. He's not pushing me away though. He's trying to pull me closer. He's *taking* it because he knows he deserves it.

"Little fucker," I grit out, pushing in deeper until I'm hitting the back of this throat. "Look at me."

He does, and I almost come right then at the look in his eyes, the tears streaming over his cheeks while I steal all the air from his lungs.

I don't usually give a shit about getting my dick sucked. I get bored with the foreplay and get it done as quickly as I can. Or just skip it altogether. Guy or girl, as long as we both get off quick, I'm happy. But with Xavi...

I could stare at his pretty lips stretched around the base of me all night.

I stop moving before I come too soon, running my thumb over the black ring at the edge of his mouth. He moves his hands around to my ass and throats my dick all by himself.

"Fuck," I choke out, wrapping my fingers around his neck to stop him.

He smirks, and I push him down on his back, crawling up onto the bed between his legs. He wipes the spit from his mouth with the back of his arm, and I take the second to take in his naked body. He's small, but not as scrawny as he once was. He's filled out a little over the last couple years, still lean but with more muscle. More dips and ridges I want to sink my tongue into until he's desperate and begging for me.

Next time, I tell myself, pushing the thought away just as quick.

No.

There won't be a next time.

Xavi coughs, and I loosen my grip on his throat, removing one of my hands to grab a condom and the bottle of lube from my nightstand. Coating my fingers, I reach down between his legs and rub his hole, watching his mouth part as I push the middle one inside him. He holds on to my wrist, rolling his hips up while I finger him open.

He's so sexy.

I've always known it, and it pisses me off. Thinking about how many guys have wanted him like this, how many have *taken* him like this like he's theirs to take.

He's not theirs.

That familiar hate bleeds into my veins, and I flip him over onto his stomach, shoving his face into the pillow so I don't have to look at it. He catches himself on his forearms, spreading his legs and arching his back like a cat, rubbing his wet, needy hole over my bare dick. My body moves to meet his, my thumbs spreading his cheeks as I slide my length back and forth along the crease of his ass. My nostrils flare at how good he feels, my anger and this desperate need for him consuming me all at once.

Fresh out of patience, I wipe my fingers on my jeans and tear the condom wrapper open.

"Wait." He looks at me over his shoulder, his cheeks glowing the way they do when he's acting shy or embarrassed about something. "I'm negative. If you want to..."

I cock my head at that, my dick throbbing in my hand when I realize what he wants. He wants me to take him bare. He wants me to make him feel *special*.

"You think you mean more to me than the strangers I fuck right here in this bed?" I ask as I roll the condom on, leaning over him until my chest is pressed against his back. "You don't."

His face falls, and I smirk at the hurt in his eyes.

"You think I trust an easy little slut like you?" I push the knife in even deeper, coating myself with lube before I rub the tip over his clenched hole. "Not a chance in hell," I whisper into his ear.

He cries out when I sink into him, gritting his teeth and shoving his face back into the pillow. His tight heat surrounds me, burning me from the inside out. I swallow the groan creeping up my throat, laughing when he reaches up and tries to yank on the short hair at the top of my head. He's upset now, trying to hurt me like I hurt him.

"I'm gonna fuck you so hard you're gonna feel me for a week. You ready?"

"Fuck, just...give me a second, Nate."

"You've got five."

He whines and uncurls his tight fist, raking his nails over my scalp as he takes a few long, deep breaths. I have to fight another groan, pressing my face against the side of his neck to hide the way my body reacts to his. I could blame it on the fact that I'm drunk, but I'd be a liar. The way I feel about him...that's not the alcohol. It's all me.

"Time's up, party boy," I murmur into his warm flesh, and then I do exactly what I said I would.

I finally let go and fuck him as hard as I can, locking one arm beneath his stomach with the other resting next to his shoulder. He tips his head back for me, exposing the erratic pulse thumping beneath his skin. Unable to help myself, I sink my teeth into the spot. He writhes and moans beneath me as I mark him for all to see. Carter, Easton, Frankie's horny little friend who thinks she's got a chance at taking a piece of him. They'll know who's been here next time they see him. They'll know who he belongs to.

"Mine," I whisper into his neck. "All fucking mine now."

"Jesus Christ, Nate," he whimpers my name, curling his fingers around the sheet.

"What?"

"Nothing, I just...I never thought this would happen," he admits. "Not in a million years."

"But you wanted it to," I point out, remembering all the times I caught him staring at me while he'd be hanging out at my house, the looks he'd give me when I passed him in the halls at school. "You've always wanted this, haven't you, party boy?"

He flushes but nods, sucking his bottom lip into his mouth.

"Is it better than you thought it'd be?"

"Yes."

"Better than my best friend?" I ask, my lip curling with a snarl as I rock into him faster.

"*Yes*," he rushes out, his voice strangled. "So much better."

"Good boy." I bite down on his earlobe, feeling him shiver against me before I pull my dick out of his ass. "Turn around."

He rolls over onto his back and wraps his legs around my hips, his eyes hooded as he runs his hands up my chest over my shirt. He looks so pretty and desperate, laid out naked and bare beneath me while I'm still fully clothed.

He lifts his ass up, seeking my cock, but I grab his inner thighs and squeeze, pushing him back down into the mattress. Bending over him, I slowly lick his body from the tip of his big dick to the base of his throat, then dip back down to swirl my tongue around the metal bars in his nipples. He moans loudly and grabs the back of my head to hold me down on him, his other hand sneaking up beneath my shirt to rub my abs. Our sweat slicked bodies slide together as he tugs on the hem, impatiently shoving it up my body and over my head. That's probably not a good idea, but I'm too much of an evil bastard to stop him.

Once he's got my shirt off, he tosses it on the floor and spreads his fingers out across my back, hooking them over my shoulders to sink his blunt nails into my flesh. He finds the chain around my neck, just like I knew he would, then freezes, staring at the ring resting on the center of his chest—*his* ring. The ring with my jersey number on it.

His lips part, but no words come out. Then his teary eyes hit mine, and my cock aches with the need to be buried back inside him.

I love it when he cries.

His gaze darkens, and he sneers like he heard me, quickly reaching for the necklace like he's about to rip it off. I snatch his wrists to stop him, pinning them to the sheet above his head. "Don't touch."

"You fucking prick," he rasps through his teeth. "That's mine."

"Not anymore."

Another glare, his breath quickening with a mixture of sorrow and anger. "I hate you."

I chuckle and press my lips to his, smirking when he locks his jaw and turns his head away from me. I release his hands and grab his face, pulling him right back. "Kiss me back or I'll make it worse."

A pained noise leaves his throat, and he opens his mouth, allowing me to suck on his tongue. I reach for my cock and push back into him, our tongues and teeth clashing while I wrap my hand around his neck and use his ass like it's my own little fucktoy.

All the nights I watched him sleep, *this* is what I thought about. Pinning him down and taking what I want from him. Making him pay. Making him break. Fucking with his head and his heart and his body all at once. It's what I crave most in the world. To see him fall apart, piece by piece until there's nothing left.

His entire body shaking, he digs his heels into my ass and his fingers into my sides, encouraging me to take him deeper. Knowing he's close, I slide my hand down between our bodies and wrap it around his dick. He's leaking all over us, moaning at every rock of my hips as I hit his sweet spot over and over again.

"Oh my *God*," he chokes out. "Shit, Nate."

"I know," I say softly, watching his body move as he grinds his ass up, fucking me back. "Fuck. Keep going just like that. You look so hot like this, baby."

He blinks and stares at me for a second, then he grabs my face and kisses me like he's starving for me. His cock pulses in my hand, his ass clamping down on my dick so hard I see stars. He cries out into my mouth and comes all over himself, locking his hands around my neck and his thighs around my waist, clinging to me like he never wants to let go.

I don't know why that's what sets me off, but it does. With our foreheads touching and our moans mixing together, I pull out and get rid of the condom, jerking my release onto his cock and abs, dirtying him up and marking him again.

I run my thumb through our cum and lift it up to his lips, pushing it into his mouth to feed it to him. He licks and sucks on it, swirling his tongue around to ensure he doesn't miss a drop.

"Dirty boy," I tease, pulling my thumb out before kissing him again, swallowing the taste of us both.

I smooth my hand over his outer thigh as we come down, nuzzling into him and keeping our bodies as close as possible. He lets out a long, tired sigh, his smile slipping as he grazes his fingers over the chain on my collarbone. Softening my eyes, I brush his hair from his forehead.

"You still hate yourself?"

He nods, chewing the inside of his cheek.

"Good," I whisper, feeling him tense beneath me. I tighten my fist in his hair and yank his head back, my mouth pressed against the hard line of his jaw. "Now get the fuck out."

CHAPTER SIXTEEN

Xavi

I *'m an idiot.*

Leaning my elbows on the kitchen counter, I hang my head and rake my hands through my hair.

It's been three days. Three days and I can't stop thinking about it. Can't stop replaying the entire night in my mind, trying to pinpoint the moment I lost my head and started falling for his shit.

I should have known better. I *did* know better.

Right up until I didn't.

I try to think about something else—college, Katy, literally *anything* else—but it doesn't work. He's made himself at home deep inside my head and I can't shake him. Pathetic, considering he hasn't said a word to me since I left his room on Friday night. I guess he wasn't lying when he said I was no different than anybody else he fucks. He used me like the easy little slut he called me and then tossed me out on my ass like I mean nothing. *Less* than nothing. It hurt, but that was his plan all along, wasn't it? To hurt me...

And I practically begged him for it.

Feeling nauseous, I close my eyes and run my hand over the hollow pit in my stomach, my other hand cupping the mark he sucked onto my neck. I hate the way my heart beats faster every time I remember it's there, which is all the goddamn time.

A throat clears behind me, and I turn my head to find Frankie standing there, widening her big blue eyes at me like I'm stupid.

"Dude, you're in the way," she says, tilting her head at the coffee machine I'm blocking.

I back up out of her space, and she stretches to grab a mug from the cupboard overhead. She'll be there a while if she's sticking her fat ass out like that to get a reaction out of me. She's probably not doing that though. I'm just pissed because she slept in Nate's bed last night—again—while I spent the night alone in the next room, knocking my head back against the headboard and wishing I was her.

She side-eyes me with a blank look on her face as she sips her coffee, her gaze dropping to my throat. I know I'm being petty, but I don't bother trying to cover it up. If I have to listen to her getting drunk, watching horror movies, and doing who knows what else with him through the wall, she can stand there and look at the hickey her fuck buddy gave me.

She purses her lips, and I'm pretty sure she's trying really hard not to laugh at me, the little bitch. I glare at her, and she rolls her eyes before she starts to say something, but then—

"Frank," Nate says from the doorway, and he *does* look at her ass, his eyes eating up the tight ripped jeans she's wearing. "You ready to go?"

"Go..." She frowns.

A beat passes, and she shakes her head with a knowing little smile on her lips. She finishes her coffee in record time, probably burning her mouth in her haste to go with him, then rinses her mug before putting it in the dishwasher.

Nate won't even look at me. He fucked me so hard that I can't sit down without *getting* hard thanks to the ache in my ass, and now he's acting like I'm invisible, like I'm not standing right here in front of him.

He wasn't exaggerating when he told me I'd feel him for a week. It feels like he beat me up again, only this is better—or worse—because it's not just my face. I can feel him *all over* me. His teeth marks on my neck, the bruises on my hips, the knife he left in my heart...

He and Frankie move to leave, and I just stand here like a dumbass, working my jaw when I catch a glimpse of the chain he's wearing around his neck beneath his t-shirt.

"You're an asshole, you know that?" I call after him, watching his back as he walks away from me. "I can't get you out of my head!"

Oh my God, you idiot.

Cheeks burning, I lean over the kitchen island and drop my face in my hands, wishing the floor would open up and yank me under. When I find the courage to look at him through the gap in my fingers, I find him grinning at me over his shoulder as he pulls his jacket on and follows Frankie outside.

Looks like *in my head* is exactly where he wants to be.

CHAPTER SEVENTEEN

Nate

"You wanna tell me why you're giving me a ride to campus when I've got my truck right there?" Frankie asks, a cigarette pinched between her teeth as she digs around in her pocket for a lighter.

"Just get in the car."

Opening the passenger side door, she climbs inside.

She knows why she's here. I wanted to piss him off, to get under his skin even more than I already am. Plus I just wanted to get her away from him. I don't like it when he's around her too much. It makes me nervous.

Once I'm seated next to her, I reverse out of my spot on the driveway and drive out through the gate. Frankie can't find her lighter, so I grab mine from the inner console and light the cigarette for her, raising a brow when she takes an exaggerated drag and pretends to mind her own business.

A minute passes, and I can't take it anymore. "Aren't you gonna ask?"

"Oh, I'm pretty sure I already know," she says with a grin,

blowing her smoke out the window. "Friday night, after you tossed that pretty cheerleader off your lap and disappeared, you were with him?"

I nod, then frown at the reminder of the way I acted when Carter grabbed Xavi and dragged him away from me. I was so drunk, all the moments leading up to me kissing Xavi are a little fuzzy, but I can't forget the look Carter gave me as he put his hands all over Xavi's body and his mouth by his ear. The look that said, *you want him? Come and get him.*

So fast I probably gave her whiplash, I ditched the girl I was with without a single word or explanation and followed them upstairs. I saw Xavi with his back against the wall and his hands on Carter's chest, so close they were almost kissing. Then I heard them talking about *last time*, and all I saw was red after that.

Glaring at the swollen cut on my knuckle, I flex my hand on the steering wheel, making it split and bleed again.

So worth it.

"Was that the first time?" Frankie asks, pulling me back from the satisfying memory of jamming my fist into Carter's nose.

"You're saying that like it's gonna happen more than once," I mutter, stealing the cigarette from her mouth.

"Boy, who are you kidding?" She laughs, shaking her head as she snatches it right back and passes me my own. "He thinks you fucked me last night."

"I know." I smile slyly, tilting my head to light up.

"Is that why you let me sleep in your bed? To make your little toy jealous?"

"No," I say honestly, turning my head to look at her so she knows I'm serious. "That's just a bonus."

She snorts and rolls her eyes. "Xavi was right."

"What?"

"You are an asshole."

I grin and smoke my cigarette while I drive, using my knee to steer so I can reach for her with my free hand, palm up, spreading my fingers out until she threads hers through mine.

My girl puts on a brave face, and she can fool pretty much anyone into believing she's the carefree, wild party girl she pretends to be, but she's not fooling me. I can see the pain she's been hiding beneath the surface, even more so over the last few days. That's why I let her sleep in my bed. Because even though she'll never admit it, she hates being alone when the demons come for her and try to drag her down.

I've only ever seen one other person look as broken and devastated as she did the night I met her four months ago. I found her on the street in the city, sitting back against the wall of the gay bar I was at with Carter. He was inside, getting spit roasted in a bathroom stall, and she was out there—an eighteen-year-old girl with no cash, no clothes, and no place to go. She told me to fuck off at first, but I eventually got her to talk when she realized I wasn't trying to pay her for sex. She asked if I was gay, being at a gay bar and all, and I hesitated before I told her I was bi, which is something I hardly ever tell anyone. After that, she cracked wide open and told me everything. And when she almost passed out on my shoulder, exhausted after being too afraid to sleep on the sidewalk for three days, I picked her up off the ground and took her home with me. I told myself I only did that because she reminded me of Katy, but that's not exactly true. She reminded me of Xavi more. The way she looked up at me with black makeup and dried-up tears smeared all over her face, but still managed to laugh her way through the pain. The way the cocky little thing still managed to give me attitude despite the shit she'd just been through. She had me wrapped around her little finger from the get go.

"Nate," she says quietly, almost like a warning, and I blink back to the present. We're in the parking lot now, just sitting here in silence with our joined hands in her lap. I run my thumb over hers, and she clears her throat, flexing her fingers to try to get free. "I'm gonna be late to meet Taylor."

"Frankie, stop."

She slumps back in her seat, gnawing on her bottom lip to hide how much it's quivering. "I told you I'm not gonna talk about it again. *Ever* again."

"Why not?"

"Because it hurts," she admits, which quickly stuns me into silence. I don't think I've ever heard her say something so honest before. "Jesus, forget I said that," she whispers. "I just...don't want to, okay?"

"No, it's not okay. You think it's better to keep shoving it down and pretending it doesn't exist?"

She cocks her head at me, narrowing her eyes with a look that makes me shift in my seat.

Fuck. Here we go.

"Why do you hate Xavi?" she finally asks, just throws it right out there, and I clench my jaw, trying to ignore the way my heart is pounding. "You're not gonna tell me, are you?"

"That's different."

"I don't think it is," she quips, yanking her hand away before she climbs out of the car. "If you get to bury your shit, you can back the hell off and let me bury mine."

"Frankie," I call, deflating when she whirls around to look at me. "If you need me..."

"Yeah, yeah. I'll call you." She waves me off, her heels clacking across the ground as she walks toward the coffee shop by the music building.

The urge to chase after her is there, but I force myself to stay put, knowing it's for the best but hating it all the same. I came on too strong with Katy, tried to force her to talk to me and control every move she made to keep her safe, and look where that got me. I lost her to the party boy. I won't make that mistake again.

Now that I'm thinking about him—*again*—I decide to sit in

my car and wait for him to show up like the stalker he's turned me into. I like watching him. I've memorized his schedule so well that I pretty much always know where he is and where he's going next. Apart from when he sneaks away at night for hours at a time. Like the night he got that cut on his thigh. And on Friday after the game, when I got home and he was nowhere to be found. It pisses me off that there are some parts of his life that don't revolve around me, but I can fix that. I just need to figure out where he's going, what he's doing, and who he's doing it with...

He finally pulls up on the other side of the parking lot, and I glare at the back of his helmet, my hand curling into a tight fist on my steering wheel. If I find out he's been sneaking out of *my* house to fuck someone else, I'm gonna choke him until he pukes.

I'm sure he spotted my car on the way in, but he doesn't see me sitting here as he climbs off his bike and takes his helmet off, scrubbing a hand through his hair until it falls over his eyes a bit. I like it when he does that. His hair's a little longer on top than it was a couple years ago, and I hope he doesn't get it cut any time soon. More to hold on to next time I'm sucking his neck and riding his ass from behind.

A light laugh leaves me, and I shake my head, dropping it back against the seat with a soft thud.

And here I was trying to convince myself and Frankie that it's never happening again.

I'm so full of shit.

CHAPTER EIGHTEEN

Nate

Xavi's gone again. It's after ten at night, and I have no clue where he is. At first, I thought maybe he's out getting high, back to his party boy ways, but then I thought better of it. He wouldn't do that. At least, I don't think he would...

Worried I might be wrong, I decided to grab my ball and go blow off some steam on the court in the backyard, but then I stopped as I was passing Xavi's room in the hall. That's how I ended up in here, snooping through all his shit to try to find a clue. There's nothing in here though. Just his clothes and a few textbooks sitting on his desk that look like they've never been touched. He brought next to nothing with him when he moved in. He could pack all his stuff and leave this house in under two minutes if he wanted to.

Slamming the top drawer of his dresser shut, I try to ignore how that thought fills me with enough unease to make me feel sick.

I don't want him to leave.

Which is stupid because when he first got here, I thought that was *all* I wanted. But now...

Jesus, what is wrong with me?

And why does he keep fucking leaving?

Dropping down on the edge of his bed, I glance at the mirror across from me as I roll my basketball between my palms, grinding my teeth when I find Carter watching me from the open doorway.

"Don't."

Ignoring the warning, he pushes himself off the door jamb, stalks inside, and plants himself right in front of me. He's got a black eye, but it hasn't taken away that stupid looking grin of his. "Whatcha doin', bestie?"

"Carter, get out of my face."

"Make me," he says cheerily, muttering, "if you can," while he snatches the ball from my hands.

Before he can make another move, I shoot up to my feet and grab him by his shirt. Even though I just told him to get out of my face, I advance on him until I'm in his, so close our noses are touching. "You've got some fucking nerve."

"Yeah. We know this. Now skip to the part where you forgive me so we can play ball and swap sex stories."

This motherfucker.

"I'm gonna kill you."

"So you keep saying." He chuckles, licking his bottom lip as he stares at mine. "I miss you—"

"Stop playing!" I bite out, so fucking mad at him that my hand is shaking on his chest, my voice cracking with rage and torment when I say, "This isn't a joke. He's the reason my sister is dead, Carter. You *know* how I feel about him and you fucked him anyway."

"Feel about him," he echoes. "As in...how much you hate him, or how much you don't?"

"Fuck you."

"Are you really mad because you feel like I betrayed you and Katy by fucking the enemy?" He tilts his head, bouncing his eyes between mine. "Nah," he whispers before I can say anything, answering the question for me. "You wouldn't have fucked him yourself if that was the reason. You're just jealous I had him first."

That gets me, just like he knew it would, and the next thing I know, we're on the bed and I'm on top of him, straddling him with my hands around his neck. I'm no bigger or stronger than he is. He could shove me off without breaking a sweat if he wanted to, but he doesn't. This is what happens when we fight. He lets me win, lets me get it all out until I start to feel better. I'm not gonna feel better this time though.

"You never *had* him, Carter." I lean over to crowd his space, digging my thumbs into his throat. "He was never yours."

"Does your boy get hard for you when you throw him around like this?" he asks as if I never spoke, taking my left hand to move it down to his dick over his sweats. "I do. You're so hot when you lose your shit."

"Touch him again," I warn, squeezing it hard enough to make him groan. "I'll rip it off and shove it up your ass."

"You kinky fucker."

"You think I'm kidding?"

"Shut up and kiss me," he rasps against my lips, and I pull back a bit, frowning at him like he's crazy.

"What?"

"We both know you're not gonna do shit to me," he says like it's a fact, using our hands to adjust himself. "I'm one of the only people you have left. One of the only ones you haven't driven away yet—"

"I've *tried* to drive you away, you idiot."

"Not hard enough. You're stuck with me, whether you like it or not. So if you're not sitting on my lap to *kill me*, which you're not, you can at least get me off and make it worth my time."

I stare at him for a few seconds, then let him go and sit back on his thighs. "There's something wrong with you."

"You love me."

I don't—not right now, at least—but I can't deny he's right about the rest of it. I can do no wrong in Carter's eyes. It doesn't matter how much of a prick I am to him, he never leaves. I don't think he'll *ever* leave me. I could kill someone in cold blood, and he'd probably high five me on his way to grab a shovel.

"Are we doing this or what?" he asks impatiently, shifting beneath me, and I frown some more.

"C, we haven't fucked since we were in high school."

"Like I said," he teases, leaning up on his elbow to cup the back of my neck. "I miss you."

"Is that why you won't stop making my life hell?" I bend down to meet him halfway, sneering. "Why you slept with the guy I've been obsessed with for years and then brought him here, dangled him in front of me and called him a *gift*, then rubbed it in my face the first chance you got? Because you *miss me* so much?"

"Okay, now you're making me look bad," he grumbles. "I never *planned* on letting you find out. It just happened."

Before I can knock his teeth out, movement in my peripheral catches my attention. Carter and I look over at the door as Xavi walks inside, his steps faltering when he sees us in here. In his room. On *his* bed. His hood is so low that it's almost covering his eyes, but I can tell by the way his face falls that he's assuming we're hooking up, that I brought Carter in here and climbed on top of him just to fuck with him. I can't say I blame him. That's definitely something I would do if I'd thought of it first.

Xavi blinks as if he thinks we might vanish into thin air, then blinks again. "Are you serious right now?"

That sick feeling in my stomach returns. I have no idea why I feel compelled to tell him I didn't plan this. Just as I'm about to do just that, Carter opens his big mouth and makes it fifty times worse.

"Baby boy," he teases, gesturing to the narrow space between his body and mine. "You want in on this? I'll let you ride his dick if you give me your mouth."

I shove him back down by his chest, and Xavi works his jaw, forcing a smirk that feels more like a death glare burning two holes into the center of my face. Dropping his phone and keys on the dresser, he walks toward us like he's ready to go for it, and I glare right back at him. "Don't even th—"

Carter smacks me in the ribs to shut me up, whispering, "Relax. He doesn't have the balls."

"I wouldn't be so sure about that, C," I mutter under my breath, rolling my eyes when Xavi kneels up on the bed.

His leg comes over Carter's body in front of me. He straddles him, his back to my chest and his ass on my dick. Carter gapes up at him, and I roll my lips together to hide my sudden amusement. I don't think I've ever seen Carter speechless before, but there it is.

Taking Xavi's waist with one hand, I lift the other one to lower his hood, but he snatches his head away before I can do it, not letting me touch him.

Brat.

Grabbing him harder this time, I go for his hood again and pull his head back on my shoulder, my mouth on his neck as I rake my fingers through his hair. His mouth opens with a silent moan, and he shivers before he can stop it, melting for me when I graze his hip bone with my thumb.

Yeah. He can be pissed all he wants. He's still mine.

"You think you're funny?" I ask, my lips playing with the hickey just above his collarbone.

"What? He offered," he rasps, putting his hands behind his back to feel for my cock. Finding it hard and ready for him, he wraps his fingers around the base through my sweats, squeezing it and making me jerk. "This is mine, yeah?"

Fucking hell.

"All right, you little slut, we get your point." I lock my arm around him and lift him off Carter, setting him down on his feet once I'm standing.

"Dude, we totally could have won that game if you weren't such a pussy," Carter complains.

I ignore him, watching Xavi as I tuck my dick under my waistband. "Where have you been?"

He gawks at me, looking from my face to my crotch, then back to my face. "Why?" he asks suspiciously.

"Just answer the question," I grit out, and he frowns like I've gone and lost my damn mind.

"No."

I step toward him, and he flinches, swallowing when his back hits the wall next to his nightstand.

"Why are you talking like that?" I ask, my irritation growing as I study his full, pink lips.

"Like what?"

"Like your tongue's too big for your mouth."

"What's with all the questions?"

Huffing out a breath through my nose, I decide to change tactics because this clearly isn't working.

Resting my arm on the wall above his head, I carefully touch his chin with my knuckles, playing as nice as I can with him while I run my thumb over his lip ring. "Tell me where you were."

He tries to keep his mouth shut, but it doesn't work. This is the first time I've given him any attention in days, and I think he likes it, *craves* it just as much as I do.

"I went to a tattoo shop in the city."

That trips me up, and I search the few parts of his skin not covered by his clothes. "You got a tattoo?"

"No."

"Then why the fuck were you at a tattoo shop?" I'm losing my temper again, but I can't help it.

The boy's infuriating.

Rolling his eyes, he opens his mouth and sticks his tongue out, showing me the new piercing there. My lips part, and I feel my dick getting even harder, my eyes darkening as I examine the little silver ball.

"That's hot," Carter says, and we turn our heads to where we left him on the bed.

"Get out."

"I'm good right here." He grins at me, resting back on the pillows with his arms folded beneath his head.

Not in the mood to deal with him right now, I pretend he's not there and look at Xavi again. My thumb's still resting on his lip, and it keeps inching up like it wants to touch his tongue. "Why'd you get this?"

He hesitates before he answers, only for half a second, but I catch him. "Because I wanted it."

"Why?" I repeat, praying for patience I don't have when I hear Carter chuckling beside us. Sighing, I ask, "What are you laughing at?"

"You little shit." He playfully shakes his head at Xavi, sitting up on the edge of the bed before he decides to answer me. "You realize he can't suck your dick for a month now."

"What?" I ask, and Xavi seals his lips together, failing to hide his amusement.

"Not until it heals. I asked."

"You *asked* the guy how long it'll be before you can suck dick?"

"So what?" He shrugs. "He doesn't know me."

"You never tell anyone you're gay."

"Apart from all the guys I fuck..." he adds, raising his brows as if that should be obvious.

"What do you mean *all* the guys?"

"I..." He cringes. "That came out wrong."

Carter laughs for real this time, his shoulders bouncing up and down as he lowers his face into his hands, clearly enjoying every minute of this. I'm about three seconds from shoving both their heads through the goddamn wall.

"Why are you so mad—Wait, you're leaving?" Xavi asks, the disappointment written all over his face as he watches me pick up my ball off the floor.

Grabbing Carter by the arm, I pull him off the bed and shove him into the hall ahead of me, slamming Xavi's door shut on my way out. Scrubbing my hand over my face, I wait a few seconds, my shoulders dropping when I don't hear the sound of him locking me out.

Goddamn him.

"You forgive me now, right?" Carter asks, grinning when I lift my gaze to his.

"No."

"Hey, Nate?" he calls as I walk away, and I close my eyes as I stop, already regretting my decision to listen to whatever he has to say. "Remember that guy I told you about a few months ago? The sexy little twink with the big dick and the nipple piercings? That was Xavi."

Spinning the ball in my hands, I turn around and throw it at the side of his head. Easton chooses that exact moment to walk around the corner, his eyebrows shooting up as he catches the ball on the rebound. I can tell by the look on his face that he heard what Carter said, but he wisely doesn't ask questions. Instead, he looks at Carter, who's holding his temple and laughing so hard he almost pisses himself.

Who needs enemies, right?

I TRIED NOT to be here tonight, but I couldn't stay away from him. Not when he made a point to leave the door open for me after weeks of locking me out.

Sitting on his bed next to him, I roll one of his cigarettes between my fingertips, copying what I saw him doing in the backyard yesterday while I was watching him through the kitchen window. It confused me when he first got here, but I know why he does it now, why he carries these around with him but never smokes them. It clicked the morning after I fucked him, after he told me why he got sober.

Because I deserve it. Because it hurts more...

Snapping the cigarette in half, I toss the broken pieces on his nightstand, resting my elbows on my knees as I turn my head to look at him. His hair's still a little damp from his shower, and it smells like coconuts of all things, making it nearly impossible for me to resist leaning over and pushing my nose into the strands. He's wearing the tightest pair of Calvins I've ever seen and one of those sexy little crop tops, the curve of his back and ass exposed where he's got the blanket wedged between his legs. It's freezing in here, but it seems he doesn't care.

He knew I'd come.

He wants me to be here. To see him like this.

Just as I think it, he stretches, pushing his ass out even further. I know his game, so I let him do his thing for a few more seconds before I decide to burst his bubble.

"I know you're awake."

He freezes, then asks, "How?"

"Your breathing sounds different," I murmur. "Faster."

He makes an effort to slow it down, turning his head my way when I don't say anything else. Silence stretches between us, and I can tell it's killing him. He's getting impatient, his toes wiggling on the sheet beside me.

"You watch me sleep," he finally says. "Steal my cigarettes... Snoop through my shit..."

"I touch you sometimes too."

"What? Where?"

"Wherever I want."

"Dude, that's kinda creepy."

"I told you to lock your door," I remind him. "Three times. It's not my fault you don't listen."

"I didn't say I didn't like it."

I raise a brow at that, a small smile touching my lips before I can stop it.

He's such a freak.

Unable to help myself, I take his thigh and pull him down the bed, making his shirt ride up even further. He opens his legs without having to be told, and I crawl on top of him, my hands grazing his sides as I admire his outfit. "Did you put this on for me?"

"Yes," he admits, his breath hitching when I run my finger over the crease between his hip and his thigh.

"Did you think about me in the shower?" I ask, and he nods, looking damn near delirious as he moves his hands up to my shoulders. "But you didn't get off," I guess, not missing how hard he is or the wet spot on the front of his briefs. "Is that why you're leaking all over yourself when I haven't even touched it yet?"

He moans quietly, and I hook his leg around my waist and drop my lips to his neck, my jaw ticking when he pulls himself away from me like he did earlier.

I hate that.

"What were you and Carter doing in here tonight?"

"Fighting," I tell him, grabbing him by his hair and pulling him back.

"About what?"

"You."

He shuts up for a second, and even though I can't see his expression with my face under his jaw, I can tell he's smiling before he mutters, "Didn't look like you were fighting to me."

I chuckle and lick his neck, enjoying the way his pulse is thumping against my tongue. "I was in here trying to figure out where you were, okay? He saw me and thought it'd be fun to piss me off. That's all it was."

"But if I hadn't walked in..."

"Nothing would have happened," I say honestly, unsure why I'm even telling him all this. "Carter and I haven't hooked up since before we moved in here."

"Why not?"

"Because I don't like him like that."

"Do you..." He clears his throat, hesitating as if he's afraid to ask. "Do you like me...like that?"

"I don't *like you*, period," I grumble, spreading my fingers out and smoothing my hand over his outer thigh. "Seeing your face... Even thinking your name makes me wanna hit something. I hate you, Xavi."

"Then why are you making out with my neck right now?" he asks, and I close my eyes because *fuck*, I don't know. "What are you doing here, Nate?"

I groan helplessly and move my lips up to his jaw, sticking with honesty. "I wanna break you."

Just as I'm about to give him another hickey, he grabs me by the neck and pushes me away with more strength than I knew he possessed, stopping me again. "Is Frankie in your bed right now?"

"No."

He stares up into my eyes, then swallows before he whispers, "Do it then. Break me."

"Yeah?"

"Yeah."

"Can I kiss you?" I ask, and he shakes his head.

"Not with tongue."

I'll just have to kiss him everywhere else then.

I let him choke me a bit while I start with his lip ring, confused as to why my dick likes it so much. Piercings don't really do it for me on anyone else, and neither does a hand around my neck, but when it comes to Xavi...I'm so hard right now it hurts.

I graze my lips over his cheek and then back down to his jaw, licking the scar I gave him before I move up to his chin. "Show me again."

He opens his mouth, and I reach for the lamp on his nightstand, flicking the switch so I can see it better.

"Tell me you didn't get this just to drive me crazy." I lean over him to lick the seam of his lips, gently nipping them with my teeth.

"I didn't," he insists. "It's not about you."

"Whatever you say," I mumble into his mouth.

Maybe he's telling the truth, but I know he's hiding *something* because his eyes keep shifting away every time I talk about it. I don't care though—or at least I *shouldn't* care—so I decide to let it be.

Slinking down his body, I move on to the piercings in his nipples. I suck one into my mouth and play with the other with my fingers, grinning up at him when he moans again.

"You like that?"

He nods, and I bite him harder, clamping my teeth around it until he shoves his fist into the bed. Once I've got him writhing beneath me, I slowly kiss my way down to his navel and run my lips over the soft skin just above his waistband. His dick is poking me in my chest, but I still don't touch it, smoothing my hands over his thighs, then down his legs to his ankles.

"I thought you wanted to break m-me," he stutters, his hips automatically bucking up into my face. "Why are you taking so long?"

Glancing up at him again, I breathe a laugh and drop my face into his hip to hide it.

Why does he think I'm doing this?

"Turn around," I say, and he lets out a sigh of...relief, I think, pulling his brows in when I shake my head at him. "I'm not fucking you, party boy."

"Then why...?"

"Because I want you to," I say simply, grabbing his waist and flipping him over onto his stomach. "Bend over for me so I can eat this pretty ass."

He curses and shoves his face into the sheet, moving up to his knees and arching his back. I run my hand over his spine and then down to his ass, pulling his Calvins down to the tops of his thighs. He starts to move like he's expecting me to take them off, but I smack him to keep him still.

"They stay on."

Another curse, louder this time when I spread his cheeks with my thumbs. Kneeling behind him, I gather the spit in my mouth and let it drip down to his hole, lowering my head to spread it around with my tongue. He sucks in a breath and holds it, reaching for the pillow above his head and pulling it to his chest.

"Don't even think about moaning into that," I say, opening my mouth and flicking the tip of my tongue over his opening. "I wanna hear you."

"Jesus Christ. Nate..."

"What?"

"You're a fucking tease."

"Says the boy who dressed up like this and waited for me to come play with him," I mutter, spitting on him again before I sink my tongue into his hole.

He whimpers when I start fucking him with it. Groaning into the smooth, hot flesh under my mouth, I wet my finger before I ease it inside him next to my tongue. His dick is still trapped inside his underwear, and when he tries to reach for it, I smack his wrist and lock his arms behind his back, making him faceplant.

"Sit up," I say, and he whines as he does it, letting me position him until his legs are spread wide and his ass cheeks are resting on his feet. "That's good. Now lean forward a bit and rub your dick on the bed."

He rolls his hips, and I go back to his hole, letting him ride my tongue while I twist my finger back inside. He cries out when I find his prostate, then add another one, his toes curling up tight as his movements get a little more frantic and less controlled.

"Keep going," I urge, grabbing his ass to help him grind his cock on the sheet. "Harder, baby."

"Shit, Nate, please," he chokes out, his thighs shaking as he tries to stop himself. "I don't wanna come like this." He sounds desperate, like it's too much and not enough all at once.

Like he doesn't want it to be over yet...

"You wanna come with my dick in your ass?" I ask, curling my fingers inside him and licking between them.

"Yes," he gasps. "I want it."

Reaching for his nightstand, I open the drawer and grab the lube I saw in here earlier. I toss a condom on the bed next to him, and he pauses for a second before he snatches it up and tears it open.

"Take my dick out."

Quick to obey, he reaches back and slides his hands into my sweats, groaning when he realizes I'm freeballing. "Fuck, Nate, that's so hot," he says, wrapping his warm fingers around the base of my cock.

Kissing the back of his head, I start fingering his ass with lube, watching him roll the condom on me before I squirt some into his open palm. With both hands wrapped around my dick, he gets me wet while I do the same to him, holding on to his hip while I run my nose over the hair at the back of his neck. He smells so sweet, and it pisses me off. Xavi Hart isn't *sweet*. He's poisonous.

I'm not finished with him yet, but it seems he's done waiting, rubbing the tip of my dick over his hole next to my fingers. "I'm ready, Nate."

I don't think he is, but if he wants it to hurt, which I'm pretty sure he does, then so be it.

Knocking his hands away, I pull my fingers out, line myself up with his ass, and push inside. He sounds like he's in pain as he grunts through his teeth, but he doesn't ask me to stop. Instead, he sits on my dick until he's got me balls deep, breathing hard and heavy as he drops his head back on my shoulder. "Take your shirt off."

"Why?"

"I wanna feel you."

I take it off and chuck it on the floor, pulling him back to my chest as I roll my hips up into him. I know he can feel the ring on my chain scraping along his skin, but he doesn't say anything about it. He takes it like a good boy, mouth open as his eyes roll back in his head. Holding him by his throat, my free hand finds his abs and travels up to his chest, the tips of my fingers brushing the hem of his crop top. He moans loudly when I pinch his nipple, holding my wrists to keep my hands where they are.

"Look at you," I rasp, turning his face toward the mirror across from us. "Such a needy little whore for me."

He blinks at himself, then tears his eyes away with a look I can't read, grabbing the back of my head to pull my mouth down to his neck.

"You want more of my marks on you?" I ask, running my tongue over the spot.

He nods fast. "Make it hurt," he reminds me, making us both groan when I sink my teeth into him.

He jerks in my hold, his entire body shuddering as I suck the bruise into the side of his throat.

"Keep still," I mumble into his flesh.

He forces himself to stop moving, and I do it again. I'm not nice about it, biting him so hard I'm close to breaking the skin, marking him five times in a zigzag shape from his jaw to his collarbone. He's had enough by the time I'm finished, squeezing his eyes shut as he pulls away and cups his hand over his neck. I pry his fingers off to look at my handiwork, tilting his face up until our lips are touching and we're sharing the same air.

"Fuck, baby, you look so pretty," I whisper, possessively grazing my thumb over the hickey beneath his ear. "You look like mine."

"Don't," he pleads, and I cock my head, watching him look up at me with sad eyes and a fragile heart. "Don't make me fall for you."

I couldn't stop the smile curling my lips if I wanted to. I shove his head away, and he falls forward on his hands, whimpering when I grab his hips with a punishing grip and fuck my dick into him as hard as I can. "Is this what you want?"

"Yes."

I give it to him, with nothing but the sounds of his cries and my hips slapping his ass filling the room. He's moaning so loud I'm sure the entire house can hear him, but that only makes me smile more and fuck him faster.

"Get back up here," I say, grabbing his hair to pull him up when he takes too long to move.

He winces when I tip his head back, my mouth on his ear as I grab his dick through his underwear. I squeeze it through the soft fabric, and he cries out again. "Fuck. Nate..."

"What?" I ask, one hand on his waist as I grind into him from behind, pushing him into my fist and jerking him off hit for hit. "You ready to come for me?"

He's coming before I even finish the question, his ass squeezing my cock while he soaks the inside of his Calvins. I groan into his hair, and he falls back into me, heavier now that he's resting his dead weight on my chest. His cheeks are bright red and his eyes are watering. He looks *wrecked*, and it does something to me I'd rather not think about.

Shoving him forward one last time, his head hits the bed as I pull out and get rid of the condom. I spread his cheeks with my fingers and watch my cum shoot out over his crease and hole, biting my lip as I spread it up and down with the tip. The urge to push it into him is there, but I don't because that would be dumb.

Don't let him make you dumb, for fuck's sake.

Letting out a breath, I grab the waistband of his briefs, pull it up over his ass, and snap it into place, tapping his hip before I climb off the bed.

"Are you gonna kick me out again?" he croaks into the sheets, and I chuckle as I put my dick away.

"Xavi, we're in your room."

"Oh yeah." He lifts his head, squinting at the light on the nightstand before he looks around.

"Are you good?" I ask, amused, using my shirt to wipe the sweat from my neck and abs.

"Do you care?" he mutters, but then he cringes and drops his face on his forearms. "Don't answer that."

My eyes run over the length of his body, and I step back over to the bed before I can talk myself out of it. I gently roll him onto his back, my fingers brushing his inner thigh. "What were you doing the night you got this cut right here?"

He frowns, his eyelashes fluttering as he stares at me like I've grown two heads. "I...can't tell you."

"What about the night of my game?" I ask, moving his hair from his eyes. "I came home and you weren't here."

"Were you looking for me?"

"Were you with someone else?"

"No."

I watch him for a moment, searching his face for the lie, but I don't think there is one. Trailing my fingers over his abs, I stop to draw a circle on his navel. "Don't ever let me catch you with someone else."

His frown deepens as he watches me straighten up, grabbing

the condom off the bed before I toss it into the trash can in the bathroom. When I get back, he looks like he's trying to force his body to move, scooting to the edge of the bed, then standing and lifting his top like he's about to strip off and head for the shower.

"Don't," I say, and he lets his arms fall to his sides.

So obedient when he wants to be.

"Don't shower tonight."

"Why?"

I take his chin between my thumb and forefinger, pulling him in and speaking over his lips. "I wanna go to bed knowing you're sleeping in our cum."

I kiss him once, softly, closing his gaping mouth with my knuckle before I move to leave.

CHAPTER NINETEEN

Xavi

"How do you look like that when you never stop eating?" I ask Easton, watching him damn near inhale the breakfast in front of him like it's his last meal.

"It's called the gym, emo boy," he answers around a mouthful of pancakes, cocking a brow as he runs his eyes over my form. "You should try it sometime."

"Fuck you." I chuckle, and he shakes his head.

"I'm kidding," he says, his eyes lingering on my body as he adds another piece of bacon to my plate. "You don't need to go to the gym. You look good as you are."

I feel my cheeks heat up but try my hardest to act like I don't notice his attention on me. Same way I'm pretending not to notice the angry amber eyes burning into me from across the island.

Nate cooked breakfast this morning—something he does a lot when he gets up at the crack of dawn. I was planning on staying away like I usually do while he eats with his friends, but then Easton dragged me in here, sat me down next to him, and demanded I eat the food he put in front of me. I thought Nate would put me in my place and tell me to get lost, but he didn't. He just looked up at us from his phone, gaze zeroed in on Easton's hand on my shoulder, and I'm pretty sure it's been there ever since.

After he left me in my room last week, he went right back to ignoring me. I hated it. But now that he's looking again—that he's *glaring* at me again—I think I'd rather go back to being invisible. Honestly, I don't know *what* I want and it's making my head spin.

"Yeah?" I mutter to Easton, using my fork to play with the pile of food on my plate that keeps getting bigger. "Then why are you trying to fatten me up?"

"I'm not trying to fatten you up." He laughs. "Dude, you don't eat. I know because the only time I ever see you put something in your mouth is when I feed it to you."

Jesus Christ.

Does he really not realize how hot it sounds when he says things like that?

Without thinking, I risk a glance at Nate to check his reaction, immediately wishing I hadn't when I catch the look in his eyes. I can't tell whether he's pissed at me, pissed at Easton, or just pissed, period. He's so hard to read sometimes.

"I eat...the muffins from the coffee shop on campus," I say, my face burning when Easton grins at me like I'm adorable.

Seriously, Xav. Be more awkward.

"Sure you do, man." Easton carries on eating, and I force myself to do the same just to have something to do with my hands.

Nate pushes himself up from his seat, and I follow him with my eyes, my shoulders hiking up when he comes up behind me and puts his mouth near my ear. "You know he's fucking with you," he whispers so only I can hear him.

"Fuck off," I whisper back. "No, he's not."

He's not, right?

I feel his lips curl up into a smirk before he wraps his big hand around the back of my neck, his fingers brushing the hickeys there before he moves away. My shoulders sink back down at the loss of his touch, and I kick myself for wanting it back.

"You should come to the game tonight," Easton says to me, and I clear my throat, rubbing the spot where Nate's hand just was.

I'm planning on going anyway, but Nate doesn't know that, and I'd like to keep it that way.

Luckily, I don't have to think of something to say before Frankie walks in, dressed in black leggings and a hoodie that's four sizes too big for her. The ball cap she's wearing covers half her face. "Hey, guys," she says on her way to the coffee machine.

I frown, trying to get a better look at the mark I thought I just saw on her mouth. I glance at the boys to check if they saw it too, but I don't think they did. I should probably mind my own business, but it's too late for that now. I'm already looking at Nate, and he's looking at me, pulling his brows in when I tap my lip and jerk my head at Frankie.

She's bleeding, I mouth, and he blinks, narrowing his eyes at the back of her head.

"Frankie."

"Yeah?"

"Look at me," he says, and she sighs, turning around to glare at me instead of him.

"You little snitch."

I flip her off, and she snorts, rolling her eyes when Nate steps toward her and takes the hat off her head. She's got a cut on her bottom lip and another just above her eyebrow. They're not that deep, and she looks fine to me, but he still looks mad as hell.

I know it's messed up, but I can't help the way my heart sinks at how protective he is of her.

"Who the fuck—"

"Nate, relax," she cuts him off, snatching her hat to shove it back on her head. "I had a fight with my sister last night. It's not a big deal. Trust me, she looks worse than I do right now."

He stares at her, and they seem to have some type of silent conversation that I can't hear, another thing that has my insides twisting with jealousy.

I hate her.

"You have a sister?" Easton asks, wiggling his brows to lighten the mood. "Is she as hot as you are?"

Frankie lets out a light laugh and shakes her head at him, turning around to grab herself a mug. "Yeah, I guess. But she's a raging cunt. You boys should be thankful you don't have sisters."

Easton's grin slips as his focus drops to his plate, and I cut my eyes to Nate's, just in time to watch him swallow and look down at the tiles beneath his feet, his hands white-knuckling the counter he's leaning back on. I'm just about to ask Frankie what the fuck is wrong with her, but she doesn't seem to notice the tension brewing between us while she jabs a few buttons on the coffee machine.

Does she really not know about Katy?

She starts talking to Easton about the game tonight, and I stand up to scrape my plate and rinse it at the sink. Placing it into the dishwasher, I get as close to Nate as possible without making it obvious.

"Nate?" I ask quietly.

"Shut up, Xavi."

"But I just—"

"I said shut up," he hisses, glaring vicious daggers at me as he bumps his shoulder into mine. "Don't come tonight," he grumbles, then grabs his keys from the side next to my hip and heads for the door.

CHAPTER TWENTY

Nate

I'm playing like shit tonight. We're down by six when we should be *up* by that much, at least. And we probably would be if I hadn't fucked us all over at the end of the first half by fouling Jackson Banks, the other team's shooting guard and my biggest rival. He was being a mouthy asshole, and I lost it.

I'm *losing* it here.

Coach is yelling, *again,* but I ignore him and catch the ball Easton passes to me. Getting into position, I shoot my shot from the three point line...and miss it.

"Shake it off," Easton murmurs as he passes, and I nod fast, scrubbing my hands over my head as I try to get it back in the game I used to live for.

It's a weird feeling, both loving and hating something so much. This stadium used to be my sanctuary, the one place where nothing could touch me and all my worries went away, but now it feels...tainted. I haven't felt at peace on this court in over two years.

Every time I look at the stands, I remember the look on Katy's face the night I won my first championship back in freshman year. She hated me the way little sisters hate their big brothers most of the time, but in here, she was my biggest fan. She was so proud of me when I won that game, I wasn't even mad that Xavi got to be the one to tell her. I'm no lip reader, but the second I made that winning shot, I'm pretty sure the first words out of his mouth were, "He did it. Holy shit, he did it."

I smiled right at him before I knew what I was doing, and the grin he hit me back with was the biggest I've ever seen on him. I quickly glared to save face, and he laughed and bit his lip before he wrapped his arm around Katy's neck and wiped her happy tears away.

I hated him being here at first. I told Katy a million times to leave his ass at home, but she was a stubborn little menace and never listened to me. Besides, it's not like anyone else would have done what he did for her. My parents said bringing her here was a waste of time. *What's the point? She can't see you. Everyone stares at her and it's embarrassing.* Katy and I never cared though, and neither did Xavi. Every game, he'd bring her and be her eyes, never taking his off me as he recounted every move I made. I never told anyone—I don't think I even admitted it to myself at the time—but I started to like it after a while. Even though he was mostly here for her, it kind of felt like he was here for *me* a little bit too.

But then Katy died, and everything went to shit.

Every time I play and my little sister isn't right here with me, it rips my heart out all over again.

"Grayson!" Coach shouts, and I cringe, watching Jackson hop up and sink the ball into the hoop.

Carter signals for a time-out as soon as he steals the ball back, and I breathe a sigh of relief even though I know Coach is about to rip me a new one.

The buzz of the stadium fills my ears, setting my teeth on edge while I receive the ass-chewing I deserve. I try to tune out the noise of the crowd like I always do, but I can't help the way I keep peeking up at the stands every ten seconds.

Coach shakes my shoulder, and I nod even though I'm not listening to a damn word he's saying.

He's not here, you idiot.

Get him out of your head.

Just then, a fight between two frat guys breaks out in the crowd, and I do a double take, squinting at the boy in the hoodie sitting at the far end of the back row. He winces and drops his head, trying to hide his face from me, but I already saw him.

"Little fucker," I whisper.

Carter tosses the ball at my abs and pushes me back onto the court. "Ignore him."

"Who's the guy?" Jackson taunts me.

Carter shakes his head before I can say anything, pushing me again. "Him too."

We get back to the game, and I try to do as he said, but it's not easy when I can *feel* Xavi watching me. It's distracting, fighting the urge to look up there.

Time goes on, and it only gets worse when Jackson scores again, putting us down by nine with two and a half minutes left on the clock.

"Where's your head at tonight, fag?" Jackson asks, smirking and sticking his arms out as he backs away from me. "Sure as shit ain't on this court."

He's getting on my last nerve, but I force my mouth to stay shut because he's nothing but a spineless little punk, calling me a *fag* like it's gonna rattle me.

There are rumors going around about me being bi, but no one really knows for sure because I've never confirmed or denied it. I've never let anyone catch me with a guy because my dad would flip his shit if he found out I've been broadcasting it.

"Seriously, Grayson." Jackson keeps talking, pushing his luck.

"I mean, you suck anyway, but I haven't seen you suck *this* bad since your dumb sister accidentally offed hers—"

My feet move before he's even finished, my vision blurring at the edges as I grab him by his jersey. I'm about to smash my head into his, but then Carter steps between us to get in my face, walking me back by pushing his forehead into mine. "Stop letting him get to you," he growls. "You *know* he's only doing it t—" He stops and studies every inch of my face, whispering, "Jesus, did you drink today?"

"Get off me, Carter." I shove him back, averting my eyes when he glares like he's about to beat my ass.

"Yeah, Carter." Jackson laughs as he bounces around us, tipping his chin up in Xavi's direction. "You're makin' his pretty little boyfriend nervous."

"Nate!" Carter shouts, but he's not fast enough to stop me this time. I'm already punching Jackson between the eyes, fighting against the arms around me as I try my hardest to get a second hit in. "Fuck!"

The next thing I know, every guy on my team is surrounding me, pulling me back to keep me away from Jackson. Carter's shouting something in my face, but I'm looking up at the stands, watching Xavi duck out through the tunnel while the ref yells at Coach to get my ass off the court.

I FEEL numb as I climb out of my car, shoving my frozen hands into my pockets while I follow the dark path that leads to my sister's grave.

I haven't been up here in a while. I used to come whenever I could, but then I stopped. Not because I don't want to see her, but because every time I do, all I feel is rage. I rarely feel sad when I think about Katy. I'm not sad she's dead. I'm livid.

I know it's not right, but I can't help it. The fact that she's gone when she shouldn't be...that I'll never see her again, or hear her laugh, or listen to her sing...it makes me want to smash everything in sight until it's all as broken as I feel.

Standing a few feet away from her headstone, I stare at the back of Xavi's head. He's sitting cross-legged on the ground in front of her, picking at the grass while he whispers something I can't hear.

I knew he was here because I'm parked next to his bike, but looking at him now, I can't stop thinking about the last time we were here together.

It's Katy's birthday next week, meaning it's been almost two years to the day. She would have been twenty. She would have been living with us at the house by now, halfway through her sophomore year at Hawthorne, probably getting into as much trouble as possible and driving me crazy.

I dream about it sometimes—a life where she's not dead—but then I wake up, and I wish I hadn't. Just for a minute, I wish I was dead too so I wouldn't have to feel the loss of her and the pain that comes with it.

I think Xavi knows I'm behind him, but he doesn't move or look back at me. He just waits, like he's expecting me to pick him up and kick his ass.

Maybe I should do that. It would probably make me feel a hell of a lot better, but I don't. I watch him instead, only just realizing my hand has crept its way up my chest, my fingers subconsciously brushing the ring that gave him the scar on his jaw.

Nate

I don't know how long I've been standing here, not moving or saying anything, just watching him—*staring* at him, unable to tear my eyes away from the person I hate most in this world.

Katy was supposed to turn eighteen today. We were supposed to go to the beach like we always do, and then I was planning on surprising her by taking her to the Lakers game in LA. Instead, I'm spending her birthday at the cemetery, glaring at the boy passed out face down in front of her headstone.

It's dark and raining, and he's lying on the ground on his stomach, using a bottle of vodka as a pillow, wearing just a filthy pair of ripped jeans and a black t-shirt that's stuck to his skin. His nails are painted black, but they're chipped and his cuticles are ripped to shit, probably where he's bitten them so much he's made them bleed. I've watched him enough over the years to know that's something he does when he's anxious.

I've fantasized about killing him so many times in the few weeks since my sister died, but now that he's right here in front of me, vulnerable and alone, killing him seems to be the last thing on my mind. Maybe it's because I'm drunk, but all I can think about is how sad and lonely he looks down there. Pathetic, like a broken toy no one wants to play with anymore. It makes my heart race with...I don't know what it is. All I know is that it doesn't make me feel as good as it should.

My phone vibrates in my hand, and I turn it over, only taking my eyes off Xavi to glance down at the screen. Carter's calling me again, but I send him to voicemail, just like I've been doing for the last...*Jesus, have I really been standing out here in the rain for an hour?*

> **CARTER**
> Nate, come on. I'm getting worried.

I snort at that, using my numb, freezing cold thumbs to type out a reply.

> **NATE**
> Since when do you worry about anyone but yourself?

> **CARTER**
> That's exactly my point! You're spiraling and it's making me nervous. I don't like it.
>
> Will you just come home? Please?
>
> Back to ignoring me, huh?
>
> Fuck this. I'm coming to get you.

> **NATE**
> Don't.

He doesn't respond, and I sigh, knowing he'll drive all the way down here if I don't give him a reason not to.

> **NATE**
> Xavi's here.

The phone rings almost as soon as I hit send, and I reluctantly hit the answer button. "What?"

"He's with you?" Carter asks. "At the cemetery?"

"No—I mean, yeah, he..." I lick my lips, looking down at the wet hair falling over Xavi's eyes. "He's asleep."

"What do you mean he's asleep?"

"I mean *he's asleep*, Carter." I roll my eyes, flicking a hand at Xavi even though he can't see him. "He's passed out on the ground in front of Katy's grave."

"Did you knock him out?"

"No," I grumble. "I found him like this."

Carter falls silent for a moment, then asks, "Dude, are you sure he's not dead?"

Shit. I hadn't even thought of that.

Crouching next to his body, I roll him onto his back and press two fingers to the side of his neck, not feeling anything at first. My heart starts beating wildly inside my chest, and I drop my phone, quickly lifting his head up and slapping his cheek. His eyelashes flutter, and I let out a heavy breath.

Fucking hell.

"Shit, Nate, is he dead?" Carter's low voice reminds me he's still there, and I pick up the phone.

"No," I mutter, doing my best to sound disappointed by the fact. "Don't come here. I'll be home soon."

"Wait—"

I hang up and shove the phone into my coat pocket. A rain droplet rolls over Xavi's puffy bottom lip. Still holding his head in my hand, I catch it with my thumb and wipe it away, ignoring the sudden urge to do the same thing with my tongue.

"Xavi," I say, taking his jaw and shaking it. "Get up."

His forehead crinkles, and he slowly cracks his eyes open, wincing like he's in pain as he drops down on his back. "Fucking lovely," he rasps when he sees it's me. "What are you doing here?"

"This is *my* sister's grave, you little prick."

"What?" he asks, looking around like he's confused.

Fresh out of patience, I grab a fistful of his hair and pull him up to his knees. I yank his head back and force him to look up at me, waiting for his eyes to hit mine. "I told you not to come back here."

"Yeah, I remember," he says boredly, like my presence has no effect on him at all. "You gonna kick my ass and make me leave like you did at Katy's funeral?"

Nostrils flaring, I shake my head and shove his away from me. "Just go, Xavi. Go crawl back into the hole you crawled out of and fucking stay there."

"You know what? Fuck you," he slurs, brave enough to look me dead in the eye. "You don't get to decide who comes here and who doesn't."

"The fuck I don't. *I'm* her brother, not you."

"Nobody gives a shit, asshole," he fires back. "She'd rather have me here than you and you know it. She hated y—"

I don't even realize I'm about to punch him until it's already happening, until I'm on top of him with one hand holding him down by his chest and the other slamming into his face. My blood runs hot through my veins as I hit him again, saying goodbye to what little self-control I had left.

I hate him.

I hate his cocky, no-fucks-to-give attitude and his big mouth. I hate the fact that he can never keep it shut and just do what I tell him to do.

Most of all though, I hate that he's right.

She chose him over me, night after night, over and over again, and there was nothing I could do about it.

My hands and his face are covered in blood, his eyes closed as he lies limp beneath me.

Fuck. I didn't mean to hit him that hard.

Still straddling his waist, I growl his name, pulling him up by his shirt when he doesn't respond. Just when I think he's really dead this time, he lets out a pained noise that turns into a breathy laugh, his pearly white teeth bloody, his head bobbing around on his shoulders as he grabs the vodka from the ground beside us.

"What are you *laughing* at?"

"You," he answers, tossing the cap away before he tips it back to swallow a sip. "You can hit me all you want, Nathaniel," he teases, my full name rolling off his tongue like silk. "I can't feel a damn thing."

My teeth clench, and I swallow as I stare into his swollen, bloodshot eyes. "Xavi, what are you on?"

"What do you care?" he asks, a sloppy, lopsided grin on his mouth as he runs his hand up over my chest, his eyes following the path he's taking with his fingers. "You worried I'm gonna OD?"

I snatch his wrist and glare at him. "You think that's funny? What the fuck is wrong with you?"

He smirks, shrugs, and then takes another sip, choking on the vodka in his mouth when I steal the bottle from his hand. Setting it down behind me, I sit on my heels and pull him back up to his knees, catching him around the waist when he sways like he's about to fall.

The rain has died off, but he's still soaking wet and freezing, his fingers making me shiver as he wraps them around my neck under my hoodie. His legs come around my hips, and I keep hold of his waist as he sits his ass down on my lap.

"What do you think you're doing?" I ask, but he's so far gone, I'm not sure he knows. I'm not even sure he'll remember this when he wakes up tomorrow.

Instead of answering me, he makes himself at home and buries his face into the crook of my neck, humming as he pushes his nose into my throat. "You smell like weed. You got any?" he asks, his small hands invading the front pocket of my hoodie. He finds what he's looking for, sticking my joint in his mouth with another one of those lazy grins. Tilting his head, he flicks his thumb like he's trying to light it, frowning when it doesn't happen. "Fucking thing," he grumbles, trying again.

There's no lighter in his hand, so I take mine out and light it for him, mesmerized by the way his pouty lips move as he inhales the first hit. He holds it inside his lungs for a few seconds, then lets it out slowly. He doesn't bother to turn his head away, so the smoke blows right into my face.

"She promised me, you know?"

"Promised you what?"

"That she'd never kill herself," he says quietly, his tired eyes filling with tears as he explains. "She made me promise the same thing. Now I'm stuck here without her. My dad blames me. My mom doesn't give a shit. Your parents don't want anything to do with me. Everyone at school thinks I'm a pill-pushing freak. And you..." He swallows, the tears finally spilling over his cheeks as he blinks slowly. "Every time you look at me, I see how much you hate me. How much you wish it was me instead of her," he adds, pulling in a long breath before he continues. "I ruined everything, Nate. I've got nothing and nobody left."

My jaw ticks at the raw truth in his words, my nostrils flaring as I watch him smoke my joint. "Am I supposed to feel sorry for you?"

"No."

"Then why are you telling me this?"

"I don't know," he mutters, shrugging. "Thought it might make you feel better."

It doesn't.

But I still nod and take the joint from his mouth, looking away from that vacant expression on his face as I put it between my lips. He shivers against me, and I take my coat off without thinking about it, pulling my brows in when he stops me from putting it on him. The ballsy little shit buries himself into my chest, choosing to warm himself up with my body heat instead. I should move him, toss him on the ground and leave his sorry ass out here to freeze, but I don't do that. Instead, I cover his back with my coat like a blanket, his warm breath tickling my neck while I run my hand through his hair.

I don't know what's happening. We don't touch unless we're fighting, but we're not fighting right now, and we couldn't be any closer to each other if we tried.

My gaze catches my hand on his hip, and I flex my fingers, glancing at the blood covering the ring I'm wearing on my little finger. It's Xavi's, and his hands are tiny, so that's the only finger I can fit it on.

I study the blood on his jaw, carefully running my thumb over the edge of the fresh cut there. "Does it hurt?" I ask, and he nods slowly, as if even moving his head up and down is too much effort for him. "I thought you said you couldn't feel anything."

"I lied," he mumbles against my collarbone, and it's only now I realize he's looking at Katy's headstone beside us. "Everything hurts, Nate," he chokes out.

My heart twists, then cracks into more pieces, my hand holding his battered face as I wrap my arm around him and tuck his head under my chin. "I know," I say softly, barely recognizing the sound of my own voice as I follow his line of sight.

As I stare at my sister's name, I hear the sound of someone coming up behind us, not even bothering to check who it is. I'm not surprised. I knew he'd come for me as soon as I hung up on him.

I can feel him looking at me—at *us*—at the blood and the tears and my arm wrapped tightly around Xavi's small waist, but he manages to keep his mouth shut.

For all of thirty seconds.

"Is he all right?" Carter asks softly—*carefully*—as if he knows I'll snap if he pushes me even a little bit.

I shake my head.

"Are *you* all right?"

Clearing my throat, I shake my head again, closing my eyes as

I bury my hand into Xavi's wet hair, my cheek resting against the side of his head.

"What's he on?"

"I don't know, C," I whisper. "He wouldn't tell me."

He falls silent again, and I take another look at Katy's headstone, discreetly shoving the tear off my cheek before he notices it.

Swallowing, I move to stand, keeping Xavi's legs wrapped around my back as I carry his limp, sleeping body.

"You need help?"

"No, I got him," I answer, stopping at Carter's side so he can fish my car keys out of my pocket.

He walks ahead of us toward the gates, and I press my lips to Xavi's neck, catching his head in my hand when it almost falls off my shoulder.

"It's okay, baby. I got you."

CHAPTER TWENTY-TWO
PRESENT

Xavi

The silence is killing me.

He's been standing there for I don't know how long, saying absolutely nothing. The only reason I know he's there is because I heard his footsteps when he came up behind me. I haven't heard him move since. I haven't even heard him breathe, so I don't breathe either.

I wish I knew what he was thinking right now, wish I could see the look on his face so I know what to expect when he finally decides to acknowledge me.

If he ever decides to acknowledge me.

Too nervous to sit still any longer, I risk a peek at him over my shoulder and find him staring into space. He's looking right at me, but I don't think he's actually seeing me. It's like he's in another place, like he's here but not *here*.

"Nate?"

He blinks at the sound of my voice, his eyes narrowing as he forces them to focus. "What?"

"What's wrong?"

"Nothing," is all he says, followed by more silence.

Okay...

He moves closer and stands beside me, his hands in the pockets of his jeans, towering over me while I sit on the ground at his feet like a puppy.

"How did you know where to find me?"

He raises a brow at that, sliding his eyes from Katy's headstone to me. "Who says I was looking for you?"

My jaw ticks, and I drop my gaze to the ground, unable to stop picturing the way he looked at me right before I left the stadium earlier. Just for a second, I swear it looked like he didn't want me to go. Like he needed me to stay.

"Did you...?"

He nods. "I got suspended. We lost the game."

And there goes his undefeated season.

"I'm sorry."

"What are you sorry for?"

"Well, I..." I hesitate. "It was my fault, wasn't it?"

He breathes out a cruel laugh, not even bothering to hide how pathetic he thinks I am. "You give yourself way too much credit for someone I couldn't care less about. You're not the reason I played like shit tonight. You don't have that kind of power over me, party boy."

Of course I don't.

"Whatever," I mutter, and then because I'm a loser who got his feelings hurt, I add, "You really did play like shit. And you let Jackson get all up in your head, just like he set out to do. Katy would be kicking your dumb ass right now if she were here."

"You told her about that?"

"I tell her everything," I admit, not missing his intense stare on the side of my face.

At first, I think he's about to make me feel like an even bigger loser for talking to a rock, but he doesn't.

"Did you tell her I fucked you?"

"Where do you think I went after you kicked me out of your bed?" I ask, shrugging when his face falls a little bit. "If you don't want her to know what an asshole you are, maybe you should stop acting like one."

"You think I'm *acting*?"

I don't answer that, tensing when he crouches down to put his mouth right next to my lips, his thumb and forefinger cupping my jaw. "Did you shower first?"

"What?"

"Before you came here and ratted me out to my sister, did you wash off the mess I made on your dick?" he asks, smirking when I shiver. "You didn't," he guesses. "You love walking around with my cum in your clothes, don't you? Feeling me every time you move..." He keeps teasing me, his teeth nipping my lip piercing. "I bet you'd love it even more leaking out of your ass."

I don't know who moves first, but suddenly he's the one sitting on the ground and I'm on his lap, him grabbing my waist as I wrap my legs around him. I lean in, but he stops me with his hand on my throat, that knowing smirk still resting on his lips as he holds my mouth away from his. He shakes his head at me, and I glare at how stupid he makes me feel. He slides his free hand into the front pocket of my hoodie, stealing one of my cigarettes. He lights it up, and my glare slips as he smokes it, his eyes on mine as he blows the smoke into my face.

"I..." I trail off, feeling something scratch at the corners of my mind. I try, but I can't get a good enough hold on it. "Nate?"

"What?"

His expression doesn't change, and I frown, bouncing my eyes between his dark ones.

I don't remember much about the last time he found me here. I remember coming here on Katy's eighteenth birthday, miserable and alone. I remember Nate hitting me so hard he left a permanent mark, but all the details in between are a blur. I woke up in a hospital bed the next morning with no memory of how I got there, with my dad and a psychiatrist staring at me from across the room, three stitches in my jaw, and a pumped stomach. When I asked the nurse what happened, she told me my *brother* dropped me off, gave her the bag of pills he found in my pocket, and then vanished before the police could ask him any questions. The only brother I have is dead, but I didn't bother telling her that. I knew in my heart that it was Nate, but I was too afraid to call him and ask why he did it. We didn't speak again until I showed up on his driveway two years later.

Just as I'm about to ask him what happened here that night, he asks, "Is your brother here too?"

I frown harder, not only because I was *just* thinking about my brother, but because in all the years I've known Nate, he's never once asked me about Blaine.

Nodding, I gesture to the left with my head, my movements limited with my throat in his hand. "He's over there."

"Do you miss him?"

I nod again, my brows pulled in tight. "Yeah."

"Not as much as you miss my sister though, right?" he asks, catching me off guard. I stumble over what to say, and he pulls back, shaking his head at me with a disbelieving grin. "You're a real piece of shit, you know that?"

I grind my teeth and shove him away before he can do it to me, taking one last look at Katy's headstone before I stand and brush the dirt off my knees.

"Where are you going?"

"Home," I grumble, and he lets out another one of those cruel, breathy laughs.

"Where's *home*, party boy?"

My heart sinks down to my ass, and I shove my hood over my head and keep on walking.

"Hey, Xavi?"

"What, Nate?" I sigh, spinning to face him and throwing my arms out wide. "What else?"

"I'll see you later," he teases, and I scoff, flipping him off as I back away from him.

"Not a chance, asshole."

He smirks again, so fucking sure of himself as he repeats, "I'll see you later."

I turn around, and those four words follow me all the way... back to the house that isn't my home and never will be.

CHAPTER TWENTY-THREE

Nate

When I get home, I sneer at the car parked in my spot. Leaving my car parked diagonally across the driveway, I grab my shit from the back seat and walk up to the front door. The music's pumping inside the house, and there are people everywhere, dancing and drinking and doing drugs on my counters.

I find Carter out in the pool, his arms wrapped around some guy's waist while he sticks his tongue in his mouth. When Carter sees me looking, all he does is grin, rolling his eyes when I take a few steps toward him. "Come here," I demand.

"No."

"What?"

"You fucked us tonight, Nate," he says, grabbing the guy's ass to encourage him to keep grinding on him. "You don't wanna party with us? Go somewhere else. I'm not shutting it down."

"Carter," I say, and he wets his lips, whispering something to the guy before he swims to the edge where I'm crouching down to level with him. "I..."

"You what?"

"I'm sorry, okay? I don't know what happened."

"I do," he says with a shrug, propping his chin on his forearms. "You let him get in your head."

I don't bother to ask who he's talking about. I already know it's not Jackson Banks.

"You're supposed to be in *his* head, Nate. Not the other way around. I didn't bring him here for that."

"Exactly," I hiss, jumping at the chance to blame him. "*You're* the one who brought him here. What did you think was gonna happen?" I lower my voice, raking my hands through my hair. "Ever since he got here, he's all I can think about and it's fucking me up," I confess. "I hate him, C."

He says nothing at first, but then he nods like he's decided something and moves to climb out of the pool. "I'm gonna make him leave."

"What?"

"Right now. I'll go tell him—"

I push him back in, blowing out a breath when he pops up, spits the water from his mouth, and levels me with a look that's both amused and annoyed.

"I didn't wanna get my hair wet."

"He's not going anywhere," I grit out.

"Okay, what are you gonna do with him then?"

I just look at him, struggling to keep a straight face when his mouth stretches into a slow, knowing smirk. I smirk back, and he laughs, bouncing up to press his wet forehead against mine.

"That's my boy," he whispers.

"Fuck off."

"Nate?" he calls as I move to leave. "If you ever show up to a game like that again," he warns, *like that* meaning drunk, I'm guessing, "I'll beat your ass."

"Will you?"

"Hard," he adds, grabbing the guy he was kissing before and pulling him back to his mouth.

I walk back into the house, heading straight for the kitchen to pour myself a whiskey. It occurs to me then that I might have a problem, but I shove that thought away just as quick, swallowing it in one go before I make myself another.

Zoey, the cheerleader I used to make Xavi jealous last week, appears beside me. She's dressed in a sexy, blood red dress, her shiny brunette hair pulled up into a tight, high ponytail. She's gorgeous, and if I wasn't so fucked up, I think she's the type of girl I could fall for. Someone fun and sexy and confident in her own skin. Someone my parents might actually like, if I offered them a chance to get to know her. Someone who wouldn't make my heart feel like it's being torn to shit and falling out of my chest every time I look at her.

"Hey, Nate," she says, trailing her eyes over my form the same way I did her just now, stopping when she gets to my face. "You look...pissed."

A rare laugh bubbles out of me, and she smiles a little, leaning into my side as I wrap my arm around her neck and pour her a drink.

She saw what happened on the court tonight, so she doesn't bother asking me *why* I'm pissed.

We knock glasses, throw them back, and then she asks, "Wanna talk about it?"

"Nope."

"Wanna fuck about it?"

I raise a brow, and she shrugs, not looking at all embarrassed or offended that I'm not interested.

"Worth a shot," she says, grabbing the whiskey bottle to help herself. "So, who is it?"

"Who's what?"

"The girl you keep blowing me off for." She squints at all the people around us, scrunching her nose when she catches Frankie looking over here from across the room. "Don't tell me it's Frankie."

"What's wrong with Frankie?"

"Nothing, except she's fucked half the boys on your team and half the girls on my squad," she grumbles. "She's a whore."

"Careful, Zoey," I tease, though I'm not entirely joking. "That's my best friend you're talking about."

"I thought Carter was your best friend."

"I've got two."

"Lucky you," she mutters, but she's not looking at me and hasn't been for the last thirty seconds.

With their gazes locked, Frankie makes a point to stick her tongue out and lick the rim of her shot glass, grinning when Zoey sneers at her.

"Zoey," I say.

"What?"

"You ever had hate sex before?" I ask, taking the bottle she's white-knuckling like she's considering bashing Frankie's head in with it.

"No, why?"

"It's hot," I inform her, leaning over to speak in her ear like a little devil on her shoulder. "You should try it."

"Maybe I will," she rasps.

I smile wickedly at Frankie while I back away from them, feeling awfully proud of myself as I leave the kitchen and take the whiskey with me.

Speaking of hate sex...

When I get upstairs, I'm about to go straight into Xavi's room to *see* him like I told him I would, but it seems I don't have to. He's already waiting for me outside my door. Leaning back against the wall, he's got his arms folded across his chest, his moody little stare following every step I take toward him. My lips curve before

I can stop it, and I hook my fingers into the waistband of his jeans, pulling him into me as I open my door and walk him inside my bedroom. "Good boy."

CHAPTER-TWENTY FOUR

Xavi

G ood boy.
Fuck, why does he have to keep saying things like that?

My heart is racing, my useless attempt at anger forgotten as soon as he closes the door behind us. His knuckles brush the base of my cock as he uses my jeans like a leash, guiding me with him before pushing me down on the bed.

"Get naked," he demands and takes a swig of whiskey. "Now, Xavi," he says when I don't move. "I don't have all night."

"You got someplace else to be?" I ask bitterly, my nose twitching at that stupid, smug look on his face.

"Get naked," he repeats slowly. "Or get out."

Fine.

Grabbing the hem of my hoodie, I pull it off and toss it down by his feet like a brat, doing the same with y t-shirt before I work on my jeans. My hands shake with a mix of anxiety and anticipation as I push them down to my ankles, yanking them off my feet before I drop them on the pile.

"That was real sexy," he deadpans, and I force a glare.

"You didn't say *strip tease*, asshole."

"You can leave those on," he says when I hook my thumbs into the tight briefs I'm wearing.

"Why?"

"Because you look hot in them," he tells me, shrugging like it's no big deal as he takes another drink. "You want some?" he asks, holding the bottle up when he catches me looking.

I quickly avert my eyes, shaking my head with a scoff. "You're such a dick."

He chuckles darkly and sets it down on the nightstand, then climbs up onto the bed and pushes my thighs apart. Lying down on top of me, he stares into my eyes and carefully runs his thumb over the corner of my mouth, playing with my piercing. "You're pathetic," he informs me, not for the first time, and I already know what's coming next before he says it. "Do you know how desperate you looked tonight? Showing up at my game like you're my boyfriend or some shit."

"It wasn't just tonight," I blurt out, my heart twisting with more anxiety when he pulls back to look at me.

"What?"

"I said it wasn't just tonight," I repeat, quieter this time. "I come to them all. I'm always there, Nate."

Silence follows, and his eyes flash with anger. I don't know what he finds when he looks into mine, but whatever it is, he doesn't like it.

"That's why you went to the cemetery after. So you could tell Katy about it," he guesses, his jaw tightening. "You do that every time?"

The backs of my eyes start to sting, and I drop my gaze to his chest, sealing my lips shut to stop myself from pouring my heart out to him. That won't do me any good. If anything, it'll just piss him off even more.

He starts to say something, then changes his mind, his voice softer than I've ever heard it when he says, "Xavi, that's not healthy."

"Don't talk to me about what's healthy, Nate," I whisper, flicking my eyes at the chain I know he's wearing under his shirt. "You're just as much of a mess as I am."

"You think so?"

"You gonna tell me I'm wrong?"

He doesn't, his head tilting to the side as he stares at my big mouth. "Can I kiss you yet?"

I blink at the sudden change of subject, frowning. "No."

"I want to," he admits in a single breath, once again thumbing my lips to pull the bottom one down. "I wanna spit in your mouth. Get it all wet and fuck that little tongue ring with my dick."

"That's disgusting."

"You like it?"

I nod, wishing he could do it right now.

"What do you want, Xavi?" he asks, making me moan when he lowers his hips and grinds on me.

He's still wearing all of his clothes, so the rough material of his jeans scrapes the sensitive flesh between my legs, but I don't care. It feels good.

It feels amazing.

"Whatever *you* want," I rasp. "Just take it."

"You sure?"

I nod again, and he drops his mouth to mine, taking my hands to place them on both sides of his neck. He doesn't spit in my mouth or go anywhere near my tongue piercing. He plays with my lip ring instead, tugging it between his teeth and flicking it with his tongue. I can almost taste the whiskey he was drinking, seeing the bottle on the nightstand in my peripheral every time I open my eyes. It's making me a little skittish, but I don't think I'm lying to myself when I realize I don't want it. I *don't*. I've got something even better right here on top of me.

He's just as addictive as any drug I've ever taken, just as destructive and dangerous to my health. He fills every corner of my mind until all I can think about is getting him inside me again.

"Nate..."

"Hm?"

"Why are you being so..."

"So what?" he asks, kissing his way from my mouth to my jaw, licking the scar he likes so much.

"Slow," I finish, huffing out a breath on his cheek.

His lips curve against my skin, and he moves down to my neck. "Whatever I want, right, baby?"

I swallow, sinking my fingers into his hair and digging my nails in, hoping that'll set him off and encourage him to move faster, rougher.

It doesn't.

If anything, it makes him even slower. I swear he's trying to kill me with his mouth and his tongue, not leaving an inch of my upper body untouched. When he gets to my stomach and slides his wet tongue down through the valley of my barely there abs, my thighs are clenching, my dick is leaking, and I'm losing my goddamn mind.

"Nate," I growl, but it turns into a whimper when he tilts his head and sucks on my hip, leaving a hickey just above the waistband of my underwear.

God.

My hips buck, and I find the chain around his neck. Without thinking, I yank on it and wrap the excess around my fist. He's on me in a flash, his nose touching mine as he holds himself up on his hands.

"If you break that," he says calmly, "I'll strangle you with it and shove the ring down your throat."

"Jesus." I let it go, flinching before I can stop it when he lifts his hand up.

Instead of hitting me, he takes my hand, an amused little gleam in his eyes as he puts it back on his chest, carefully wrapping my fingers around the chain again. "Are you afraid of me?"

"No," I deny, and he raises a brow at my too quick answer. "Okay, maybe a little bit, yeah," I admit.

He laughs like I'm ridiculous and lifts up to look at me properly. "Are you for real?" he asks, his laughter dying on his lips when he realizes I'm not playing. "You never used to be," he says quietly, his eyebrows creasing as he runs his thumb over my jaw. "You used to run circles around me, remember? It didn't matter what I said or did to you, you'd just laugh and tell me to go fuck myself. You drove me crazy."

I clear my throat as several memories fill my head all at once. I can picture it just like he said; me being a brat to get his attention, him threatening me, me getting off on it and being an even bigger brat to him...

But those were two completely different people, two completely different lives. The people we were back then, they don't even exist anymore.

"That was before..."

Before Katy died.

I don't dare say it out loud, but I know he hears me all the same. He nods, and then in the next second, he's grabbing my waist, flipping me over, and shoving me face down into the bed, something I know he does when he can't stand to look at me.

I swallow my shame, burying it for another time, and he fists my briefs with both hands, tearing them down the middle for easy access to my hole.

"Fuck," I whisper into the sheets, lifting my ass up for him when he grabs my hips and tugs.

He spreads me open with his thumbs, and I welcome the distraction, moaning freely when his mouth finds my hole. He spits on me, then spreads it around with his tongue, his rough hands rubbing the backs of my thighs while he eats me out. I'm damn near shaking, arching my back as much as I can without pulling something. My fingers twist the sheets next to my face, and I have to squeeze my eyes shut, fighting the urge to reach back for his head and hold him down on me. He seems to know what I want without me saying it, grabbing my right hand and pulling it back until it's resting on the back of his head.

"Fuck," I say again, my mouth falling open when he pushes a finger and his tongue into me at the same time. "Shit, Nate, keep doing that," I plead, ignoring how unhinged I sound. "Give me another one."

"Greedy whore," he says, but it sounds more like a praise than an insult, his voice muffled by my flesh on his mouth. "Ride it, baby. Hold me still and push your ass back into my face."

Baby.

Goddamn him.

He adds another finger, groaning like he's enjoying this as much as I am. I roll my hips back and forth, up and down, fucking myself on his face.

"I need to come," I pant. "I need it…"

Unable to think about anything but release, I reach into the band of my briefs and fist my dick. Using my precum as lube, I stroke it hard and fast, matching the pace with my ass on his tongue and fingers, stealing pleasure from both sides. Within seconds, I'm already *right there* on the edge. But then he stops and bats my hand away from my cock, straightening up and pulling me up with him by my hair.

"Not yet."

"Nate—"

"I said not yet," he growls in my ear, rubbing my heaving chest with his palm as he brushes his lips over the pulse in my neck. "Stroke it slow."

I pause and look at my dick, not missing the way his is hard and pressed up against my ass through his jeans. "Yours or mine?" I ask dumbly, sensing his grin on my flesh before he answers.

"Yours, Xavi."

I stroke it like he told me to while he grabs what he needs from his nightstand. I feel him unbuttoning his jeans behind me and pulling his dick out, not letting go of my chest as he opens the condom and slides it on. I still want him to fuck me bare, but I'm not about to offer again, not after what he said to me the first time.

He pops the cap off the lube with his teeth, and then his wet fingers are at my hole, pushing and twisting inside to open me up even more. He fingers me for a while, playing with the metal in my nipples as he does it, nipping my earlobe, licking the hickeys on my neck, driving me insane with need.

"Nate, please, just fuck me."

"You gonna come as soon as I put it in?" he teases, pulling his fingers out to rub the head of his dick over my hole, sliding it up and down.

"Probably."

"Don't," he warns, and then he's shoving it inside me in one quick move, punching the breath out of my lungs, pulling me back by my waist until he's buried balls deep in my ass. "God, you're tight."

"Fuck," I grunt at the same time, squeezing my dick so hard I'm sure it's turning purple.

Don't.

Don't come, don't come, don't come.

He groans against my cheek and starts rolling up into me, the position we're in causing his dick to hit my prostate on every move of his hips. He fucks me slow and deep at first, then hard and deeper, then back to slow. Every time I feel like I'm about to come, he changes the pace, backing off my sweet spot to fuck me with just the tip.

"What are you doing?" I complain, rolling my head back on his shoulder to look at him.

"Edging you," he answers, smirking when he catches the look on my face. "You like it?"

"I hate it."

I'm such a goddamn liar.

I love that he's playing with me like this, dragging it out like he's just as desperate as I am to make it last.

He kisses me and moves down to my neck, holding me still with his fingers wrapped tightly around my throat. He's choking me, but it's not hard enough to stop me from breathing, my dick leaking all over my knuckles while he sucks on my bruised skin, leaving fresh hickeys right on top of the old ones.

When I start to rub my dick again, twisting the thick base with my fist, he takes both of my hands and slides his fingers through mine, locking them together at my sides. My breath catches, and I close my eyes, hiding from him, biting my lip when he kisses the back of my neck and slides his thumbs over my knuckles.

He fucks me just like that for a while—*holding my hands*—our bodies covered in sweat and sliding against each other. It feels so good, but all I can think is...this isn't hurting me. This isn't *breaking* me like he said he would.

Or maybe it is.

Maybe this is his punishment for me, his own twisted brand of torture.

A whimper slips out of my mouth at the thought, and he smirks against me as if he can see inside my head, like he just *knows* even though I haven't said a word.

He knows exactly what he's doing.

"I hate you," I grit out. "I hate you so fucking much."

"I know, baby," he whispers, and I whine pathetically.

"Say something mean."

"You want me to be *mean* to you?" He sounds amused,

refusing to let go of my hands when I try to take them back. "Why, because you think I might start to like you if I fuck you for long enough?" He flexes his fingers between mine, and I swallow, not liking where this is going. "It doesn't matter how hot you are or how good you are at taking my dick, party boy. You're still the reason my sister is dead." The words he's saying are harsh, but his voice is soft, his lips gentle as he runs them over the back of my neck, and I think that's the part that hurts more. "You're still the reason we have to wake up every day and live this shitty life without her," he goes on. "You're still the reason we're alone."

Tears roll down my cheeks, but I can't even swipe them away. All I can do is take it while he keeps fucking me, using our joined hands to pull my hips back into his.

"You're an asshole," I choke out, hating myself for the way my voice cracks on the last word.

You asked for it, you idiot.

He chuckles. "I'm not holding a gun to your head, you know? You don't have to be here and put up with my shit. You can leave." He tilts his head at the door to emphasize his point, and I narrow my eyes at it.

"What if I don't?"

"Then you're mine," he says simply, lowering his head to lick the marks on my neck. "Whenever and wherever and however I want you, you're mine."

"And when you don't want me? What am I then?"

He shrugs like it should be obvious. "Nothing."

My teeth clench, and I twist my body around in his grip, a cross between a growl and a cry escaping me when he starts railing the fuck out of my ass with no remorse. I give up fighting and fall back into him, bracing myself against his chest as I balance on that fine line between pleasure and pain.

"I hate you," I remind him.

He stops, pulling out so fast it makes my head spin. He picks me up and flips me over like a rag doll, shoving me down by my chest and pinching my nipple so hard I let out a squeal.

"Motherfu—"

"Look at me when you say that," he demands, teasing my ass with his cock before he shoves it back in. "Come on, party boy. Say it again."

"I hate you," I rasp, trying my hardest to mean the lies pouring out of my mouth. "I hate you. I...hate...you."

"Good boy," he says softly, praising me for real this time, his eyes darkening as he drops down on top of me, presses his mouth to mine, and pounds into me as hard as he can. "So good, baby. Fuck."

"Nate, can I—"

"*Yes*," he hisses, shoving his hand down between us to get to my cock. "Do it now. Wrap your legs around my waist and come all over me."

God.

He's acting crazy, and it's only now I realize he hasn't just been edging *me* this whole time; he's been edging himself too.

It's how manic he looks right now that finally sets me off. Grabbing both sides of his head, I cry his name into his mouth and fall off the edge he's been dangling me off for what feels like hours, my cum soaking his fingers as he fucks it out of me.

He's breathing hard and fast as he pulls out, batting my arms out of his way before he kneels up and straddles my chest. His dick is in my face, the condom tossed aside, and then he's pushing my head back into the sheet.

"Close your mouth," he says, using his clean hand to rake his fingers through my hair, pulling it tight.

I breathe through my nose, eagerly waiting for what's coming. He comes all over my lips and chin, his hips stuttering as he squeezes the tip, giving me everything he's got. I feel it dripping down my neck, but he doesn't give it the chance to hit the sheets.

He bends over and cleans me up with his tongue, sliding it over my face until he's caught every last drop.

I tip my head back for him, granting him better access. "And you call *me* dirty."

He licks my lips last, sucking and toying with my lip ring a moment before he straightens back up. Looking right into my eyes, he puts his fingers in his mouth and sucks my cum off of each one, still holding me down by my hair to ensure I keep watching him.

"Can I stay with you tonight?" I blurt out, kicking myself as soon as the words leave my mouth.

"No," he says, climbing off me to tuck his dick away.

"Why not?"

Jesus Christ, shut up.

He grabs his whiskey off the nightstand, making me wait while he takes a drink. "Stop acting like this is more than what it is. You're a hole to stick my dick into, party boy. That's it."

I sneer. "Like a sex doll?"

"Sex dolls don't talk," he grumbles, and I glare, sitting up to snatch my jeans off the floor. "They don't get dressed after they get fucked either."

He's got to be kidding me.

But when I look up at him, I see he's dead serious. He's not gonna let me get dressed before I leave this time. There's a massive tear in the back of my Calvins, and he wants me to walk out into the hall like this while there's a raging party going on downstairs. I know no one's allowed on this floor, but Carter, Easton, or Frankie could be coming up any second now. They could already be up here for all we know.

"You think I won't do it?" I cock my head at him, forcing that bratty little grin I know he hates so much. He doesn't even blink, so I decide to push him, bending over to pick my clothes up off the floor. "Watch me. Maybe one of the boys will see me like this and let me sleep in *their* bed."

His face falls, and I push up on my tiptoes to kiss his mouth, my small victory almost as sweet as the taste of our cum on his lips.

"Xavi," he warns, but I'm already leaving.

"Later, asshole."

Still grinning, I open his door and step out into the hall. No one's out here, but I don't miss the way he's watching my back just to make sure, waiting until I'm safely back in my own room where I belong. Making a point not to look at him, I close the door behind me and fall back against it, dropping my clothes on the floor before I knock my head back with a quiet thud.

My feigned happiness vanishes as soon as I'm alone, and I feel fresh tears filling my eyes, pissed at myself for letting him get to me, for hoping it might have ended differently this time.

I asked for this.

I deserve this.

Aching all over, I crawl into bed, pull the blanket up over my head, and silently cry myself to sleep, just like I do every time he fucks me.

CHAPTER TWENTY-FIVE

Xavi

I like Easton, I really do, but sometimes I wish he'd just shut up and let me drown myself in misery.

It's Katy's birthday today. I haven't seen Nate yet, and I don't want to. I woke up this morning and didn't even bother getting out of bed. I planned on spending the day hiding from him and everybody else, but then I made the mistake of coming downstairs. I didn't think anyone was around when I snuck into the den. Didn't expect Easton to be standing behind me when I picked up the whiskey. Definitely didn't expect him to snatch it out of my grip and scare the shit out of me when I almost took a swig of it. I felt all the color drain from my face when I saw the concern on his, but he didn't say anything, and neither did I. Without a word spoken between us, he set the bottle down on the bar, dragged me to the couch in the living room, and chucked a PlayStation controller at me. I haven't been able to get away from him since. It's been two hours, and every time I try to get up, he grabs the sleeve of my hoodie and pulls me back down without taking his eyes off the TV.

"You like hot chocolate?" he asks *another* question, and I drop my head back with a silent groan.

I know he's just being nice, trying to get me to talk or whatever, but I feel dead inside.

"No."

"What's the deal with you and Nate?"

That gets my attention, and I look over at him, blinking when I catch the small smile on his lips.

He knows he's got me.

"What do you mean?" I ask, clearing my throat when I hear how scratchy my voice sounds.

"I've heard you screaming his name from across the hall, Xav," he murmurs, still smiling at the TV. "I know he's the one who's been fucking you."

I open my mouth, then snap it shut again. "I don't *scream.*"

"You're totally a screamer," he says bluntly, laughing when he catches me hiding my burning cheeks with my sleeves. "I thought he hated you."

"He does hate me."

"So, what, you just let him chew you up and spit you back out whenever he feels like it? Like you're his bitch?"

"I'm not his bitch," I lie, resisting the urge to rotate my hips and run my hand over my dick through my sweats.

I'm getting hard. It's as if my cock only has to hear its owner's name and it wakes up ready.

"Dude, I hate to break it to you, but those hickeys on your neck say *bitch.* Loud and fuckin' clear. I saw the one on your hip as well." He lets go of his controller to poke my side, making me jump. "Right there."

"What? When?"

"Your shirt rode up when you grabbed a glass in the kitchen last night." He shrugs, side-eyeing me when I go back to saying nothing. "You know he wants us to see them, right? He's marking you, letting us all know you belong to him."

Sinking further back into the couch, I pull my knees up and cover my lips with my knuckles, fighting the stupid smile trying to break free.

He's talking shit, but I can't help the way my heart feels a little fuller when I pretend what he's saying is true.

Easton glances at something behind me and does a double take, sighing quietly as he lifts his arm up on the back of the couch. I follow his line of sight to find Nate watching us from the doorway, my face falling when I see the dark circles under his eyes. He looks rough, leaning his shoulder against the door jamb with his arms folded over his chest. He doesn't seem angry or amused or anything in between. He's just staring at me.

He's such a stalker.

Why do I like it so much?

"How much of that did you hear?" Easton asks, but Nate ignores him.

I don't miss the slight tick in his jaw while his eyes move from my face to Easton's arm resting behind my head, almost touching me but not quite.

"Come with me," Nate says.

I blink, my eyebrows hiking up as I look across at Easton, then back to Nate. "Me?"

"Yes, you, party boy. Hurry up."

He doesn't even acknowledge Easton, waiting for me to pass him before he turns and follows me out of the room. Feeling his eyes on my back, I stop and spin to face him. "I haven't showered today yet."

Not that I was planning to at all, but if he wants to fuck, he's gonna have to wait for me to get ready.

"You don't need a shower for this," he says after a beat. When I don't move, he grabs my upper arm and walks me outside to his car. "Get in."

I blink at him again, stunned because not once has he ever let me inside this car. Even when Katy was alive, when I'd take her out and get too fucked up to drive her home, he'd pick her up from wherever we were but he always left me to fend for myself. Every single time.

"Really?"

He lets out a long, heavy sigh, hitting me with an impatient look that has me sealing my lips shut and moving my ass.

Okay, then. We're getting in the car.

CHAPTER TWENTY-FIVE

Nate

EASTON

> Go easy on him, Nate. I caught him with a bottle of whiskey this morning.

I pause on my way to the driver's side, my hackles raising as I look at Xavi through the windshield. He looks fine—sort of—but I still check his eyes, trying to decide whether the redness is because he's upset or because he relapsed.

Before I can ask, another text pops up.

EASTON

> He didn't drink any.

NATE

> You sure?

EASTON

> Yeah. I stopped him. I haven't taken my eyes off him since.

Yeah, I bet you haven't, you fucker.

He hits me back with three laughing emojis, and I pocket my phone, getting inside the car.

I wasn't planning on bringing Xavi with me today, but when I came downstairs and found him and Easton on the couch together, playing video games and talking about me like they're besties or some shit, I acted without thinking.

Fucking Easton.

He's not usually this nice. Why he's got a soft spot for Xavi of all people, no fucking clue.

I eye Xavi's form while I drive, pissed at how hot he looks today even when he's a broken mess inside.

That's why.

CHAPTER TWENTY-SIX

Xavi

We're sitting in complete silence, without even the radio to keep us company while I stare straight ahead at the busy highway.

"You know where I'm taking you?" Nate finally asks.

I nod and continue biting my nails in the passenger seat, my anxiety growing as we pass the sign for the beach off the next exit.

"She told you," he guesses, and I nod again.

"She told me—"

"Everything," he finishes, then adds, "I get it, Xavi."

I look out the window and stab my fingernail into my bleeding cuticles, whipping my head around when he snatches my left hand and yanks it over to his side. Keeping his eyes forward, he locks our fingers together like he did the other night, his thumb moving over the edge of mine.

I swallow and sit still for as long as I can, which isn't even a full minute. When I can't take it anymore, I test the waters and try to slip my hand free, but he doesn't let me, tightening his grip and sealing his fingers over my knuckles. He doesn't say anything, but I can tell he's up in his head, deep in thought while he drives us to where we're going.

"My parents are assholes," he says randomly.

"Okay..."

"You know my dad's been calling me nonstop since Friday night?"

"To give you shit about getting suspended," I assume, not really surprised by that.

I bet he's furious. All that guy cares about is his image. He has to be the best at everything, have the most money, the biggest house, the most expensive car, the most successful, straight and narrow kids, emphasis on the *straight* part.

I know he's proud of Nate for being the star that he is, not because he loves him and wants the best for him, but because it makes him look good.

Katy once told me that she thought her dad used to wish she was never born. She thought she embarrassed him by being blind. I've never wanted to punch someone more than I wanted to punch him that day.

"He called me again this morning, and I picked up just to see what he'd say. He didn't even say hello before he started riding my ass about the game." He pauses, his jaw tightening as he swallows. "He didn't say a word about Katy."

"He forgot."

"Yeah, Xavi. He forgot," he says quietly. "Or maybe he didn't, and he just doesn't give a shit anymore."

I clench my teeth to stop myself from saying what I really want to say, watching the scenery as we get closer to the ocean. "What about your mom?"

"I don't know. I haven't talked to her."

"Why not?"

"You know my mom, Xav," he grumbles, still not looking at me. "She's my dad's little minion. It doesn't matter what he does, he's never wrong. Everything was always Katy's fault. It was Katy's fault she was born blind, Katy's fault she got bullied in middle school, Katy's fault they made her so depressed that she started fucking around with you, got hooked on drugs and ruined their reputation." His wrist is resting on top of the steering wheel, his hand curling into a tight fist. "My mom will defend my dad until she's blue in the face, but she could never stand up for her own kids. She took your side over mine the day Katy died, you remember that?"

"Yeah," I whisper, unsure what else to say.

He parks the car and finally lets go of my hand. "Leave everything you have on you in here."

"Why?"

"Just do it, Xavi." He sighs, dropping his stuff into the inner console before he gets out.

Worried he'll leave without me, I quickly take my phone out and toss it in, checking my pictures and Katy's list are tucked safely inside my wallet before I place it down on top of his. I get out of the car and hurry toward him, pulling my hood over my head and shoving my hands into my pockets, shielding myself from the cold. The sky is gray, and there's hardly anyone up here, maybe two or three people walking on the sand.

Nate walks to the end of the pier, just like I knew he would. I sit on the edge beside him, hesitating a moment before I slide my ass over and bump his hip with mine, getting as close to him as I can without being on top of him.

Silence stretches between us, but it doesn't feel awkward. It's almost nice, just being here with him, feeling the warmth of his body at my side, our legs dangling over the edge as we look out at the water.

"My parents used to do it every year, for both of us," he says after a while. "Throw these ridiculous birthday parties at the house, invite all their friends and their kids to show off how much money they have." He doesn't sound angry as he talks about it, just distant, and even though I've heard this story a few times before, I'm hanging on to every word as he tells me his version. "Katy was thirteen the year she finally told them she didn't want a big party with a bunch of people she didn't know. She just wanted to go to the damn beach, and they couldn't even give her that. I found her crying in the bathroom just before we were about to cut the cake. I was so pissed, I picked her up and told her to go wait for me in the garage. I swiped my dad's keys when he wasn't looking and we stole his car. Katy was so excited and hysterical at the same time, terrified I was gonna get arrested." A small grin breaks free, but he scrubs a hand over his mouth to bury it. "Anyway, I took her to the beach, and we sat right here, talking shit about our parents. And then she told me she wanted to swim..."

"Jesus," I whisper, feeling nauseous just thinking about it as I peek at the ocean beneath us. "And then she just...*jumped*? With all her clothes on?"

He laughs at the look of horror on my face, nodding as he rubs his hand over the back of his neck. "The little shit knew I'd follow her, but still, I've never been so scared in all my life. I could have killed her."

I smile and wrap my arms around my knees, quiet a minute before I ask, "You come here every year?"

He nods, and it's only now I realize how vulnerable he looks, still rubbing that same spot on his neck like he's embarrassed. "I know it's stupid," he says.

My lips part as I stare at the side of his face.

I've known this heartless asshole for five years, and I've *never* seen him act like this before.

"I don't think it's stupid," I say softly, resting my cheek on his arm. "I think it's sweet."

He turns his face to look at me, scrunching his nose. "I'm not sweet."

"Yeah, I know," I grumble, pointing in the general direction of my jaw and throat.

He smirks and shoves my head away, standing up to tilt his head at the ocean. "Come on."

"Y-you want me to go with you?"

"Why not?" he teases, grabbing my wrists and pulling me up to my feet. "You scared?"

I pale, and he narrows his eyes, staring at me like I've grown two heads.

"I've seen you swim a hundred times, party boy. I know you're not afraid of the water."

"It's not the water, it's what's *in* it," I stress, a shudder rolling through me as I shake my head firmly. "I don't do the fucking sea, man. It freaks me out."

"Why?"

"Because it's dark and...filthy. And there are fish in it."

"Fish."

"Yes, fish," I hiss. "Stop laughing."

But I'm grinning.

Why the hell am I grinning so hard?

I can't seem to get myself to stop, and it only grows bigger when he closes the distance between us, puts both hands on my waist, and rests his forehead on mine. Just as I think he's about to kiss me, his laughter dies off, and he searches my face.

"Do you mean it when you say you hate me?"

"No," I admit, barely even thinking about it as I wrap my arms around his neck and lean up to brush my lips over his. "Most of the time I'm just pretending."

"Wanna see if we can fix that?" he asks, and then—

"Nate!" I scream, but I'm already falling.

Falling.

Still fucking falling before I hit the water with a crash.

Oh, shit, oh, shit, oh, shit.

I squeeze my eyes and mouth shut as I sink down fast and deep, frantically kicking my arms and legs to swim back up to the surface. As soon as I break it, I pull in a deep breath and keep kicking, desperate to keep my sinking head above the freezing cold water.

Fuck. He did not just do that.

This motherfucker seriously just picked me up and yeeted me into the motherfucking sea!

"Nate!" I scream again, spluttering as more water makes its way into my mouth. "If you leave me out here, I swear to God I'll find your baby sister and we'll haunt your sorry ass—"

A huge splash scares the ever-loving shit out of me, and I panic, pushing against the water to try and get away from it. Nate's head pops up a few seconds later, and I'm both relieved and enraged.

"You asshole," I rasp. "I changed my mind. I meant it every fucking time."

He grins, and I splash him furiously despite the fact I'm drowning, squealing when my foot hits something hard under the water.

"What the hell is that?!"

"Jesus Christ." He hooks his ankle around the back of my knee. "Come here."

As soon as he's within reach, I throw my arms around his neck and lock my legs around his hips, shaking all over as I cling to his body.

"You know how deep this water is?" he asks.

"I'm trying not to think about it."

"You wanna swim for a bit?"

"No!" I say quickly, glaring when he grins again. "You're not funny," I growl.

But he still laughs and starts to swim, one big arm wrapped around my waist as he uses the other to get us back to shore. I don't help at all, and I'm still terrified, but I feel...happy for some reason, smiling like a fool as I bury my face into his shoulder and run my fingers through his short, wet hair.

I started this day feeling so broken and alone, wanting to drown myself in whiskey and whatever else I could get my hands on, but now it's turning into one of the best days I've had in a long time.

"Xavi."

"Yeah?"

"You can stand up now," Nate says, and it's only now I realize he's started to walk, still holding me up even though the water's barely up to his hips.

"No, thanks. I'm good up here," I say seriously, locking my ankles at the base of his spine to ensure he doesn't drop me and make me touch the bottom.

He carries me all the way back to his car in the empty parking lot, opening the trunk and grabbing a towel from inside. I absent-mindedly run my thumbs over the base of his neck, content to stay right here in his arms. He cocks his head at me. Huffing my disappointment, I slide off his body and set my feet on the ground, taking the towel he offers me. There's only one, so we share it, using one end each to dry our hair.

"Take all your clothes off," he says, crossing his arms over his body to peel off his wet hoodie and shirt. "I'll make sure no one sees you."

"I don't care if anyone sees my naked ass, Nate."

"Maybe not, but *I* do," he stresses, and I pause.

I get undressed, and he hands me a clean pair of black sweats and a hoodie, squeezing the excess water from my clothes while I put his on. They're huge and look ridiculous on me, but I like them.

"What about you?" I ask, moving my gaze over his half naked body.

He ignores me and grabs the towel, redrying my hair because apparently, I didn't do it properly the first time.

"You never planned on bringing me here, did you?" I ask, batting the towel away from my face so I can see him. "You just wanted to get me away from Easton."

Again, he ignores me.

Once we're as dry and as clean as we're going to get, he tosses all the wet stuff into the trunk and slams it shut. I'm trying my hardest to wipe the smile off my face as we get back in the car, but it won't go away.

Nate turns the heat up, and I wrap my arms around myself, enjoying how soft and warm his hoodie feels on my frozen skin. "I'm keeping this," I tell him.

"Go ahead," he says, holding the back of my seat as he reverses out of the space. "It's not mine."

"Whose is it?"

"I don't remember his name."

I sneer and pluck the fabric between my thumb and forefinger. "Did you fuck him on the back seat?"

"Nah," he says, smirking as he puts the car into gear. "He was bent over right where you are when I made him scream with my dick in his ass."

I glare, studying every inch of his face as he drives us back toward the highway. "You're lying."

He raises a brow at that. "What?"

"You're a clean freak, Nate. Your car's as immaculate as your house is. There's no way you had some random guy's hoodie in your trunk. It'd drive you crazy knowing it was there, with no *proper place* for it to go."

He briefly flicks his eyes my way, then mutters, "You think you're so fuckin' smart, don't you?"

I grin big, hooking my fingers over the collar and smushing my shoulders up into my new hoodie.

"I'm keeping this," I tell him again.

I'M SO CONFUSED.

We took turns showering in his bathroom when we got back to the house, and then he took me down to the kitchen. After he finished putting a load of laundry in the washer, he asked me when the last time I ate a proper meal was. I frowned and told him it was when I had breakfast with him and Easton the other day, and he glared before making us enough food to feed his entire team. I watched him while he cooked, and then we sat side by side at the kitchen island, talking and eating together like it was the most normal thing in the world.

We're back up in his bedroom now, lying on his bed and watching a movie that I'm not even paying attention to. He's on his back, and I'm on my side, my leg hooked over his thigh and my cheek on his chest, his knuckles grazing my spine as I brush my fingertips over the waistband of his sweats.

He won't leave me alone. Not that I want him to, but I've been testing him. Every time I try to slip away, he grabs me by my hair and pulls me back, silently telling me he's not done with me yet.

I smile into his chest every time he does it.

"Why do you keep looking at your watch?" I ask, tipping my chin at the black Rolex on his wrist.

"Hm?"

"You've checked it five times in the last two minutes," I inform him, my face heating with embarrassment when he doesn't say anything. "Do you...do want me to go?"

Instead of answering me like a decent person would, he rolls over and grabs the brown paper bag on his nightstand. He picked it up from a bakery in town on the way back earlier, but he wouldn't tell me what was in it when I asked.

He pulls out two cupcakes topped with vanilla frosting and rainbow sprinkles—mine and Katy's favorite—and my mouth parts as he passes me one. When he takes out two silver candles, I grab his wrist and check his watch, my throat damn near closing up on me when I realize it's almost midnight.

There's no way...

"Nate, what are you..." I trail off, closing my mouth when he pulls me up and sits in front of me.

We're facing each other on the bed, both cross-legged with our knees touching as he pops a candle in each cake. He smiles as he steals the lighter from my pocket, but it's not his usual smile. He's not teasing or making fun of me, he's just smiling, a little shyly, I think, and it's making me want to bawl my eyes out.

"How do you know about this?" I whisper, unable to speak properly as he lights the candles.

"She told me things too, party boy," he answers. "You were all she fuckin' talked about most of the time."

I let out a noise that sounds more like a sob than a laugh, my eyes glistening with tears as we wait for the seconds to tick by on his watch. At one second to midnight, he blows his candle out, and at one second past midnight, I blow mine out, signaling the end of Katy's birthday and the beginning of mine.

We remove the candles, and he takes a big bite out of his, making me laugh. I copy him, watching his mouth move as I lick the frosting off my bottom lip.

"Happy birthday, Xav," he says softly.

I throw myself at him, straddling his hips and wrapping my arms around his neck. He kisses me first, but I kiss him harder, blindly setting the half-eaten cakes down on his nightstand before I reach down and tug on the hem of his hoodie. He lets me pull it off over his head, and then he's taking my waist in a tight grip, rolling me back and forth to get me to grind on him.

I should keep my mouth shut and let him fuck me until I lose the ability to think straight, but something's been playing on my mind all day, and I need to know.

"Why are you being so nice to me?" I rasp, pushing his chest until he's lying on his back, rubbing my hard dick against his. "Why did you spend the day with me, Nate?"

"Because I wanted to."

"Why?"

He hesitates before he admits, "Because I didn't wanna be alone."

I pause when he says that, and he snatches my waist again, forcing me to keep moving.

"I didn't want *you* to be alone. Not today."

I...have no idea what to say to that, so I don't say anything.

I kiss him again, holding his face with both hands and tugging on his lips with my teeth. He loses patience after just a few seconds and takes back control, pulling my hair and moving his mouth over my neck and throat. My collar keeps getting in his way, and he growls, "Take it off."

"Take what off?"

"All of it," he rasps, pulling at the sweats I'm wearing like they offend him.

I take the hoodie off and throw it somewhere on the bed, letting him bite my earlobe as I work on getting the waistband of his sweats under my ass. My eyes catch on my wallet on the sheet next to us, and I pause. It's fallen out of my hoodie pocket, the piece of paper inside sticking out of the top. I see my name written in black ink at the bottom of Katy's list, and every hair on my body stands on end.

Fuck. I forgot I had that on me.

I must have stopped breathing because Nate pulls his head back with his brows dipped. "What's wrong?"

"Nothing," I lie, acting as natural as possible while I try to kick my wallet off the bed.

He's already looking though, his gaze narrowing when he

realizes I'm trying to hide something. He reaches for the paper, and I panic, snatching his wrist to stop him.

"Nate, don't."

But of course he doesn't listen to me. He pushes me away with ease and unfolds the paper, silently staring at the words on it, his eyes repeatedly flicking to the bottom of the page.

I know what he's reading. I know what's on that list word for word—I've only read it a thousand times—but I force myself to keep as still as possible, too afraid to spook him.

After what feels like forever, he slowly blinks his eyes up to mine.

My stomach is twisted up in tight, painful knots.

He tries to say something, fails, and then looks back down at the paper in his hand. His eyes are glassing over, and it's ripping my heart out, watching him fight it, clenching his jaw as he pushes me off him and stands to turn his back on me.

He's still holding his sister's list, and for the first time in my life, I find myself wishing I'd never met her. I wish I'd never pushed my way into her world and forced her to be my best friend.

"Why weren't you with her?" he asks, and I flinch like he slapped me. "If you were there..." He slowly turns his head my way, looking as broken and as wrecked as I feel. "You could have saved her."

God, just fucking kill me.

"I know," I manage to say.

This is something I carry around with me every day, something that haunts my dreams and keeps me up at night. It's always there, the guilt and the shame lurking just beneath the surface.

Katy sent me a voice note the night she died and told me she'd go out without me if I didn't call her back, and I did nothing. I was knee-deep in some shit I didn't want her to know about, so I let her go, thinking she'd be safer that way.

I didn't realize how wrong I was until it was too late.

The guy who rented the house she was found in told the police he'd seen her around before—a group of us used to hang out at his place a lot—but he didn't know she was there that night. He had an alibi, said he was partying at a friend's house with a bunch of other people. We still don't know whether he was lying or not. If he wasn't with her, whoever it was must have panicked and run. Katy was only seventeen, so they left her there alone and didn't look back. They didn't even bother to call her an ambulance. If they had, there's a good chance she'd still be here.

I found out a few days later that when Nate couldn't get ahold of us that night, he hacked into Katy's account and managed to track her phone to the house she was in. He was the one who found her, but he was too late to save her life. He held his sister while she died in his arms, and he didn't see me until I showed up at the hospital an hour later.

I kept waiting for it for weeks after she died, but he never asked.

Not once.

Now he's asking, and I'm terrified of how he'll feel about me when he finds out.

"Where were you, Xav?"

I could lie right now. I should. I should make something up, tell him I was passed out somewhere, too out of it to answer when she called me. *Anything* would be better than the truth.

But I still give it to him.

"I was with my dealer."

"Buying drugs?"

Kneeling on his bed in front of him, I screw my face up in agony, the tears streaming down over my cheeks and jaw.

"Not buying drugs," he guesses, a broken laugh slipping out as he steps closer. "You were getting fucked while she was calling you? While she was *dying* on some random guy's bathroom floor?"

Even though he's the one who said it, I don't think he really

believes it yet. I think he's waiting for me to deny it, but I don't. I
can't.

"Jesus Christ." He laughs again. "No wonder you can't look at
yourself in the mirror, you piece of shit."

"Nate."

"Stop saying my name like that!" he shouts, making me jump
and flinch away from him.

"Like what?"

"Like you're *sorry.*" He sneers, pulling me off his bed and
shoving me down to the rug on my ass. "I'm so sick of you being
sorry."

I wipe my eyes with the back of my wrist and pull myself up
with his bed frame, unable to look at him head-on. "What do you
want me to do?"

Shaking his head at me, he shoves Katy's list at my chest hard
enough to make me fall back a step. "Just get the fuck out of my
face."

"Nate, please—"

"Get out, Xavi."

—don't kick me out.

Clutching the paper, I pick up my wallet and the hoodie he
gave me, using it to cover myself while I open his door and walk
out into the hall. When I get to my room, I drop my things on the
bed, head straight into the bathroom, and lean over the sink.

The small mirror on the counter feels like it's taunting me,
and I curl my lip at it, picking it up and smashing it against the
tiled wall. A piece of glass bounces back and hits me in the face,
cutting my cheek just under my eye. Touching the blood there,
my lips tremble as I crouch down to pick up the pieces, picturing
the half-eaten cupcakes on Nate's nightstand while I glare at my
broken reflection.

CHAPTER TWENTY-SEVEN

Nate

"Where the hell have you been?" Frankie asks as soon as I walk inside the house, following me with Carter and Easton on her tail.

"I told you I was going for a run." I throw my t-shirt over the back of my neck, white-knuckling both ends as I walk into the kitchen.

"Nate, that was three hours ago," she draws out. "Jesus, did you run that entire time?"

I don't respond to that, keeping my back to them while I grab myself some water from the fridge. I feel their eyes on me while I drain half the bottle, my chest burning as the sweat pours over my chest and back. My entire body feels like it's on fire, which is exactly what I wanted. *Needed.* I'll take physical pain over the other kind any day.

When I turn around to go grab a shower, I find Carter watching me intently, squinting at my head like he's trying to see what's inside it. "What happened?"

"None of your business."

He raises a brow at my tone. Just as I'm about to tell him not to fuck with me today, he steps away from me and calls out, "Baby boy!"

He walks down the hall to the living room, and I can't not follow him, hearing Easton and Frankie coming up behind me as I stop to watch from the open doorway.

"What did you do?" Carter asks Xavi.

Xavi's looking back at him from his spot on the couch, confused, but then he sees me, and his confusion morphs into something more painful and raw.

I shouldn't have opened my mouth last night. I knew I shouldn't have asked him what I've been wanting to ask him for years, but I did, and now here we are. I'll probably never be able to look at him again without picturing him bent over for some faceless prick, moaning into his sheets, ignoring my baby sister calling his phone because he was too busy getting his slutty hole filled.

Whatever look he sees on my face makes him flinch, his shoulders sinking as he buries himself into the blanket he's got wrapped around his body. He looks exhausted, like he didn't sleep at all last night, the dark circles under his eyes even darker than usual, his messy hair sticking up and out in every direction possible. He's wearing the hoodie I gave him yesterday. I feel something pull at my chest, but before I can figure out what it is, the feeling fades away and I go right back to wanting to throw him off a roof.

Carter sighs and sets his sights back on Xavi. "Are you just gonna spend your entire birthday sulking or what?"

Xavi's eyes widen a fraction, and his cheeks turn pink with embarrassment when Easton and Frankie look at him, probably because now he looks like an even bigger loser than he already is.

"It's your *birthday*?" Frankie asks, frowning. "But you've been sitting there by yourself all day. Where are your parents?"

"Hey, it was me who didn't wanna do anything with them, not the other way around," he snaps defensively, and she frowns even harder.

"Dude, I was just asking."

He rolls his eyes, and I subtly move mine between the two of them. That's not the first time he's said or done something to piss her off, but Frankie never seems to react to him the way she usually does. If anyone else talked to her like that, she'd be threatening to shove her fist down their throat by now. I wait for it, but she doesn't say anything to him. Instead, she hides a smile behind her knuckles, and it makes me want to hit something.

Great. The psycho girl has a soft spot for him too.

"We should take him to the gay club," Frankie suggests out of nowhere, and Carter grins.

"Yes."

"No," Xavi and I say together, our gazes colliding at the exact same time. I glare at him, and he glares right back.

"I'll go if I want to."

"The fuck you will."

Easton clears his throat and runs a hand through his hair. "I'll go," he says to Frankie and Carter, clearly uncomfortable and ready to get out of here.

"Wait, *you're* gonna go to the gay club?" Xavi asks, perking up as he turns around on his knees and rests his arms on the back of the couch.

"Why not?" Easton shrugs, smirking a little as he wraps his arm around Frankie's neck. "The bi girls are there."

She playfully shoves his face away, and Xavi chuckles, his face falling when he catches my eyes again. "Why can't I go?"

"Probably because you're a recovering junkie," Carter says bluntly, still grinning at all the drama as he pops a piece of gum into his mouth. "Too much temptation."

Frankie's eyes widen slightly.

Xavi's cheeks glow even brighter as he spits out, "Fuck you, Carter."

"Just tell me how you want it, baby boy," he teases, grabbing the base of his dick through his pants.

I pull him back by his collar before he can take a step, facing Xavi as I put myself between him and Carter. "You're not going."

Folding his arms over his chest, he raises his eyebrows like a brat. "You don't think I can do it?"

"I know you can't."

His eyes narrow, and he pushes himself off the couch, looking both humiliated and determined as he folds the throw blanket exactly the way I like it.

"What are you doing?"

"Proving it to you," he answers, speaking to Frankie and the boys as he passes. "Give me an hour."

I step in front of him again, and he stops just shy of bumping into me, his eyes slowly moving up from my shorts, over my abs and chest, and then finally landing somewhere around my mouth, not quite brave enough to look me in the eye when we're this close. My hands move without my consent, and I curl my fingers around his waist, pulling him in and thumbing his hip bones beneath the hoodie. He melts against me almost instantly, like a little bitch who can't get enough, desperate for my attention.

Cupping the side of his soft face, I force him to meet my gaze while I brush the small cut on his cheek. He swallows, clamping his lips shut tight and refusing to answer my unspoken question.

I can't get a read on what he's thinking right now. His head is too messed up for me to even attempt it, but I can tell he's nervous, and I love it. I love the way he acts when I'm around, like he's constantly on edge, waiting for me to punch him. Or fuck him.

I let my hands fall off his body, then step aside, tilting my head at the door to give him permission. He blinks, ducking his face to hide his expression as he walks out of the room.

"Well, shit."

"Shut up, Carter," I mutter, gripping the t-shirt around my neck while I watch my boy go.

AFTER MY SHOWER, I dry myself off, wrap a clean towel around my waist, and walk out of the bathroom, my bare feet drawn toward the corner of my closet. Reaching up to the top shelf, I find the black box I'm looking for and slide it out, carefully setting it down on the vanity. I glare at it for a solid minute before I bite the bullet and take the lid off.

I don't look at these pictures often, mostly because I hate them, but also because every time I do, the temptation to tear them all up and set them on fire almost wins. I still want to do that, maybe force Xavi to watch while I rip out the last piece of his heart, but I know it wouldn't change a damn thing.

I used to think that if I tried hard enough, if I pushed hard enough, I could turn Katy against him and tear them apart, but I never stood a chance. She used to tell me they were *platonic soulmates* or some shit, and it turns out she was right. It didn't matter what I did, there was nothing I could do to keep them away from each other.

I pick up one of the Polaroid pictures on top and stare at it. They're at the carnival in this one, sitting at the top of the Ferris wheel. He's got his arm wrapped around her neck, and she's got her tongue on his cheek, her arm outstretched in front of them to take the picture. He looks like he's both grinning and cringing, and she's laughing so hard her hand must have been shaking, blurring the shot a little.

Turning it over, I read the words she scribbled on the back. Katy's handwriting was a disaster even on good days, but I've read this so many times that I can make it out just fine.

I licked it so it's mine.

Smiling a little, I toss the picture back into the box and gently set the lid on top. "Too bad, little sister," I whisper. "He's mine now."

JUST AS I'M leaving my room, Xavi walks out of his with ten minutes to spare, pulling the door shut behind him and shoving his wallet and phone into his back pocket.

I curse when I get a good look at him, quickly closing the distance between us and making him jump, his eyes wide as I cage him in against the wall.

I don't know whether he's trying to piss me off or impress me, but either way, he's succeeded at both.

He's wearing the tightest pair of jeans he owns and a black fishnet crop top. It's long sleeved, but the hem is high, sitting just below his nipples. His piercings poke through the material, and my fingers glide over his ribs and then up to his chest to graze the metal. He gasps, and I kiss him without warning, squeezing his nipple hard enough to make him moan into my mouth.

"Fuck."

Yeah. Fuck.

I don't know what's wrong with me.

I hate him, but I can't stay away from him.

The way I'm pulled toward him...I'm fucking powerless to stop it.

There's a silver chain with various pendants on it around his narrow waist, and I hook a finger under it, my dick jerking behind my zipper while I imagine how hot he's gonna look when I'm fucking him later.

I tug on it while I kiss him, and he whimpers, opening his mouth and offering me his tongue. He's not supposed to give it to me until it's fully healed, but I still take it, teasing just the tip and the edges with mine, careful not to touch his piercing.

He pushes himself up on his tiptoes to try to get closer, like he wants to climb inside my skin and live there. I help him out, hooking his thigh around my hip and sliding my free hand into his back pocket. I steal his things and shove them into my pockets instead, only taking my hands off him for a second before I put them back on his body.

"What are you doing?"

"They're in the way," I tell him, spreading my fingers over his ass and squeezing. "I wanna see the shape of this ass every time you move tonight."

"Nate," he whines, locking his arms around my neck, rubbing his big dick on my thigh. "I changed my mind."

"About what?"

"I don't wanna go out," he says quickly, his hands shaking as he tries to unbutton my jeans. "I wanna stay here with you. Fuck me right here. Please."

Suppressing a groan, I snatch his wrists and pin them to the wall. He tries to wriggle free, so I slam his hands back again. He looks up at me then, and I kiss him softer this time, teasing him.

"Fucker," he whispers, and I laugh, looking left when Carter's door opens beside us.

He stops walking when he sees us, his eyes immediately landing on Xavi's body, his mouth forming that stupid smirk of his as he devours him with his gaze. "You really gonna let him wear that?"

"He can wear what he wants." I run the backs of my fingers over Xavi's waist chain, looking at him again. "No one's gonna get near him."

His eyes seem to darken and light up all at once, and I nip his bottom lip, my touch just as soft as the words coming out of my mouth.

"If you even try to make me jealous tonight, I'll fuck you so hard and for so long, you'll never want dick again by the time I'm done with you."

"I'm not gonna try to make you jealous." His arms come around my neck, his breath tickling my jaw. "I'm not trying to make you mad, Nate. I just wanted to look good for you."

My groan slips free, and I grab his hips, rubbing myself on him to show him how hard he's making me. "You look so good, baby," I rasp, cupping his face to study the eyeliner he's wearing. "So pretty."

He flushes and bites his lip. "I wish I had a choker to wear," he says, and I drop my eyes to his throat.

Taking his wrist, I ignore the way Carter's gaping at us while I walk Xavi down the hall. He looks confused when I knock on Frankie's bedroom door, not taking my eyes off him as she calls out, "Okay, okay, I'm almost done!"

I open the door wide and step out of the way, gesturing for Xavi to go on in and ask her for one. He doesn't move, scrunching his nose as he cranes his neck to peek inside the room. "I'm not going in there."

I push him in anyway, and he hits me with a wide-eyed, panicked look over his shoulder. Just as he's about to run back out, Frankie appears wearing nothing but her underwear and a pair of red bottoms on her feet. "Damn," she says, her huge grin aimed at Xavi. "Boy, you look hot."

His eyes are still wide, and he's turning red from his cheeks to his abs, unable to hide it with all that bare skin on display. He's looking anywhere but at her, and she's straight up eye-fucking him right in front of me, snorting when she catches my glare.

I move to leave, then stop when something occurs to me. "Did you eat today?" I ask Xavi, and he hesitates before shaking his head.

Grinding my teeth, I walk down to the kitchen and cook him some food, pretending Carter isn't drilling his eyes into my back, worried I've gone crazy.

CHAPTER TWENTY-EIGHT

Nate

Xavi keeps touching his neck as if he can feel my eyes on it, looking at me sideways every so often to check I'm still watching him.

The choker Frankie let him borrow is silver and tight, just a finger's width of space between it and his flesh, the tiny butterfly pendant dangling on his throat matching the ones on his waist chain. It looks so good on him, I'm tempted to tell him he's never taking it off.

He smiles as if he can hear the incessant thoughts running around in my head, his hand flexing in mine as we near the main entrance of the club we're taking him to. I grabbed him when we got out of the truck and refused to let him go, making a point to position myself between him and Carter when I caught Carter staring at his ass.

"Why didn't we take an Uber?" Xavi asks, tipping his chin at Frankie's truck over my shoulder. "I don't trust myself to drive that thing, Frankie. It's too big."

"You're not driving my truck," she says, outraged he'd even say such a thing.

"Then how are we supposed to get back?"

"In my truck..." she says slowly. "That I'll be driving."

He frowns. "Are you not drinking tonight?"

"None of us are," Frankie tells him, fluffing her hair in a car window as we pass it.

He looks at the boys, blinking at them when Easton shrugs like it's no big deal. Xavi side-eyes me with his brows drawn in, the accusation clear, and I subtly shake my head. I didn't tell them they couldn't drink tonight. That's on them.

We get to the club to find it just as busy as it always is, body to body, the rainbow-colored strobe lights flashing across the huge space. Looking around, I immediately spot two guys passing pills with their tongues against the wall in the corner, which is exactly why I didn't want Xavi coming here, but he's not even looking at them. He looks more concerned about my hand being in his, his fingers twitching every few seconds as if he wants to let go.

"Stop," I say, and he stops, chewing that goddamn lip ring again while I turn him to face me.

Frankie and the boys leave us to it and head down to the dance floor, and I walk Xavi back into the glass balcony overlooking the lower level. Still holding his hands, I push myself into him, shamelessly letting everyone around us know that he's mine. There are so many eyes on him right now, but he's either ignoring them or he genuinely doesn't notice, not once looking away from me.

I don't even know why I'm so worried. I might not be the only guy he's ever let fuck him, but I'm the only guy he's ever looked at like that. I've never seen him look at anyone the way he looks at me. Not even Katy, and he used to look at her like she was his entire world.

"Nate..." he warns, swallowing when my lips brush his piercing. "Nate, someone could recognize you."

"Would you believe me if I told you you're worth it?" I ask, and he narrows his pretty eyes into slits.

"No."

A light laugh leaves me, and I finally let him have his hands back, taking his waist before running my palms over his stomach. "No one's gonna recognize me, but if they do, Carter's here. He's got my back."

He turns his head to follow my line of sight over the balcony, seeing Carter looking up at us as he dances with some pretty, dark-haired boy who looks a lot like Xavi from a distance. I glare, and Carter grins, the fucker.

"There are rumors going around about you, you know?" Xavi asks, pulling my attention back to him.

"Yeah, I know."

"But you don't care?"

"My dad's the only one who cares, Xav. I don't give a shit what people say about me. The only reason I'm not out is because I just want—"

"An easy life," he finishes for me, nodding. "I get it."

His smile is more sad than comforting, and it suddenly makes me want to make him smile for real.

"Come dance with me."

"What?"

Ignoring his shock, I take him downstairs and guide him through all the bodies on the dance floor, taking his waist and hooking my fingers under the chain resting on his hips. He hesitantly reaches up and links his hands behind my neck, allowing me to move his body and roll our hips together.

Carter raises a brow at me over his shoulder, and I smirk, lowering my head to put my mouth near Xavi's ear. "You remember the last time I caught you and my sister in a place like this?"

He nods, and I don't miss the smug look on his face before he tries to hide it in my neck.

I remember walking into that club with Carter and finding Katy with some guy I'd never seen before, him standing in front of her like a human shield while Xavi was fighting with another guy just a few feet away. Furious with both of them, I grabbed my sister and told Carter to watch her, then moved to grab her idiot best friend, pulling him off the guy he was on top of by the back of his neck. Xavi tried to take a swing at me, so I grabbed him by the throat and yanked his little body into mine, daring him with my eyes to do it. All the color drained from his face when he saw it was me, and he finally calmed down, wincing when I yelled at him to stop fighting in front of my sister. I lost count of how many times he'd gotten into it with some guy who tried to put hands on her. I probably would have thanked the little shit if he wasn't the one putting her in danger like that night after night.

Just as I was about to drag them both out of there, the guy on the floor stood up and tried to go for Xavi again, and I lost it. I knocked him out right there in the middle of the club, my knuckles bloody as I grabbed Xavi's arm and dragged him to the exit. He couldn't stop smiling, even as his lip was bleeding, dripping all over his chin and neck, I'd never seen him look happier. It pissed me off, and I ended up pinning him to the wall outside. That was as close as I'd ever gotten to him before, and I knew he liked it just as much as I was pretending not to. His dick was hard, and he didn't even try to hide it from me. It was only when we both noticed that I was hard too that I finally let him go and took ten steps away from him.

Carter and I took Katy to the car, and Xavi stayed against the wall I'd pushed him into, still smiling as he watched me leave him behind.

"Cocky little asshole," I mutter, and Xavi laughs in my ear, tightening his arms around my neck as we roll our hips to the beat of the music.

His breath catches when I run my hands down to his ass, his cheeks glowing beneath the lights. Cocking my head, I discreetly rub my middle finger over his hole through his jeans. He moans, sinking his nails into the back of my neck.

"Baby..."

"Hm?"

"What have you got in your ass?"

"A plug."

I curse, and he grins proudly, his eyes closing as he continues dancing against me.

"You're such a slut." I take his face in my hands, waiting for him to look at me again. "Did you put it in for me? So you're nice and ready for my dick as soon as we get home?"

He nods.

"Good boy," I say, and he arches up onto his tiptoes to kiss me.

I kiss him back and take him to one of the empty couches in the corner of the club, sitting down and guiding his legs over my thighs. He straddles me and rubs his ass on my dick to get comfortable, his teeth playing with my lips. "You think anyone will be able to tell if I make you come in your jeans?"

"Probably, yeah."

"I'll take that risk if you will," he teases, and I snatch his hands before he can grab my cock, making him pout.

"Tell me about the list."

All the playfulness slips off his face, and he swallows, dropping his eyes to avoid mine.

"Tell me, Xav."

So quietly that I have to read his lips to catch it, he says, "I don't want to."

"Xavi."

"I said no, Nate." He tries to pull away from me, but I don't let him, grabbing the backs of his knees and yanking him right back.

"I won't get mad." I loosen my grip, sighing when he gives me this *look* as if to tell me I'm full of shit. "I promise."

"You won't punch me either?"

I shake my head, and he squints at me, pursing his lips as he thinks about it for a minute.

"I'm not telling you anything," he finally says. "You can ask me and I'll answer if I feel like it."

"Fine." I play along. "Did you write it out for her?"

He nods once, giving me nothing else.

I raise a brow, unable to resist asking the question I want to know the answer to most. "And the last one?"

"Fuck me," he mutters under his breath, rubbing a hand through his hair as his face heats with embarrassment. I tilt my head, waiting, and he rolls his eyes, dropping his arm back down on his lap. "Okay, look, that was Katy, not me. I didn't even know it was on there until I broke into your house to get it."

"You broke into my house?"

"You beat me up and kicked me out of her funeral," he snaps at me, his teeth clenching at the lack of remorse on my face. "I was pissed at you and I knew you'd all be at the church for a while, and I just..."

"You just what?"

"I just wanted something that was hers, okay?"

No, it's not okay.

I'm just about to tell him he didn't deserve anything that was hers, but I stop myself, doing my best not to get mad like I promised.

"And now what?" I ask. "She's not here to do those things herself, so you're doing them all for her?"

He hesitates for a few beats, then nods again, my heart twisting in my chest at the raw emotion on his face. It looks like love, but it's tainted, his guilt over what happened to her cutting him up inside.

I don't tell him I know exactly what that feels like.

"That's why you got your tongue pierced?"

"Yeah."

"Whose pool did you skinny dip in?"

"Bryson West's," he answers, and I think back to the party Easton brought him to the night he moved here, the night I dragged him out of the kitchen after he told me Katy always liked him more than me. "That's how I hurt my leg," he goes on, looking down and running a finger over the spot on his inner thigh. "I cut it on the fence when I was running away from his dad."

"He chased you?"

"Yeah, while I was butt naked." He scoffs out a laugh, shaking his head at the memory. "I shit myself."

"You know he owns a gun, right?"

"What?"

"Xavi, he's crazy," I stress, not finding this even a little bit funny. "Did he pull it on you?"

"I don't know. I was blindfolded."

Jesus Christ.

"Wait, why were you...?"

And then it hits me.

He's doing it all blind.

Fuck. There's something wrong with my heart.

Xavi clears his throat and averts his gaze, watching Easton and Frankie dance with a girl covered in tattoos a few feet away from us, her in the middle while my friends grind on her from both sides. Easton winks at Xavi, and Xavi's lips twitch, his head whipping back around to me when I say, "Go dance on the bar."

"What?"

"You heard me." I lean back on the couch and run my hands over his tight stomach, my fingertips teasing the skin under his crop top. "That's number seven, right? Dance on a bar."

"Yeah..."

"So go dance on the bar."

"I can't."

"Why not?"

"I didn't bring the blindfold."

Glancing around at all the shirtless people walking around the club, I reach behind my neck and pull my t-shirt over my head, twisting it a few times before I use it to cover Xavi's eyes. He gapes at me as I tie my shirt at the back of his head. Standing us both up, I walk him through the crowd and back onto the dancefloor.

Easton and Frankie have ditched the girl they were with, just the two of them dancing together now, so I walk up behind Frankie, leaning over her to shout over the music. "Distract the bartender for me."

She grins wickedly over her shoulder, and I take Xavi over to the least crowded spot by the bar. Not that it's gonna make any difference. He's not even up there yet, but people are already looking at him, curiously following him with their eyes as he adjusts the makeshift blindfold.

"If you're gonna fall, fall forward," I say in his ear, picking him up and setting his ass on the edge.

He lets out a squeak and reaches out to touch my shoulders, checking where I am. I tap his outer thigh, signaling for him to get up, and he doesn't even hesitate, pulling his legs in and pushing himself up to stand. "Come & Get It" by Selena Gomez is playing through the club, and Xavi doesn't miss a damn beat, drawing a crowd of people within seconds.

I can see Frankie and Easton in my peripheral, starting an argument with each other at the other end of the bar to get the bartender's attention. I'm sure Carter's around here somewhere too, but I don't take my eyes off Xavi to find out. I'm like a hawk stalking its prey, my fists resting on the edge of the bar in front of his feet, my fingernails cutting into my palms.

He looks so fucking sexy up there. He's moving like a stripper, slowly rolling his hips from side to side with his hands on his waist, his stomach, up over his neck and into his hair. His grin is huge, but I bet he doesn't realize how many people are watching his little show right now, drawn to him like moths to a flame.

It's kind of funny. Cocky little thing like him has no idea how beautiful he is.

I see a guy pointing his phone up at Xavi next to me, but before I can even think about my next move, Carter appears out of nowhere and casually takes it from his hand, pressing it to the guy's chest and telling him to beat it. He says something back to him, getting in Carter's face, and Carter shoves him harder than necessary. He stumbles back into someone else, and then a fight breaks out between Carter and a few of the other guy's friends.

Time to go.

Reaching up to grab the back of Xavi's thigh, I gently tug him toward me and catch him when he jumps into my arms, wrapping his legs around my waist as I take my shirt off his face. He grins at me like I just hung the goddamn moon for him, and I grin back, holding him up with my arm under his ass while I pull on the back of Carter's shirt. Pushing him to walk in front of me, I follow him to the exit, rolling my eyes when I see Frankie in a fight with a guy twice her size by the main doors. Carter grabs her from behind, and he and Easton carry her out of the club, avoiding getting knocked out by her long legs as she kicks them out at the guy she's still screaming at.

"They're your family now, aren't they?" Xavi asks me, and it's only now I realize there's a weird smile on my lips.

I nod, shrugging when I catch the pathetic look he's hitting me with. "Don't feel sorry for me, party boy. I've got more people I love than you do."

He presses his lips together and tightens his hands into fists on my shoulders, trying and failing to hide the hurt on his face. He tries to get down, so I smack his ass and squeeze it hard, pushing my fingers into his crease over his jeans. He groans and drops his face into my neck, probably regretting telling me about the plug in his ass.

"I'm gonna go home with that cute little twink who looks like

Xavi," Carter announces, and I stop walking, turning around to face him.

"I want his name and address."

"Why, so you can take my sloppy seconds again?" he teases, winking at Xavi when he sneers at him. "Relax, baby boy. I'm kidding."

"Why are you friends with him?" Xavi asks me.

"Because he pays half the rent," I answer, shaking my head at the stupid look on Carter's face.

"I love you too, bestie."

"Name and address, Carter."

"I already sent them."

I pull my phone out of my jeans to check, nodding at him when I see the message and the picture he sent me. He heads back inside the club, and I pocket my phone again, carrying Xavi back to the truck. Seemingly forgiving me for being a dick a minute ago, he wraps his arms around my neck and lays his head down on my shoulder, watching Easton and Frankie fall in line to follow us. "How did you meet Frankie?"

"If I told you that, she'd kill you in your sleep."

"Damn right," Frankie calls out.

I look back at her, stopping mid-step when I see her wiping the blood off her lip with her finger.

"Did that guy hit you back?" Easton asks, walking backward like he's about to run back in there.

"No, I bit my tongue."

My shoulders drop, and I lean back against the passenger side of her truck, allowing Xavi to slide down to his feet but not letting him go.

"What happened in there?" he asks, turning around to rest his head back on my chest.

"Nate told me to make a scene," Frankie says simply, taking a cigarette out and lighting it.

"I told you to distract the bartender," I correct her.

"Same thing." She shrugs. "Anyway. Easton and I were pretending to argue, pushing each other around and stuff, and then some guy got between us and tried to defend me. He took a swing at Easton, so I punched him in the throat."

Easton barks out a laugh, wrapping his arm around her neck and kissing her temple. "The look on his face, man. It was funny as shit."

Xavi chuckles and pulls my arms around his body, using me to keep himself warm. "Sorry," he says to Frankie.

"What are you sorry for?"

"Getting you kicked out of the club."

"Sweetie, it was so worth it," she tells him, smirking as she watches me play with his waistband. "That was one of the sexiest things I've ever seen."

"What was?"

"You," she says, smiling fondly at the confused frown on his face. "You really have no idea how hot you are, do you? It makes you even hotter."

"I...Thank you...?"

"You're welcome." She laughs, flicking the roach of her cigarette onto the street. "And don't worry about me getting kicked out of the club. I'll show the manager my tits next weekend and he'll let me right back in."

I snort, and Xavi scrunches his nose, tilting his head back to look at me upside down. "Is she kidding?"

"Probably not."

CHAPTER TWENTY-NINE

Xavi

My back hits my dresser, and I wince, clinging to him while he kisses me until I run out of air. My hands are fisted in his shirt, pulling it up over his abs, but I don't manage to get it off. I'm just trying to feel his skin on mine, arching my back to get as close to him as I possibly can.

I don't trust the way he's treating me tonight, the way he's been looking at me since the second I walked out of my room wearing the outfit I put on for him. It felt real, but I know it's not. I know I'm deliberately setting myself up for more heartache, but I'm too far gone to stop him. All I can think about right now is taking every scrap he's willing to give me. I'll deal with everything else later.

"You want it?" he asks, moving his mouth around to my ear as he works on my zipper.

"I'm an addict, Nate," I rasp. "I need it."

He pushes my waistband down over my hips and picks me up like I weigh nothing, putting me down on the dresser to pull my jeans and underwear the rest of the way off. The pressure of the plug in my ass makes me moan, the wicked gleam in his eyes telling me that's exactly why he put me up here.

"Take yours off too," I plead, spreading my legs to slide my toes over his outer thighs.

"No."

I try to glare, but I'm too worked up to make it stick. "Why do you always fuck me with your clothes on?"

"Because you want me to take them off," he says simply, his touch light as he fingers the chain on my waist. "I like the way you act like a spoiled bitch when you don't get what you want."

"I'm not a bitch."

"Those hickeys on your neck say *bitch*," he taunts me, repeating the exact same words Easton said to me yesterday. "*My* bitch."

My jaw ticks, and I stare into his eyes, fighting the urge to lean into his hand when he palms my neck and runs his thumb over one of the marks there. By some miracle, I manage to keep my head exactly where it is, not so patiently waiting for him to stop touching me like I'm his prized possession.

"Just fuck me so you can fuck off."

His lips curl upward, and he pushes me back, making me thump the back of my head on the wall. He pulls my lower half forward until I'm hanging off the dresser, his hand flat on my chest as he uses the other to rub the plug between my legs. My nostrils flare, but I don't get to call him an asshole because then he's pushing on the base, fucking me with it and making my eyes roll back in my head.

"God..."

His hand on my body travels up to my throat, and he wraps his fingers around the choker I'm wearing, holding me down as he takes the plug out. He sets it down on the side and slides two fingers inside me, hitting my prostate on every slow curl of his knuckles. It's impossible for me to keep quiet when he's teasing me like this, trying to get as much noise out of me as possible.

"Nate, please..."

I expect him to refuse, but he surprises me by picking me up again, gently lowering me down onto my bed. He makes himself at home between my legs and takes my hand, linking our fingers together as he bites on my bottom lip. "I like this," he whispers, flicking his tongue over my piercing before he sucks on it.

"Do you?" I ask distractedly, too focused on the way his hands feel in mine.

He tries to deepen the kiss, so I tip my head back and offer him my neck instead, desperate to hold on to whatever's left of my dignity. He doesn't let me, taking my jaw to pull my mouth back to his.

"*Nate*," I whine, struggling beneath him to get my hand back, but he just tightens his grip and refuses to let me go.

"What's wrong?"

The bastard knows what's wrong.

He chuckles into my mouth and feels around in my night-stand for a condom, pulling his head back when I snatch it from him and toss it across the room. He grabs another one, and I toss it again, grinning as sweetly as I can when he pins me down by my neck.

"Brat."

"I thought you liked it," I tease, rolling my hips up to rub my ass over the front of his jeans. "Have you ever put your cock in anyone without one before?"

"No."

"Do it to me," I rush out. "Please."

He lets go of my neck and grabs my dick instead, using his tight grip to stop me from grinding on him. "You don't like it when I hold your hand, but you want me to make you feel special by fucking you bare," he says slowly. "Make that make sense."

When I say nothing, he leans over me and touches my fore-head with his.

"Tell me why you want it."

"I don't know why."

Except that I do.

I've never let anyone fuck me without a condom before, but the thought of Nate sliding into me raw, feeling him inside me with nothing between us, his come leaking out of my ass...

It's driving me crazy.

"Come on, baby," he says in my ear. "Think harder."

I groan and wrap my arms around his neck. "I want to mean something to you," I admit. "*Anything*. I want you to remember me after you decide you're done with me and kick me out of your life for good. I wanna ruin you so bad that it's me you'll think about every time you're fucking the person you really wanna be with."

It's his turn to be speechless, staring at me as if he's mesmerized while I rock myself into his hand. Losing patience, I reach down to unzip his jeans, freeing his dick. Another couple seconds of silence pass before he finally snaps out of it, letting go of my cock before he spits into his open palm. "You wanna ruin my life, party boy?"

"You've already ruined mine," I mutter, lifting my ass up for him as he coats his dick with saliva. "It's only f—*fuck*," I say instead, my eyes dropping as he pushes the tip inside me.

"Is this what you want?"

"*Yes*."

He pushes the rest in with one roll of his hips, not stopping until his pelvis is pressed right up against my dick. We groan at the feel of it, my nails clawing at the sides of his neck as his fingers dig into my waist.

"God, baby," he rasps, flattening his hand and moving it over my stomach. "You need more lube?"

"No." I shake my head, my hole clenching at how big and hard he feels inside me. "I need it to hurt a little bit. Please, don't stop."

He tongues my choker as he rocks inside me, setting a steady pace that has my toes curling into the sheets.

"Oh my God, Nate..."

"Xavi, shut up."

"Harder," I beg, groaning again when he growls and pulls out fast. "Why are you stopping?"

"Because I *have* to, you little shit."

A surprised laugh bubbles out of me, and I lean up on my elbows to see what he's doing, raising a brow when I catch him squeezing the tip of his cock.

"You really can't last thirty seconds?"

He narrows his eyes, and I snap my lips shut to hide my amusement, grunting when he pushes me back down and shoves my legs apart by the backs of my knees. His mouth is on my hole before I even realize what he's doing, his tongue flicking my entrance a moment before he pushes it inside. He fucks me with it for a while, then pulls it back out to spit on me. I moan loudly, grabbing the back of his head and holding on tight. I use my other hand to reach for my dick, but he smacks it away before I can get to it, grabbing the base and pointing it down toward his mouth. My eyes widen, but he doesn't give me a second to prepare myself before he's *sucking* on it, sliding his thumb into my ass as he starts throating my dick.

"*Fuck!*"

My fingers dig into his scalp, my mouth hanging open as my legs begin to shake uncontrollably. He gags a few times, but he doesn't let that stop him. He just keeps coming back for more, looking up into my eyes with his spit and my precum dripping over his jaw.

"Jesus, fuck, Nate," I say, loving the way his puffy lips look stretched around my cock. "You look so hot with my dick in your mouth."

He eases off me, sliding his tongue over the underside and

making it even wetter. "You know I'm not the one with the praise kink, right?"

"I don't have a praise kink."

"You've got a degradation kink too," he adds, and I pull my head back, scrunching my nose.

"I do not."

"If you say so," he mutters, moving back up to his knees and slowly stroking his own cock. "Be a good little whore and show me what's mine."

The flash of heat in my eyes makes him smirk. Spreading my legs as far as they'll go, I move my hands underneath me and pull my cheeks apart, showing him like he told me to.

"That's it, baby." He moves closer, tapping my hole with his dick. "Hold it open for me."

I do, and he spits on me again, rubbing it around with his thumb before he eases his dick back inside. He fucks me slowly —*painfully* slowly—his eyes darkening as he rocks his hips back and forth.

"Do I feel good?" I ask.

"So good," he breathes out, leaning over me to speak against my lips. "You love this, don't you? Making me lose my damn mind..."

I nod, grabbing his head to pull him down to my neck. "Mark me," I beg. "I need more."

He sucks my skin into his mouth, and I shiver violently, planting my feet on either side of him to move with his body. Once he's done with my neck, he moves across to my collarbone and down to my chest, sucking on my nipple through the fabric of my top. I whimper at how good it feels, turning my head to look at the mirror on the wall. I avoid looking at my face and study our bodies instead, his still fully clothed while mine is completely naked from my chest down. He looks so much bigger on top of me like this, blanketing my small form with his huge one, his rough hands sliding over my sides, his forehead touching my chest as he flicks my piercings with his tongue.

I wish I could stay here forever. Be his forever.

He gently tugs on my jaw with his forefinger, and I look away from the mirror and up into his eyes, confused by the look on his face. It's kind of soft, and I don't like it, my hackles raising as he lowers his mouth to mine. He kisses me like he's never letting me go, and I pull away, turning my head to the other side. "Stop it, Nate."

"Stop what?" he asks innocently, still moving inside me as he feathers his lips over my face and neck.

"Stop *kissing* me." I pull away as much as I can, smacking his hand when he tries to pull me back again. "Jesus Christ. Just fuck me like you hate me."

"I do hate you."

"Then stop pretending you don't!"

The laugh he's been fighting slips free at my outburst, and he props himself up on his elbow, brushing my hair out of the way. "Does it confuse you when I touch you like this?"

"No," I deny, and he pulls his dick out of my ass and slams it back inside me once, *hard*. "*Yes*," I rush out. "Yes, it confuses the shit out of me, okay?"

He doesn't say it, but I hear the word he's thinking as he rubs his thumb over my bottom lip. *Good.*

"Nate..." I warn, my nails biting into my palms as he starts fucking me slowly again.

"You said I could take whatever I want, remember?"

"Not that," I grit out.

His lips twitch as he slides his hand over my chest, over the organ beating wildly beneath his touch.

"I want it, Xavi."

"You're not getting it."

"You're gonna give it to me anyway," he teases, pulling my mouth up to meet his.

Fuck him.

Fuck him so hard for doing this to me.

And fuck me for letting him.

Snatching both sides of his face, I kiss him back and open my mouth, letting him feel my tongue piercing for the first time. He groans and sucks on it greedily, shoving his hand down between us to wrap it around my cock. "Good boy," he says, and fuck me, maybe I do have a praise kink. "You want it hard?"

I nod, and he gives it to me, hitting my prostate and jerking me off at the same time, not stopping until I'm chanting his name and coming all over us both. The moan he lets out into my mouth makes me whimper, my fingers digging into his scalp and my legs locked around his waist, holding him down on me as I feel his hot cum filling my ass. I lift my hips up, trying to steal every last drop. He smacks my outer thigh, and I yelp, laughing lightly when he falls down on me and drops his head on my shoulder.

He doesn't move for a while after that. He's heavy, but I don't mind, easing his shirt up and trailing my fingertips over his sides while I wait for us both to come down. After a few minutes, he lifts his head to look at me, examining my face with his hand tucked underneath my jaw.

"Why don't you wear makeup anymore?"

"What?"

"I like it when you wear it," he says, swiping his thumbs over the black smudges beneath my eyes. "It's sexy when it runs down your face like this."

I chew my lip, refraining from telling him I'm gonna wear it every day now I know how he feels about it.

I know he feels my cock getting hard again, and just when I think he's about to get up and leave, he looks down and wraps his fingers around it. "Your dick is so big," he says, swirling his thumb over the cum on the tip. "I've never done that before."

"Done what?" I ask absently, my abs clenching at how sensitive it feels with him touching it like that.

"Put one in my mouth."

I chuckle, my brows jumping when I realize he's not messing with me. "You're serious? Why?"

"I don't like it. Not even when I'm the one getting my dick sucked. I'd rather just fuck and get it over with."

"You liked it when I did it," I remind him. "And you throated mine like you were starving for it."

"That's because I was." He twists his fist around the head, looking up at me again when he feels my eyes on the top of his head. "Wipe that stupid look off your face, party boy. I still hate you."

"You sure?"

"Stop talking, Xavi."

I should probably listen to him and stop before I get my feelings hurt, but I don't.

"Wanna know what I think?"

"Not really."

"I think you're full of shit," I tell him anyway. "I think you're starting to like me."

"Do you?"

"Just a little bit," I mock whisper, pinching my thumb and forefinger together.

He laughs and lets go of my dick, once again grabbing my jaw as he crawls over the top of me. "I don't fuck you because I like you. I fuck you because you're easy."

"I'm not that easy." I keep playing, smirking as I lean up on my forearms and tease his mouth with mine. "It took you five years to get inside me."

"Baby, I could have had you in five minutes if I wanted you." He closes the small gap between us, sucking on my lip. "Easy."

He's got me there.

"Why didn't you then?"

"You were fifteen."

"I lost my virginity when I was fourteen," I tell him, enjoying the way his eyes darken with jealousy.

"Who was he?"

"Who said they were a he?"

His brows jump at that, more surprised than amused. "Have you fucked a girl before?"

I nod, already anticipating his next question, trying not to laugh as I wait for his mind to catch up.

He searches my gaze, then blinks, quickly wrapping his hand around my neck, the butterfly pendant digging into my throat with his tight grip.

There it is.

"If you fucked my little sister, I will kill you right now."

My laugh tumbles out, and I place my hand over his, not to get him off me, but to hold him there. "I didn't, I promise. It was just the one girl. She was my brother's friend. We did it the first time I got high. I knew something was up with me when I didn't like it, but I just thought it was the drugs or something. I didn't realize I was gay until the first time you touched me."

He frowns and searches my face again, a dubious smile touching his lips. "You're lying."

"I swear to God. Remember the first time you caught me climbing in through Katy's window? You grabbed me by my hoodie and threatened to throw me out of it."

"Yeah, and you just stared at me..."

"That's because I was so hard I didn't know what to do with myself," I tell him, chuckling as I run my palms up beneath his shirt. "I remember it hitting me that the reason I loved riling you up so much is because I had a crush on you or some shit. I was so scared, I climbed back in after you kicked me out and freaked out while I was coming out to Katy. She didn't disown me like I thought she would though. She just laughed and told me she loved me no matter who I wanted to fuck. Or be fucked by."

He stares at me for an uncomfortable amount of time, making me regret everything I just said.

"Katy was the first person you came out to?"

"She was the only person, Nate. A few people know I'm gay, obviously, but Katy was the only person I ever trusted enough to say it out loud to. And now you, I guess..." I pause, clearing my throat. "Anyway. I avoided you for a month after I figured it out because I thought you'd be able to tell. Wanna know what happened the first time you saw me again?"

"What?"

"You could tell," I say, and he laughs.

"Xavi, I knew you were gay the first time I saw you."

"Good for you, but I didn't."

He shakes his head at me and pulls out of my ass, making me whine at how empty I feel after having his dick inside me for so long.

"Don't leave."

As soon as the words leave my mouth, I slam my head back against the pillows, wishing I could pull them back.

Goddamn it, he's got me running around in circles. One minute I hate the way he's touching me and I'm desperate for him to stop, and then as soon as he takes it away, I feel like I'll die if I don't get it back.

When I finally find the courage to peek up at him, I find him standing at the foot of my bed, smirking at me as he tucks his dick back into his jeans.

My legs are still wide open, and I can feel his cum dripping out of my ass, clenching my hole to keep as much inside me as possible. His eyes flash, but he doesn't move, not even when I reach down and rub my fingertips over the mess he made. He watches me though, taking much longer than necessary to zip his jeans back up.

Leaning over me again, he places both hands on the bed on either side of my head. "Am I your drug now, party boy?" he asks.

I nod, unashamed as I finger myself and push his cum back into my ass. I'm just about ready to beg him to fuck me again, just once, anything to convince him to stay, but he's already backing away.

"I'm sure you'll live without it," he taunts, smirking at the way my face falls just before he closes the door behind him.

I pull my fingers out of my ass, wiping them on the covers as I glare at the ceiling. I think about following him, sneaking into his room and climbing into bed with him, but manage to convince myself that would be stupid.

So stupid.

Rolling off the bed, I clean up and change my sheets, angrily shoving the dirty ones into the hamper. I take a scalding hot shower and scrub my sore body, refusing to look at the fresh marks on my neck as I towel myself dry.

Immediately regretting washing his scent away, I throw on the hoodie he gave me and grab my cigarettes, stopping mid-step when I see the present wrapped in black paper sitting on the window seat. That wasn't in here when I cleaned up just now, meaning someone must have come in and left it there while I was in the bathroom.

Eyeing it suspiciously, I pick it up and take a seat, propping my feet up while I stick my cigarette between my teeth. There's a white ribbon and a neat bow on it, but no card, no name to tell me who it's from. I set it down on my lap and tear the paper off, my heart thumping in my ears as soon as I recognize the black box that used to live at the bottom of Katy's closet.

"Holy shit," I choke out, the cigarette falling from my mouth as I cover my face with my hands.

Letting out a shaky breath, I swipe the moisture from my eyes and carefully take the lid off, and when I see all the Polaroids inside, I wrap my arms around the box and cry my heart out.

I DON'T KNOW how long I've been sitting here, going through all the photos and reliving the best three years of my life. When I finish looking at the last one, I put them all back and stand to walk around my bed, finding my wallet where Nate left it on my nightstand. I take out Katy's list and grab my marker, uncapping it to cross out number seven—*Dance on a bar.* After I put it away, I tap my phone screen to check how much charge it's got, frowning at the messages I missed.

UNKNOWN

Nice boyfriend.

Gritting my teeth, I zoom in on the picture they sent me, cursing when I realize it's one of me and Nate. He's leaning back against Frankie's truck on the street outside the club, his arms around my waist and his mouth on my neck. My head is tilted to the side, and it's clear I'm loving every second.

UNKNOWN

Your last one was hotter.

My leg kicks out into my nightstand, and I wince at the noise it makes, staying dead silent for a few minutes so I can hear if Nate decides to come and check what the fuck I'm doing. He doesn't come, so I quickly lock the door and type out a reply.

XAVI

What do you want?

It's been hours since he sent that last message, but like the stalker he is, he replies almost instantly.

UNKNOWN

You know what I want.

Before I can tell him there's not a chance in hell, blackmail or not, he texts me again.

UNKNOWN

Happy birthday, Xav. I left your present on your bike.

My eyes widen, and I move as quickly and quietly as I can, jogging downstairs and out the front door. I snatch the brick sized box off the seat of my bike. I already know what's inside, but I still take the lid off, sneering at the several little bags of pills and coke inside.

UNKNOWN

You're welcome.

His perfect timing makes me nervous, and I look around, squinting at the thick trees surrounding the property.

XAVI

Are you still here?

UNKNOWN

You don't belong with him and you know it.

The bright headlights shining through the iron gates scare the shit out of me, and I make a run for it, hauling my ass through the front door and locking it behind me. I shut the lights off and back away, hiding myself against the corner wall in the entryway. I jump at the sound of a key in the lock, and then the door opens, the lights flicking back on to reveal Carter walking inside. My shoulders sink with relief, and I blow out a long breath. I've never been so happy to see him in my life.

He grins when he sees me wearing nothing but Nate's

hoodie, the hem sitting at the tops of my thighs, but then he must see the remnants of horror on my face, and he drops the act. "What?"

I know I have to tell him, but I still hesitate, keeping my hands behind my back to hide my *present*. "Don't get mad."

"Show me," he says, so I show him. His eyes flick down to the open box in my hand and then back up to mine, his jaw clenched tight as he snatches the drugs. "Was he here?"

I nod, tilting my head at the front door. "He left it on my bike. I don't know if he's still out there."

"Damn it, Xavi," he hisses as he looks out the window, but he doesn't seem scared, just mad.

"I said don't get mad."

"You told me it was over."

"It *is* over. I haven't seen or talked to him since we..." I trail off, cringing. "You know."

"He hasn't tried to see you since you got out of rehab?" he asks, and I shake my head. "Then why now?"

"He saw us at the club," I answer, passing him my phone to show him the picture.

He glares at it for a few seconds before he passes it back. "I'll deal with it. Go back to bed."

"I'm going with you."

"No, you're not."

"Carter—"

"You think he's not gonna notice you're gone in the middle of the night?" he whispers, stepping closer to me as he throws a hand toward the stairs. "I wanted to tell him, Xavi. You're the one who's terrified for him to find out."

"I already told him a little bit," I say quietly, backing away from him when I catch the anger in his eyes.

"What?"

"Last night," I admit. "He asked me, so I...I told him I was with my dealer when Katy died."

His jaw ticks, and he cocks his head, not bothering to hide how stupid he thinks I am. "How'd that go for you?"

I huff out a breath, crossing my arms over my chest as I stare at my bare feet on the tiled floor.

"Next time he asks, do us both a favor and keep your fuckin' mouth shut," he says harshly, shoulder-checking me on his way to the front door.

"Carter."

"What?"

I wait for him to turn and face me, awkwardly rubbing the back of my neck as I say, "Thanks."

"Fuck off, Xavi. The only reason I keep doing this shit for you is because we're in too deep. If Nate finds out, my ass is on the line right next to yours."

IT'S BEEN ALMOST two and a half hours since Carter left. I've been sitting on the window seat in my room all night, staring at the dark driveway and waiting for his car to pull up. I tried calling him, but of course he didn't answer.

When he finally gets home at just after five in the morning, I sit up straight, looking down at him as he climbs out of his car. He nods up at me when he catches me watching, and I sigh out my relief.

Knowing he probably won't feel like telling me if I ask him what happened, I don't bother going downstairs. Climbing into bed, I bury myself under the covers, wishing I hadn't changed the sheets so I could use Nate's scent to get me to sleep.

My eyes refuse to stay closed, and when the first light of the sun comes in through the window, I hear my phone go off and reach out to check it.

UNKNOWN

Fucking pussy.

Send your guard dog after me again, I'm sending you his dick in a box.

I scoff and toss my phone back on the nightstand.

CHAPTER THIRTY

Xavi

Nate's shutting me out. Not that I was expecting any different after the last time we were together, but it feels different this time.

I know giving me that box of photos was more difficult for him than he'd ever let on. At the time, I figured he'd have to care about me at least a little to give them up, but ever since that night, I haven't seen him once. He's not taunting me with silence like he usually does. He's not making a point to ignore me every time we're in the same room together. He's just...not here.

He's hiding from me and I hate it.

I drop my head back against the headboard and run my fingers over Frankie's butterfly choker on my throat. I've been wearing it every day this week, putting eyeliner on every morning, walking around the house wearing the skimpiest tops I own, all in the hopes that Nate will find out and come find me to do something about it. But either Frankie and the boys aren't snitching on me, or they *are* snitching and Nate just doesn't give a shit.

Picking up my phone, I scroll until I find Nate's number.

> **XAVI**
>
> Hey.
>
> Where are you?

I cringe as soon as I hit send for the second time, even more so when I see he's read the message but doesn't bother texting me back. I wait five minutes, and then another twenty, sitting up straight when he finally decides to acknowledge me.

> **NATE**
>
> Who is this?

I huff. I know he used to have my number because he used to call me all the time and threaten me to tell him where Katy and I were.

> **XAVI**
>
> You really deleted my number?

He leaves me on read for another seven minutes.

> **NATE**
>
> I never saved it in the first place.
>
> What do you want? I'm busy.

> **XAVI**
>
> Busy doing what?

He doesn't text me back at all after that, and I can just picture him shaking his head and shoving his phone back into his pocket, probably enjoying what a stage five clinger he's turned me into.

A LITTLE WHILE AFTER NIGHTFALL, I hear his car pull up and leap off the bed like it burned me. Walking over to the window, I peek out through the blinds, relieved when I see he's alone, grabbing his gym bag from the back seat. I don't know why I thought he might be hooking up with someone else, that he might bring someone else home with him. I don't think he hates me *that* much, but I never know with Nate.

When he doesn't look up at my window like he usually does, I glance at my bedroom door, debating doing something I shouldn't.

Fuck it.

I have nothing to lose. Not even my dignity because that bitch is long gone.

Heading out of my room, I make my way to the next one over. He doesn't keep his door locked, so I let myself in and walk into his bathroom. Turning the water on, I strip out of my clothes and step under the showerhead, tipping my head back to get my face and hair wet. Grabbing his shower gel off the neatly stacked shelf in the corner, I squeeze some into my palm and put the bottle back in the wrong place to mess with him. I smile to myself as I wash my body, loving the way it makes me smell like him.

He doesn't keep me waiting for long. As if he can sense my desperation for him, he steps into the bathroom and squints at me, my eyes on his as I leisurely jerk myself off with the soap bubbles.

"What do you think you're doing?"

"Waiting for you," I answer, making myself shiver as I squeeze out a drop of precum. "Did you miss me?"

"Not really," he mutters, but he can't stop his hungry gaze from traveling over my soaking wet body.

I smirk because if he wants it, he's gonna have to take his clothes off and come and get it. But this is Nate we're talking about, and the stubborn fucker doesn't play the way I want him to. Cocking his head at me, he sets his phone and car keys down on the counter, then steps into the shower fully clothed. I pout, watching the water soak the white t-shirt he's wearing until it's completely see-through. I can see his nipples and the outline of his abs through the material, close enough for me to touch, but I don't get the chance before he's moving closer and tracing the choker around my neck with his forefinger. The smug grin on his lips makes me want to bite it off his face.

"You're such a prick," I grouch, and he kisses me, squeezing my throat with his left hand while he wraps the other one around mine on my dick.

I moan at the way he's helping me jerk myself, opening my mouth and sticking my tongue out for him, encouraging him to suck on it.

"What about this?" he asks, licking around my piercing.

"It's all better now," I tell him, teasing a finger over his abs. "You can fuck it if you want."

He lets out a breath and pushes me to my knees. Tucking his sweats down beneath his balls, he grabs the base of his hard cock and yanks my head forward by the back of my neck. If I thought he was gonna be gentle about it, I was dead wrong. Before I can even attempt to prepare myself, his dick is in my throat and I'm choking on it, digging my fingers into his hips to keep myself steady. Leaning on the wall with his free hand, he pulls my head back by my hair and forces me to look up at him, holding me still as he rocks his hips back and forth.

"Fuck, that feels good," he says, more to himself than me, fucking into me deeper.

I gag, and he lets me breathe for no longer than five seconds, pulling my face back by my jaw when I try to turn it away. The same thing happens the next time he lets me take a break, and he pulls my hair so hard I wince.

"Turn your face away from me again and I'll fuck it until you're choking on my cum."

I glare, my hackles raising at how weird he's acting. "What's wrong with you?"

"You're what's wrong with me," he grits out, and I look up at him dumbly, feeling a little dizzy.

"I don't know what that means."

"That's because you're an idiot."

I huff and open my mouth, widening my eyes like a brat and making a point to not look away.

"Good boy," he praises, laughing lightly at the heat in my eyes before he shoves his dick back down my throat.

It hurts, but I don't beg him to stop like I think he was expecting me to. I might as well be begging him to keep going, trying my hardest to impress him by taking him in as deep as I can. My lungs are on fire and I'm gagging on every hit, and just when I'm sure I'm about to puke, he yanks my head back and swipes his thumb over my bottom lip. His cock is dripping, and he rubs it all over my mouth and cheeks, coating my face with the mix of his precum and my own spit. It's messy and disgusting, and I love it.

"God, baby," he groans when I suck on the tip, tonguing his slit with my piercing. "*Fuck.*"

He pulls out and leaves the bathroom, leaving me alone and confused on my knees. I'm just about to get up, but he returns a moment later and tosses me a bottle of lube, retaking his spot in front of me and nudging my inner thigh with his foot.

"Spread your legs and finger yourself open for me. I want you ready."

I nod obediently, flipping the cap off the top to coat my fingertips. Lifting my dick and balls out of the way, I reach down and rub my hole to prep myself. He taps my lip with his cock, and I open wide, moaning around him as I slide my middle fingers inside my ass.

"Harder," he demands, and I do what he says, my jaw and arm aching as I finger myself open.

He takes it easy on me this time, letting me suck him at my own pace, stroking the back of my neck as he bounces his eyes between my face and the spot between my open thighs. He can't decide where to look, and even though I'm on my knees, it's making me feel ten feet tall, knowing he's as worked up as I am.

"I'm ready," I tell him, and even though he looks like he doesn't quite believe me, he doesn't call me out on it.

He pulls me up to my feet, pushes me back against the wall, and hooks my thigh around his hip. I cover his dick with lube, and he looks down between us, taking over to line himself up. I cry out when he slides into me, wrapping my arms around his shoulders and burying my face into his neck. Not giving me a second to relax, he fucks me hard against the shower wall, my cock trapped between our stomachs as the water rains down on us both. Without thinking too much into it, I sink my teeth into his wet flesh, biting him harder when he squeezes my ass with both hands.

"Nate," I whine, and he hauls me up, dragging both of my legs around his waist.

His phone rings on the counter behind him, but he either can't hear it or he's ignoring it, probably bruising my ass with his fingertips as he fucks me hard and fast. It rings again, and he grunts into my ear, turning us around and carrying me out of the shower. With his dick still buried in my ass, he sets me down on the edge of the counter, dries his left hand, and hits the answer button.

"What?" he asks as he lifts the phone up to his ear, narrowing his eyes at my chest as he listens to whoever it is. "What's she doing?"

He keeps fucking me, so I lean back on my hand and arch my back, rolling my hips up while I pinch my nipple between my thumb and forefinger. He leans over me to bite it, and I moan louder than I mean to, grabbing the back of his head to press my lips into his hair.

"Who do you think it is?" he grumbles against my skin, looking up at me as he drops his voice to a whisper. "Come before he hangs up or don't come at all. I've got shit to do."

My nostrils flare, and he traps my nipple between his teeth, sucking it into his mouth and making me shiver.

"Spit on my dick," I rasp, and he surprisingly does as I ask, pulling back to let his saliva drip down to where my hand is wrapped around my cock.

My thighs begin to clench when he hits my prostate, and I jerk myself off hit for hit, whimpering out a curse as I race him to the edge. He gets there first, and I'm right behind him, biting my lip to keep myself quiet as I feel him filling my ass with his cum. Mine hits my abs and waist, and he quickly scoops it all up with his fingers, choking me with it while he carries on speaking into his phone.

"Don't let her out of your sight," he says to who I'm assuming is Easton. "I'll be there in ten minutes."

He tosses his phone down next to the sink, and I collapse back on the mirror behind me, my hand still wrapped around my spent dick as I study the purple hickey on his neck. He peels off his wet clothes and takes a thirty second shower, glaring at me as he puts the shower gel back on the shelf the correct way. Stepping out, he grabs two towels off the rack and chucks one at my head.

"Get out."

"Where are you going?" I ask, grabbing my clothes to follow him into his bedroom.

"Out."

I frown, not sure whether he's telling me he's *going* out, or reiterating the fact that I should *get* out.

He doesn't acknowledge me again as we get dressed, and I work my jaw, staring at the side of his head. "Why are you being such a dick?"

"I'm always a dick."

"Not like this."

He lets out a laugh, sparing me a few seconds of his precious time to back me into the corner next to the door. "You beg me to fuck you like I hate you, and then you want me soft when I go and give it to you. You don't know what you want, do you, baby?"

I slowly shake my head, and he hits me with a look of mock pity, knocking my chin with his knuckles before he moves to leave.

"Is it Frankie?" I call as I follow him, sighing when he doesn't answer. "Can I go with you?"

"No."

"Why not?"

"Because I don't want you with me." He spins around, speaking slowly like I'm a four-year-old. "You're not my boyfriend, party boy. You're not my anything."

I'm just about to remind him he's called me *his* more than once, but then I stop, saying nothing instead because there's no point.

He walks down the hall without me, not even bothering to glance back before he disappears around the corner. Walking into my room, I resist slamming the door behind me, knowing it'll only make him laugh when he hears it.

Heading over to my window, I lean my shoulder against the wall and watch him climb into his car, the backs of my eyes stinging as he hits the gas and speeds away. Once he's gone, I strip out of my clothes and take another shower, forcing myself not to cry over him and his mind games.

I'm done playing.

I'm fucking *done* letting him break me.

CHAPTER THIRTY-ONE

Nate

Pulling up outside the house Frankie's at, I find her sitting on the grass at the end of the driveway, her arms folded over her knees with her chin resting on top. Easton's standing behind her with his hands in his pockets, worrying his lip between his teeth when he sees me walking toward them.

Frankie's blonde hair is a mess and there are black smudges under her eyes, but I don't think she's been crying. She just looks worn out, like she's been rubbing her hands over her face without giving a shit about ruining her makeup.

Easton told me she's been acting weird all night, getting wasted by herself in the corner, not acknowledging or speaking to anyone. He said he lost sight of her for a few minutes, and when he searched the house, he found her half asleep on the bathroom floor. That was right before he decided it was time to call me.

"What happened?" I ask.

"Nothing *happened*," she slurs, rolling her eyes at the look on my face. "I'm fine, Nate. Easton's just bein' a drama queen, as usual."

"Hey. I'm not a *drama queen*."

"If you say so."

He lets out a sigh and looks at me, waiting for direction. I tilt my head at the house, letting him know he can go back inside, and he hesitates.

"I got her," I assure him, and he nods, leaning over behind Frankie to kiss the top of her head.

She reaches up to rub his hair, and I wait for them to say good-bye, stepping closer once he's gone and crouching in front of her. She looks up at me with a fake, tight-lipped grin, and I let out a chuckle.

This fucking girl.

"What's wrong, Frank?"

"I don't even know." She shakes her head, laughing as if this whole situation is ridiculous. "I just feel..."

"What?"

"Like shit," she finishes, using the back of her hand to wipe her eyes. "It's been a real shitty day, Nate."

I nod, knowing exactly what she means without having to ask. I never understood it when Katy used to feel so depressed some-times for no reason in particular, but now that I've experienced that feeling myself, I get it. It sucks feeling like there's an invisible weight pulling and pushing you down at the same time, when there's nothing you can do to stop it, so you just have to suffer through it and hope that tomorrow is better.

Frankie smiles sadly, then sighs and drops her head down. "I need another drink."

"You're not going back in there."

"Don't need to," she mumbles, pulling out an unopened bottle of vodka from the inside of her leather jacket.

"Where did you get that?"

"I swiped it from the kitchen when Easton was walking me out," she says proudly, twisting the cap off the top.

Knowing she's not ready to go home yet, I sit down on the

grass beside her and mirror her position, propping my knees up and resting my elbows on top.

"Sorry I took you away from Xavi."

I can't help but flinch at the sound of his name, accepting the bottle she offers me and taking a drink to hide it. The alcohol burns as it slides down my throat, but it doesn't hurt nearly as much as my chest does. Every time I've thought about him this week, all I can picture is me standing outside his bedroom the night of his birthday, hearing his soft cries through the door after he found the box of pictures I left him. I wanted to go in there, but I didn't. I left him to his misery and proceeded to keep pretending he means nothing to me.

And the way I treated him tonight...

I don't know why I feel so guilty about it. He deserves everything I throw at him, but...

"What did you do?" Frankie asks, proving I'm not hiding shit from her.

Sighing, I take another swig of vodka. "I did what I always do, Frank."

She doesn't seem surprised by that, not saying anything else as we pass the bottle back and forth.

"Can I have a cigarette?"

She reaches into her jacket pocket, passing me one before she lights one up for herself.

"Have you ever bottomed before?" she asks randomly, and I smirk, taking the lighter she offers me to light my own.

"No."

"Why not?"

"Why are you asking?"

"I was just thinking you should let your boy fuck the sad out of you with that big dick of his," she says casually, raising a brow when she catches the nasty look I'm throwing at her. "What? You think you're too cool to be a sad fucker like the rest of us?" she asks, blowing a cloud of smoke out in front of her. "'Cause you're not."

"How do you know how big Xavi's dick is?"

"Carter's got a big mouth." She shrugs, and I clench my jaw. "Is that why you're doing this to Xavi? Because he slept with your best friend when he's supposed to be yours?"

Shaking my head, I look away, too chicken to let her see my face. I finish my cigarette, put it out in the grass, and take the vodka, filling myself with liquid courage. "Xavi was..." I clear my throat, trying again. "He was my little sister's best friend."

Frankie's expression doesn't change, but I don't miss the slight dip of her eyebrows.

"Katy," I try to tell her, but it comes out as nothing more than a rough whisper. "Her name was Katy."

CHAPTER THIRTY-TWO

Xavi

"Don't you have someone else to stare at?" Carter asks, his eyes closed as he leans his head back on the side of the hot tub. "Where's Nate?"

That's a good question.

He's been gone for over two hours. I thought he would have been back by now, but I'm trying not to worry too much. Or miss him too much. It's not working, but it's the effort that counts.

I got sick of staring out the window like an abandoned puppy, so I came downstairs and found Carter out here by himself. He didn't say anything when I sat down on the edge of the tub beside him. He just looked over at me, gave my body a casual once over, and then went right back to smoking the joint in his hand.

"Not here," I answer, gritting my teeth at the stupid smile on his face. "He fucked me and left. Again."

He looks genuinely puzzled when he opens his eyes and catches my glare on him.

"What are you pissed at *me* for?"

"Because it's *your* fault," I bite out, his smile returning as he laughs at me with his eyes. "I'm not stupid, Carter. You brought me here so he could get his revenge. You *knew* he was gonna break my heart and you didn't care. I should have told you to go fuck yourself and gone back to live with my mom."

"Because she loves you so much?"

"Fuck you."

He laughs for real this time, and I angrily shove his head away, growling when he just keeps on laughing.

"What are you *laughing* at?"

"You," he says. "You're so blind."

"What?"

"You think it's easy for him to ignore you like this?" He kneels up on the edge to level with me, snatching my wrists when I try to back away. "You think he likes pushing you away when all he wants is to keep you at his side?"

"What?" I ask again, unsure what else to say.

"He's fallen for you, you idiot," he says slowly, rolling his eyes when I widen mine a fraction.

"Don't say that." I shake my head, hating myself for the way my heart is leaping around in my chest, hopeful and desperate for what he's saying to be true. "He hasn't..." I trail off, shaking my head again. "You don't know what you're talking about."

"You sure?" he teases. "Baby, he's balls deep in love with you and he hates you for it. That's why he's treating you like shit. That's probably why he's *always* treated you like shit."

The sound of the front door slamming hits my ears, and I turn around, snatching my wrists out of Carter's grip when he tries to hold me tighter.

"Don't call me baby."

"Baby boy..." he says in my ear, but I'm barely listening as Nate and Frankie walk through the house, his arm locked around her waist to hold her up as she stumbles into the kitchen.

"Don't call me that either." I smack Carter's hand off my hip, looking back at him when he touches me again. "The fuck are you doing?"

"Just wait and see what he does," he says quietly, tilting his head for me to look at Nate while he runs his finger over my lower back.

He's barely touching me, but he's close enough for me to feel his heat, his naked, wet chest just a few inches away as he kneels behind me.

"I can't believe I'm riskin' another black eye for this," he mumbles. "You better think about me when he's fucking you tonight."

"I'll never think about you when he's inside me."

He hums next to my ear. "Say that to him next time I come up," he suggests. "Trust me, he'll like it."

Nate finally sees us, and I force myself not to squirm, waiting for it like Carter told me to. But Nate doesn't move. Not an inch.

Frankie follows his line of sight and ditches him to come outside, a lopsided smile on her lips as she picks up the joint in the ashtray.

"You're a dead man," she sings to Carter, seemingly happy about it as she sticks his joint between her teeth, strips down to her underwear, and settles in on the other side of the hot tub.

Carter pushes his luck and slides his hands around to my front, and then Nate's moving, shoving the door open and coming toward us. Without a word, he pushes Carter back into the hot tub and fists the front of my hoodie. Pulling me up to my feet, he turns us around, takes my spot on the edge, and guides me down to straddle him, one arm behind my back to drag me closer. His fingers creep up beneath my hoodie, and I put my hands on his shoulders, studying his glassy eyes and his head lolling to one side.

"Did you miss me?" he asks, and I blink at the sound of his slurred voice.

Fucking hell. He's wasted.

"Not really," I mutter, my brows dipping when Carter lets out a loud yelp behind him.

I try to look at what Nate's doing with the arm behind his back, but he stops me, using his free hand to hold me still by the back of my neck. "Don't look at him."

I stay completely still on his lap, and he rewards me by running his fingers through my hair, his nails teasing my scalp and making me shiver.

"Nate, get off me," Carter grunts, but Nate ignores him, staring into my eyes as I graze my thumbs over his jawline.

He must notice the concern on my face because he frowns and asks, "What?"

"Did you drive like this?"

He shakes his head. "We got a ride."

"What about your car?"

"You can take me to get it in the morning."

"You want *me* to take you?" I raise a brow. "On my bike?"

"Fuck, no. We'll take an Uber."

"Then why do I need to come...?"

"Because I want you to," he says simply, and I laugh.

"You really are drunk."

"I don't have to be drunk to wanna spend time with you." He sighs. "It happens when I'm sober too."

"Told you," Carter calls, then lets out a choking sound.

From the way the water keeps splashing over the side, I think Nate's drowning him repeatedly, but he doesn't once take his eyes off me. My dick is rock hard, and I know he can feel it, his hand moving down between our bodies to grab it over my sweats.

"Needy little boy," he whispers, tilting his head down to make out with my neck. "You ready for bed?"

I nod and grab hold of his hair, catching eyes with Frankie over his shoulder as I grant him better access. She looks amused, but I don't miss the way her eyes soften for me just a tiny bit. She's got a hell of a poker face, but I know her better now than I did when I first moved in here. We've become...well, not friends, exactly. I still hate her. I just hate her a little bit less since she let me keep the butterfly choker Nate loves so much.

"Bed," Nate reminds me, and I climb off his lap, looking up at him when he stands and pulls me in closer. He kisses me hard, probably to prove some kind of point to Carter, his fingers digging into my waist as he teases me with his tongue, making me moan. His grin on my lips tells me that's exactly what he was waiting for, his forehead resting on mine as he guides me back toward the house.

He suddenly stops walking and turns his head to look at Frankie. He looks a little guilty for some reason, but she just chuckles, seeming to know what's up without having to ask. "It's okay," she tells him. "I'm a big girl, Nate. I can sleep all by myself."

"You sure?"

"What if I say no?" she asks, smirking as she smokes Carter's joint, using the lit end to gesture between me and Nate. "You gonna let me sleep in the middle? 'Cause I don't think your boy would like that very much."

"No shit," I say, working my jaw when she, Carter, and Nate all snort in unison.

I push myself back into Nate's chest, and he wraps his arms around me from behind, hesitating a moment before he shares a look with Frankie, nodding at her when she shoos him away with her hand. She winks at me, and I discreetly flip her off, making her laugh.

Bitch.

I hate that I like her.

Nate takes me upstairs without letting go of my waist, which means it takes us three times as long to get to his room, but I don't mind. I know I shouldn't, but I love it when he acts like this, like he's obsessed with me and needs to keep his hands on some part of me at all times.

He backs me up until my legs hit the bed, and I look up at

him with my arms hooked around his neck, feeling all kinds of things I shouldn't be feeling.

So much for being done, I think to myself, but I don't care. My heart aches for him so bad it hurts. I couldn't walk away right now if I wanted to.

I move back until I'm lying on the bed, and he comes with me, raising a brow when I roll him onto his back and climb on top of him. Ignoring the amusement on his face, I remove my hoodie and shirt and toss them onto the floor, running my nails over his hard stomach while I push his top layers up to his collarbone. He doesn't fight me when I yank them off over his head, grabbing my waist again to pull me down to his mouth.

I pass him the lube from his nightstand, and he uses it to finger me open, his hand down the back of my sweats while he kisses me senseless. I'm still a little sore from earlier, but he's not rough with me, taking his time as he stretches me with one finger, then two.

We're grinding on each other and making out like teenagers, our half naked bodies rubbing together for what feels like an hour, maybe more.

"If you want me hard while you fuck me, we need to stop," I warn.

"Why?"

"Because I'm gonna come."

"Come then," he rasps, sucking my lip between his teeth. "I can make you hard again. All fucking night if you want me to."

He's not wrong about that.

"Deeper," I whisper, and he gives it to me, making me whimper as he grabs my ass and squeezes it, curling his fingers while he grinds up into me.

"Baby, let me see your dick."

I sit up and shove my hand down between us, pushing my sweats down to my upper thighs to show it to him. I'm freeballing tonight—not to tease him, but because it was more comfortable after the way he treated my ass earlier—and he groans when he notices, his cock visibly jerking against mine.

"Is it wet?" he asks, and I nod, twisting my fist over the precum leaking out of the tip. "Get up here and put it in my mouth," he demands. "I wanna taste it."

When I don't move fast enough, he hooks his fingers inside me and pulls me up until I'm sitting on his face, scooting his back down the bed so I can lean forward on top of him. Grabbing the headboard, I look down and feed him my dick, arching my back as I roll my hips back and forth, giving him about half of it on each hit.

"Don't be a pussy, Xav," he taunts, still fingering my ass. "Use my throat like I used yours. Fuck it hard."

God. Fucking shit.

He squeezes my ass with silent encouragement, and I give him what he wants, shoving my dick into his mouth until I'm fucking the back of his throat.

I wanted to make this last, but it's physically impossible for me to hold out while I'm watching him choke on my dick, the warmth of his mouth driving me to the brink of insanity. Pulling back at the last second, I rest the tip of my cock on his tongue, moaning as my cum shoots out into his open mouth. He closes his lips around the head and sucks, and I hiss through my teeth, pushing him down by his head to get him off me.

"Did you swallow it yet?"

He shakes his head, and I lean over to take his face in my hand, stealing a sticky kiss from his lips that has him groaning some more. He shoves my own cum into my mouth with his tongue, and I suck on it like a fiend.

"Show me," he says, so I stick my tongue out the way he likes and show him my piercing, letting our spit and my cum drip back down into his mouth.

He swallows it then, licking my lips from corner to corner to ensure he gets it all. I kiss him again before I shuffle my way down his body, stripping us both of the rest of our clothes. Lifting my leg back over his hips, I grab the lube and flick the cap off, reaching between my legs to rub some on his dick. I'm just about to put it in, but he's being oddly compliant tonight, and it makes me hesitate. "How drunk *are* you right now?"

"How much do you care?" he fires back, taking my ass to guide me back and forth, helping me tease him.

"Not that much," I admit, making him smirk as I squeeze the base of his dick, rubbing the head over my wet, open hole. "I need it."

"Take it, baby. It's yours."

Mine.

Granted, he didn't tell me *he* was mine, but I pretend that he did as I lower myself down, my mouth falling open as I cry out at the feel of it.

"Does it hurt?"

"No—I mean yeah, but I like it," I confess, feeling him stretch me open as he lifts his ass up, filling me deep with one slow thrust. "Fuck, Nate."

"I'm getting to that," he jokes, and I let out a surprised laugh, snapping my lips shut when it makes me clench around him.

Just as he's about to start moving, I stop him with my hands on his abs. "Let me do it," I plead, shamelessly taking his good mood for granted. "Let me show you how good I can ride you."

He curses, and I take that as a yes, lifting my hips almost all the way up before I lower myself down. I start off slow at first, and then I move faster, loving the way his fists clench around the sheet and his eyes darken until they look pitch black.

"Fuck, Xavi," he growls through his teeth, and then he moans, fucking *moans* when I bear down on his cock and really give it to him.

Feeling more confident than I ever have, I pull his head up by the back of his neck, teasing his lips with mine. "Spit in my mouth again."

He does, and I sit up straight, letting it drip onto my dick before I use it to jerk myself off.

"Filthy little whore," he rasps, and I can tell he loves it just as much as I do. "Come here."

Placing my free hand on his thigh behind me, I lean back even further. He grins evilly, hitting me with a heated look that tells me I'm pushing it. Running his palms over my chest, he pinches my nipples and pulls, forcing me to lie on top of him or risk him ripping my piercings out. I give in and let him play with my tongue.

"You're so good at this, baby boy," he groans, running his hands over my sides and down to my lower back. "You're perfect."

His praise lights me the fuck up, his teeth nipping my lip while I ride him harder. "Carter calls me that."

"I don't give a shit what he calls you." He grabs my ass, holding me down on him possessively. "You're not his. You're mine. *My* baby boy..."

"God, Nate, keep talking like that," I beg, working my fist over my dick between our bodies.

"You like it when I call you mine?"

I nod, rolling my head back when he moves his mouth down to my throat and brands my skin with more of his marks.

"Show me," he rasps, licking over the bruises. "Show me how bad you want me to keep you."

My heart skips a beat at the thought of him keeping me, our skin slapping together while I bounce up and down on his dick. I make him come first, moaning into his neck when I feel him pulsing inside me and filling me up. I'm just about to follow him over the edge, but he doesn't let me, batting my hand away from my cock and catching my wrists.

"You ever come hands-free before?"

"No."

"Do it for me," he demands, pressing my palms down on the bed on either side of his head. "Now."

"I don't know if I can..."

"You're not getting off my dick until you do."

I grit my teeth, and he fucks up into me, smirking when I cry out in frustration. I fist my hands next to his face, focusing on the look in his eyes while he touches every part of my body he can reach, helping me move up and down on him. Still hard inside me, he scissors his fingers and rubs them over his dick in my hole. I let out a helpless sound I've never made before, feeling myself shake and clench around him.

"That's it, baby," he says softly, somehow knowing I'm almost there. "Come on. You can do it."

"Choke me."

His other hand squeezes my throat, my eyes rolling back in my head while he rocks up into me. That sets me off, a scream tearing out of my open mouth as I come hard and loud. It feels like it goes on forever, making my entire body vibrate as I'm torn apart from the inside out.

I barely register what Nate's doing underneath me, but when he pulls me down and shoves his wet tongue into my mouth, I taste the cum and realize he's been busy scooping it off his abs and chest.

"So dirty." I croak out, falling on top of him when I'm too weak to hold myself up.

"You okay?"

"No. My legs are on fire," I tell him, smiling into his neck when he massages my outer thighs, kneading the flesh beneath his palms. "That's cute."

"Shut up."

I laugh and roll off him, staring at the ceiling above us while I psych myself up to leave. He doesn't kick me out right away, and I'm grateful, stretching my legs out while he lies silent beside me.

"You told Frankie about Katy," I say after a minute, thinking back to the look she gave me outside.

I'm not brave enough to look at him, but I see him nod in my peripheral.

"What did she say?"

"She didn't say anything. She just listened," he answers quietly, making me frown when his pinky brushes mine. "She was crying by the time I got to the end, but don't tell her I told you that."

"Why not?"

"Because she'll beat both our asses."

I nod my agreement, tensing when he takes my hand and links our fingers together, his thumb brushing mine. He's got a habit of doing that, but never after sex. I don't know what he thinks he's doing, but I'm too chicken to ask, so I don't.

"You've never fucked her, have you?" I ask him instead, finally turning my head to face him, finding his eyes already locked on mine. "You've just been messing with me to try to make me jealous."

"Try?" he echoes smugly, chuckling when he catches the slight tick in my jaw. "No, Xav, I've never fucked her," he admits. "That'd be weird. She's like a little s—" He cuts off, and we both wince at the word he almost used. "She's my best friend."

"Good for her," I mutter, sliding my hand out of his grip before I sit up and snatch my sweats off the floor.

"Where do you think you're going?"

"Bed."

"You're already in bed."

"*My* bed, Nate..." I draw out, frowning when he tosses my sweats and pulls me back by my wrist.

"No."

"No?"

"No," he repeats, grabbing my hips to yank me closer, pulling me right up against his chest. I'm too stunned to fight him on it, gawking at him as he grabs the back of my thigh and drags it over his body. "What?" he asks, amused.

"I'm not sleeping in here with you."

"Why not?"

"You know why not," I say angrily. "You just wanna fuck with me before you snatch it all away again."

"I won't," he promises. "Not this time."

I shouldn't believe a word that comes out of his mouth, but for some reason, I think he means it.

I stare at him, and he stares right back at me, raising a dark eyebrow when he sees the unspoken questions swimming around in my eyes.

"What?" he asks. "Say it."

"I don't get you," I admit, avoiding his eyes as I trail my finger over the ring on his chain. "You're so hot and cold all the time. It's like you're two completely different people. Which side are you faking, Nate?"

A small smirk touches his lips, but he doesn't answer me, his knuckles brushing my outer thigh while I lay my head on his chest. I'm exhausted, both physically and mentally, but I fight the sleep trying to pull me under, not wanting to miss a second of the comfort and warmth of his body against mine.

"You ever slept next to anyone before, Xav?"

I hesitate, and he tightens his arm around my back, probably knowing what I'm about to say before I say it.

"Just Katy," I whisper.

CHAPTER THIRTY-THREE

Nate

"You know I have my own bathroom, right?" Xavi asks, hip-checking me out of the way to rinse the conditioner from his hair. "And my own shower."

"You didn't seem to care about that yesterday," I remind him, pushing him back against the wall to take my spot beneath the water.

"Yeah, well, I wanted your dick yesterday," he jokes, his eyes on said dick as he slides his fingers through the soap bubbles there. "I'm sick of it now."

"Just my dick, huh?"

A small smirk touches his lips, and he wraps his fingers around it, pulling me into him and using his other hand to run his hand over my chest. The little liar doesn't *look* sick of it, and I know he wanted a hell of a lot more than sex when I found him in here yesterday, but I don't call him out. I'm too focused on his pretty face, reaching up to run my thumbs over the black makeup smudged beneath his eyes.

I woke up this morning to find him wrapped around me like a

blanket, his legs tangled with mine, his head on my shoulder and his messy hair covering his face. I moved it out of the way, and he smiled in his sleep, more content than I've ever seen him. He looked beautiful like that, and it pissed me off, so I turned him over, woke him up with my tongue in his ass, and then fucked him from behind until he was screaming my name.

His smirk turns into a grin, the happiness on his face clear as he pushes himself up on his tiptoes to get closer. "You can't stop thinking about me, can you?" he asks, teasing me with his mouth but never giving it to me for real. "Even when I'm right here in front of you..."

I snatch his waist and lift him up, his head knocking back against the shower wall as I take what I want by force. He laughs and wraps his legs around me, grabbing the back of my head as I deepen the kiss.

"When did you get this cocky?" I ask.

"I've always been this cocky."

Tightening my grip on his outer thigh, I pull back to look at him. "That's not what I mean and you know it." I search his gaze, pissed at the way he seems to know something I don't. "Tell me."

He hesitates, laughing again when he catches the tick in my jaw.

"Since Carter told me you're in love with me."

My face falls, and I let out a curse, fisting my free hand on the wall next to his head.

I'm gonna kill him.

"Is that true?"

Fucking hell.

"Get dressed," I order, dropping him to his feet and stepping out to throw a towel at his body.

"Wait, Nate, I was just fucking aroun—"

"I'm not kicking you out, Xavi."

He blinks at that, the hurt on his face morphing into confusion. Wrapping my towel around my waist, I walk out into my room and go to my closet, grabbing some clean clothes and two hoodies. When I walk out, I find Xavi towel drying his hair next to the bed, his sexy little ass on full display, covered in hickeys and little bruises.

"I need to do my laundry," he says, scrunching his nose at the pile of dirty clothes on the floor. "Can I wear—"

I throw one of the hoodies at him, and he grins, dropping the towel to catch it. Just as he starts to say something, someone knocks on the door and we turn that way, finding Easton opening it a crack and sticking his head inside. "Dude, are you sick or somethi—" He cuts off, doing a double take at Xavi before his wide eyes drop to my boy's dick.

Easton's mouth parts as he stares at it, and I grab my basketball, throwing it at the door next to his face. "The fuck are you looking at?"

Xavi snorts out a laugh, and I cut my eyes to him. He doesn't bother covering himself up, so I step closer and slap the side of his ass, enjoying the little yelp he lets out before I shove my hoodie on over his body.

"Nobody sees this but me," I say quietly, reaching down beneath the hem to squeeze his cock.

He bites his lip and nods his head, his bright eyes locked on mine to show me his obedience. We're both rock hard now, so I sit on the edge of the bed and pull him down to sit on my lap.

"Good boy."

He groans and parts my towel, not so discreetly rubbing himself on me as he jerks us off with both hands. I give him a pointed look, and he pouts.

"Don't stop me," he whispers. "I'll be quiet."

I doubt that, but I'm not stopping him. I might not want Easton to *see* what belongs to me, but I've got no problem letting him hear it. Again.

"What do you want?"

Easton looks from Xavi to me when he realizes I'm talking to him, clearing his throat as he picks up the ball and sets it down on my dresser. "Nothing, I just thought something was up with you. You never sleep this late and you missed cardio."

"I did my cardio," I tell him, tilting my head at Xavi. "Four times."

Easton pushes his lips together, failing to hide his smile, then lets out a chuckle, shaking his head at me while he walks out the door. Before he closes it, I see Frankie passing my room in the hall, her expression unreadable as she looks right at me. I remember telling her about Katy last night, but I must have been more drunk than I thought I was because I'm pretty sure I told her...other things too.

I'm pretty sure I told her *everything*.

Shit.

Realizing Xavi's about to come all over me, I twist him around, shove him back on the bed, and suck his dick into my mouth, swallowing his load.

"Get dressed and I'll take you out for breakfast after we grab my car." I smack his ass again and stand up, stopping when he grabs my wrist and pulls me back.

"What about you?" he asks, blinking up at me with those pretty blue eyes of his, swirling his tongue around the head of my cock.

"You want it?"

He nods, and I straddle his face to give it to him.

"WHAT ARE WE DOING HERE?" Xavi asks, eyeing me suspiciously while we walk toward the main entrance of Lucky's Diner.

"I told you I was taking you out for breakfast."

He frowns at me when I hold the door for him, and I smile behind his back before I follow him inside.

I don't hold his hand here because we're too close to campus that someone might recognize me, but I still keep him close, guiding him this way and that with my fingertips on the bottom of his back.

A pretty waitress with shoulder length blonde hair seats us at a booth, eyeing Xavi while she sets our menus down and asks us what we want to drink. We order coffee, and she looks at him before telling us she'll be right back.

"Do you know her?"

"Who?"

"The waitress," I say dryly.

He turns his head to get a good look at her. "I don't think so, why?"

I shake my head at him, laughing under my breath as I pick up my menu. "You're fucking cute."

His eyes fly back to mine. "What?"

"What do you wanna eat?"

He looks at me like he doesn't know what to make of me, then picks up his own menu. We order, and by the time the waitress comes back with our food, I think she realizes Xavi's not interested in her.

He might think no one outside of our little circle knows he's gay, but he's not as sly as he thinks he is. He doesn't take his eyes off me as he eats, and I can tell the waitress notices, a knowing smile on her face while she brings us two more coffees.

"What happened to your appetite?" I ask once she's gone, gesturing to the half-eaten pile of pancakes he's been picking at for the last half hour.

I know he used to have one because I once saw him eat an entire large pizza by himself, but ever since he came back into my life, I've barely seen him eat.

"Depression." He forces a fake smile, making a point to pop a tiny piece of bacon into his mouth. "I don't sleep much either."

"You slept with me last night."

He shrugs, hiding his expression behind his coffee cup as he leans back to take a sip.

"Do you have Katy's list on you?" I ask, making him frown once again.

"Yeah..."

"Pick something on it."

"What?"

Sighing at how difficult he's being, I lean my elbows on the table and repeat myself slowly, "Pick something on it."

Not for the first time, he looks at me like I'm a crazy person, his wary eyes on me as he pulls it out of his wallet. Opening it up, he glances at the list, then at the motorcycle shop across the street, a slow grin splitting his lips.

"Anything but that," I say, and he grins some more.

"I CAN'T BELIEVE I'm letting you do this," I grumble, glaring as I approach his bike on the driveway.

The helmet we bought for me on the way home just now weighs heavy in my hands, a solid black one to match his, as he insisted.

Shaking my head at how stupid this is, I put the damn thing on before I change my mind. He's already wearing his helmet, so I can't tell what he's thinking as he nods at me. Swinging his leg over the bike, he pats the seat behind him, and I hesitate.

"Maybe you should be the backpack," I say.

"Why? Don't you trust me?"

"Not a fucking bit."

He laughs at that, grabbing the front of my hoodie and pulling me closer. Just when I think he's about to say something reassuring, he pushes himself up to level with me and says, "Pussy."

I shove his head away and get on behind him, grabbing his waist and pulling him back to me. Leaning forward to grab the handlebars, he scoots his ass back a little more, and I wait for him to get comfortable, sliding my arms around his middle to reach into his front pocket.

"Just so you know," I start, taking his blindfold out and stretching it over his helmet, securing it at the back. "If you had let my sister drive this thing, it would have been the last thing you'd ever done."

His hands grab mine to flatten my palms on his stomach. "And you wonder why we kept so many secrets from you."

"What secrets?"

"I'm no snitch, baby," he teases, giving the throttle a little twist before he inches us toward the end of the driveway. "I'm taking those to my grave."

Baby.

"Who the fuck are you calli—"

He twists it again to bump me into his back, and I let out a curse, forcing myself to shut up and concentrate on what I'm supposed to be doing. I guide him through the gates, and he turns left, speeding up once I give him the all clear and driving out onto the street. My arms are locked tight around him, my heart rattling inside my chest, and I can't tell whether it's with fear or ecstasy. Probably a little of both, although I'll never tell him that.

"Two miles of open road and then we go back."

He nods to let me know he hears me as he speeds up even more, and I can tell he's grinning when he calls, "Whatever you say, baby."

"COME HERE, YOU LITTLE SHIT."

He runs away from me, and I chase him through the front door and up the stairs, grabbing his ankle half way up and making him squeal. He shoves me off him and carries on running, heading straight for my bedroom and trying to shut the door in my face. I catch it just in time and swing it open, grabbing him by his hips to throw him down on my bed. He lands on his back with a grunt, and I straddle his little waist, pinning the squirmy fucker by his arms.

"I said I was sorry!"

"You hit my *car*," I growl, ripping the helmet off my head before doing the same with his.

"I *tapped* it," he rasps. "It was an accident!"

He bucks his hips up into me, and I narrow my eyes at the pure delight on his face.

"You think this is funny?"

"No," he lies.

He's still struggling and twisting his body around, and I'm letting him play his little game, allowing him to spin us over and push me down on my back. He climbs on top of me, his forearms braced on either side of my head, and then the weirdest shit happens. I realize I'm laughing just as hard as he is, our bodies vibrating together at the adrenaline running through our veins. But then, as if it hits us both at the exact same time, the moment dies and the grins slip off our faces.

We're not supposed to be this happy.

"Where's the list?"

Sitting up on my lap, he reaches into his back pocket and pulls out his wallet, unfolding the paper and smoothing it out on my chest. Leaning up on my elbows, I look at it upside down, reading the second thing he wrote on it.

Ride a motorcycle.

He crosses it out with the marker, anxiously chewing on his lip while he glances at me. I lie down again, moving his hand away from his mouth when he starts biting away at his nails.

"She used to come to me for stuff like that, you know?" I mutter after a while, gently flicking the corner of the paper. "She used to come to me for everything. And then one day she started going to you instead, and I..." I trail off, taking a shallow breath as I lift my eyes up to the ceiling. "I lost her."

Xavi doesn't move or speak, a deep crease forming between his eyebrows as he tries to stop his lips from trembling. His eyes are glistening, and I can tell he wants to tell me he's sorry again, but he wisely chooses not to.

Folding my arm beneath my pillow, I move my other hand down to his thigh, playing with a loose thread at the rip in his jeans. "Wanna know one of the reasons why I hated you so much back then?"

"Why?"

"Because I was jealous of you," I admit, swallowing my pride. "She didn't keep a box of pictures of me and her in her closet, Xav. I hated you because she loved you more than me."

His mouth parts, and I slowly shake my head, stopping him before he can say it.

"Don't tell me it's not true. We both know it is."

He drops his shoulders, rolling his lips to ensure they stay shut, chewing the bottom one so hard it's starting to swell. Reaching up, I use my thumb to tug it out from between his teeth.

"I was a shitty brother," I add, letting my hand fall to my stomach. "I didn't listen to her. I didn't *see* it. And then she died and...it was too late. I'd give anything for one more day with her," I whisper, looking away so I don't have to see the pain in his eyes, knowing he feels the same. "Just to tell her all the things

I'm sorry for...To hear her voice...To hear her sing one more time..."

"I have videos."

My eyes cut back to his, and I lift my head, propping myself up on my elbows. "What?"

"Nothing," he backtracks. "Nothing. Just forge—"

"Will you show me?" My voice breaks, my feigned resolve breaking right along with it. "Please."

CHAPTER THIRTY-FOUR

Xavi

Swallowing, I nod mutely and pull my phone out of my pocket. Opening the album I made just for me and Katy, I scroll up to the top and click on one of the earlier videos, hesitating a moment before I press the play button and pass it to her brother.

Katy's voice comes through the speaker, half way through the chorus of "Scars to Your Beautiful" by Alessia Cara. As soon as Nate hears it, he sits up fully, his eyes glistening with emotion while he scans my pale face on the screen.

"Where is she?"

"Right in front of me," I whisper.

His left arm trembles as it comes around my back, and I run my fingers through the short hair at the nape of his neck, trying to comfort him as well as myself.

There's a lazy smile on my face in the video, my head tipped back on the seat while I smoke a joint on the balcony at my mom's house.

Before the next chorus starts, Katy stops singing just to say, "Xav, turn it up."

When the camera flips around, it zooms in on her lying sideways on the chair opposite me, her bare legs and feet dangling over the arm. She's wearing one of my faded black t-shirts and a pair of shorts, her dark, tangled hair pushed back into a messy bun, the loose strands framing her pretty face.

The black ring I used to wear comes into view as I reach for the speaker on the coffee table between us, turning the volume down instead of up, wanting to hear her over the song. Katy stops singing again and drops her sunglasses, narrowing her eyes in my direction. "Are you recording me again?"

"Mhm."

Her feigned annoyance disappears, and she pretends to flip her hair. "How do I look?"

"You're beautiful, babe."

"But?"

"But nothing," I say automatically. "Keep going."

She grins and starts singing even louder than before, her eyes closing, her feet tapping in time with the beat of the music. The way she sings is effortless. It's as if she's not even trying to sound that good, she just *is*. I must have watched this a hundred times, but even now, her voice still catches me off guard and takes my breath away.

The video ends with the song, and after a few seconds of staring at Katy's frozen smile on the screen, Nate says, "Fuck." He drops his head, and I catch it in my hands, wrapping my legs around his waist and my arms around his shoulders, burying his face into my neck.

"Nate, are you okay?"

He nods firmly, saying nothing.

Setting Katy's list aside to ensure we don't rip it, he turns me away from him, sitting me down between his legs and pulling my back to his chest.

He doesn't give me my phone back, and I don't have the heart to ask him to. I know this is a bad idea, but I ignore my nerves and settle back against him anyway, letting him scroll through the hundreds of pictures and videos as he draws random patterns across my stomach with his fingers.

I've got hours and hours worth of footage—some of her singing, some of us just messing around—and we spend the rest of the day watching it, not moving even when the sun starts to fall beneath the horizon.

"Would she be pissed at you for letting me watch these?" he asks, his voice a little rough after not speaking for so long.

"She's probably cursing me to hell right now." I nod, and he lets out a weird sounding laugh.

I'm too much of a pussy to look up at him, too afraid to see whatever expression is on his face, so I look down at our hands instead, spreading my fingers out for him when he links his with mine.

As he gets closer to the more recent videos, I get more and more anxious about what he'll see if we don't stop soon. But every time I try to lift my hand to touch the phone, he wraps his around mine, pinning them to my chest to stop me.

When we get to the one of me brushing my teeth in Katy's bathroom with her singing in the shower behind me, her body hidden behind the frosted screen, I feel his glare on the side of my face and let out a scoff, surprising myself as much as him with my shitty attitude. "Get over yourself, Nate. How many times have you seen Carter naked?"

"That's different."

"Oh, yeah. You're right," I say sarcastically. "You fucked Carter. I never fucked Katy."

He clenches his teeth, but I can feel his amused smile on my cheek before he nips it. "Brat."

I let out a soft noise and arch back into him, reaching up to grab his head and guide his mouth to my exposed neck. "You're making me hard."

Running his hand over my front, he reaches for my dick over my sweats, fisting the base and pointing it upward like he's examining it. I wasn't lying, but I think he knows I'm trying to distract him.

Letting go of my cock, he grazes his lips over the pulse in my neck and asks, "You wanna tell me what you're so freaked about?"

No. No, I do not.

I try to take my phone without making a big deal out of it, but again, he doesn't let me, snatching both of my wrists and pinning them to my body.

"Nate, that's enough," I whisper. "I mean it."

"No, I wanna see it," he says firmly, pulling his knees up to trap my lower half between his thighs.

"See what?"

"Whatever's making your heart beat so fast."

I try to twist my way out of his arms, but he's so much stronger than me, I'm not going anywhere. All I can do is watch while he swipes to the next video, cringing when Katy's face fills the screen, her pupils blown wide and her matted hair falling into her face.

"Xav, is this thing on?" she asks, kneeling on the floor of my bedroom. "I can't tell if it's on..."

"What are you doing?"

"You're always taking videos of me," she grumbles, angling the phone up toward the sound of my voice. "It's my turn."

"That's you," I say, stumbling into view above her, cursing when I hit my hip on the dresser.

"Oh." She frowns, then purses her lips and holds the phone out in front of her. "Do I look hot?"

"You're beautiful," I tell her, just like always.

"But?"

"But nothing," I drop to my knees behind her, wrapping my

arms around her and pressing my mouth to her cheek. "You're always beautiful, babe."

"Aw. You're so sweet and pretty."

"How do you know I'm pretty?"

"Lucky guess," she teases, palming my face and snickering when I move down to her neck.

I'm grinning in the video, but right here and now, my nerves are shot and I'm panicking. "Nate—"

"Shut up."

I tear my eyes away so I don't have to watch what comes next, but I can't help but picture what he's seeing. He's seen us both high a few times today, but we're out of it in this one, all over each other and rolling around on my bedroom floor. After Katy props the phone up against the base of my dresser, she ends up on top of me, and my head hits the rug with a soft thud, my hands on her sides as she lowers her face to mine. Silence follows for a few beats, and then she lowers her face even more, clicking her tongue when I smile and turn my head away at the last second.

"Ugh. You little tease," she jokes, placing a finger on my cheek to pull my eyes back to her. "Why can't you just fall in love with me already?"

My smile grows bigger as I shake my head at her, and she lets out an exaggerated sigh, lying down on my chest and resting her chin on her hands.

"Is it because you're in love with my brother?"

"Fuck off." I laugh, my cheeks stained pink as I reach for the vodka bottle next to us. "I'm not in love with him. I just want him to fuck me."

"You liar."

I pinch my lips together as hard as I can, and she reaches up to touch my mouth, feeling for my expression. She bursts out laughing when she realizes, and I laugh too, rolling us over and caging her head in with my arms. "Don't tell him."

"I would never," she promises. "So long as you promise I can be maid of honor at your wedding."

I snort at that. "You realize he hates me, right?"

"Wanna know what I think?" she asks, not giving me a chance to answer before she says, "I think he's full of shit. I think he's gonna snatch you up someday and he's gonna love you just as much as I do. *More* than I do," she corrects, pouting as she lifts her hand and presses her thumb and forefinger together. "Just a little, teeny tiny bit more."

"Are you done?"

"I think you're gonna flip his world upside down and there'll be nothing he can do to stop it." She grins, looking awfully proud and excited about it.

Sitting up with my knees on either side of her waist, I uncap the vodka and take a drink. Katy can't see me, but Nate and I can't miss the pathetic, hopeful smile on my face. "Even if all that shit you just said happens, which it won't, I'm pretty sure your parents won't be happy unless he ends up with a girl, babe. He's not gonna end up with me."

"Fuck that." She shakes her head, stealing the bottle from my hand to point at my face. "He's gonna risk it all for you. You'll see."

"You're out of your damn mind."

"And right," she adds. "I'm always right."

Laughing again, my eyes catch the phone I forgot about propped up beside us, my face falling as I reach over to snatch it.

The video finally ends, and I swallow around the tightness in my throat, wiping the tears streaming from my eyes as discreetly as I can.

Katy made me promise I wouldn't delete this one, but now I'm wishing I'd broken that promise and gotten rid of it as soon as I picked my phone up.

Nate's arms have loosened around me, and I manage to slip out without a fight, not looking back as I swipe my phone from his hand and all but run out of his room. Frankie stops walking when she sees me out in the hall, but I ignore her, keeping my head down as I slip inside my own room.

My tears are falling fast and hard, and I feel like I'm choking on them, trying to make myself as quiet as possible while I crawl into bed. I glance at the door a few times, but he doesn't come for me.

I'm an idiot for thinking he would.

CHAPTER THIRTY-FIVE

Nate

Not moving from my spot on the bed, my eyes glaze over as I stare at the empty space between my legs, unsure what to think or do with myself.

The backs of my eyes are on fire, and I can still hear my sister's voice, her words replaying inside my head over and over and over again.

Is it because you're in love with my brother?

My bedroom door opens, and I snap my head up, unsure whether I'm relieved or disappointed when I realize it's not Xavi.

Frankie lets herself inside and walks over to me, her jaw set tight as she props her hands on her hips. I blink my eyes up to her face, silently praying she can't see the agony lingering on mine. I must have a better hold on it than I thought I did because she doesn't look like she feels sorry for me.

She just looks pissed at me.

"What are you doing?"

My mouth parts, but I say nothing, frozen in place.

"Don't just sit there, you idiot. *Go after him*," she demands, gritting her teeth when I make no move to get up. "What the hell is wrong with you, Nate?"

Again, I say nothing, refusing to show her even an ounce of emotion or remorse. She sneers at me, and I force a smirk, using every ounce of strength I have to look like the heartless asshole I am.

"You know what?" She laughs bitterly, backing up a few steps. "I thought it was hot at first but I was wrong. What you're doing to that boy is sick."

I pull my head back at that, finally finding my voice to bite back at her. "You don't know shit, Frank."

"If you don't wanna lose him," she goes on, "you'd better get off your ass and go get him."

With that, she leaves my room just as quick as she came in, making a point to slam the door behind her. I scowl at it for a moment, dropping back against the headboard and listening for any sounds coming through the wall between Xavi's bedroom and mine. I don't hear anything, just the sound of my own heart ringing in my ears.

I think you're gonna flip his world upside down and there'll be nothing he can do to stop it.

Swallowing, I reach out and grab Katy's list off my nightstand, feeling myself crumble while I read what she wrote at the bottom of the page.

She knew.

She always fucking knew.

A COUPLE HOURS LATER, I'm sitting in the dark hallway by myself, slouched back against the wall next to Xavi's door with a bottle of whiskey dangling between my fingers. It's the middle of the night, but I know he's not asleep because I can hear him moving every now and again, probably tossing and turning around in bed.

I want to be in that bed with him. I want to hold him and touch him while he sleeps. I want to wake up next to him in the morning and never let him out of my sight. But I can't. *Won't.* So I just sit out here and pine for him, staring into the blackness while I try to drink all my problems away.

I hear more movement inside his room, the sound of his closet door opening and closing followed by the jingle of his keys, and then the door opens quietly beside me. Xavi walks out, closes the door, and trips over my widened legs. He curses, and I grab his waist to stop him from falling over me.

"Nate. Jesus," he hisses, righting himself before he bats my hands away. "What are you doing?"

My nostrils flare as I study him, trying to decipher his mood in the dark. "What are *you* doing?"

"Going for a ride."

"Without your helmet?" I snatch his waist again when he tries to walk away from me, pulling him down to sit on my lap. "The fuck you are. Take your clothes off and ride me instead," I demand, grabbing a fistful of his hair to kiss his neck.

I glide my tongue over the marks I know are there, and he pushes my face away, his fingers digging into my jaw as he holds my head back against the wall. I hit him with a lazy, drunken grin, and I don't miss the slight cringe on his face before he tears his eyes away, climbing off my lap and taking my hands in his. "Come on. Get up."

I cooperate as well as I can, and he manages to pull me up to my feet and wrap my arm around his neck, snatching my whiskey when I try to bend down to pick it up. I raise a brow but don't say anything, letting him play nurse and guide me back to my bed. As soon as I'm sitting down on the edge, I grab his ass and pull him in to stand between my legs, pushing his hoodie up to kiss his hip and the soft skin above his waistband.

"You're so warm," I say. "Hot."

"Nate..." he warns. "I'm not doing this."

"No?"

"No."

"Then why are you holding me down on you?" I tease, smirking against him before I slide my tongue over his abs.

He shivers and lets go of my hair, taking a full step back. Before he can get too far, I stand and crowd his space, backing him up and caging him in against the wall next to the dresser.

"Nate..." he says again.

"Don't go," I rasp, damn near pleading. "I need it."

"It."

"You," I amend, sucking his lip into my mouth. "I need *you*, baby."

"I said no," he grits out, pushing me back with more strength than I knew he had.

I move closer again, and he glares, stopping me in my tracks with just that one look.

"You're mad," I say, shifting my eyes between his.

"No shit."

"*Why* are you mad?"

Another glare. After a long moment of silence, the two of us trapped in an intense staring contest, he caves first and knocks his head back against the wall. "You were supposed to chase me."

Searching his face once again, I give him my best incredulous look, forcing a laugh when his expression doesn't change. "You can't be serious."

He closes his eyes briefly before he moves to leave, and I catch his arm, pushing him back into the wall and pressing my forehead into his.

"You really gonna be a little bitch about this?" I ask, holding him tighter when he tries to fight me off. "What, did you think I was gonna find out you've been in love with me for years, hear you cry and run after you to tell you I love you too?"

"Something like that," he mutters, and I shake my head.

"That's never gonna happen."

"Why not?"

"You know why," I growl. "Do you really expect me to forget what you did?"

"I don't want you to forget," he whispers, holding my gaze as he blinks the fresh tears from his eyes. "I just want you to love me anyway."

Pulling in a slow, deep breath, I inhale his sweet scent and slide my thumbs over his wet cheeks. He looks so sad and broken, and it hits me then that this is exactly what I wanted. I have his fragile little heart in the palm of my hand, I just need to crush it. And even though there's something inside me screaming at me not to, that's exactly what I do.

"I don't love you, party boy," I say, channeling every ounce of hate I have left. "It's just a game."

He nods, expecting that, his eyes darkening as he works his jaw. "You're a fucking liar."

I open my mouth, but he doesn't give me the chance to tell him he's wrong, shoulder-checking me so hard that I stumble back a step.

"I'm done," he tells me, grabbing Katy's list off my nightstand and sliding it into his back pocket.

"With what?"

"You," he answers, his voice just as empty as the vacant look on his face. "You win, Nate. I hate you just as much as you hate me."

My stomach bottoms out, and I narrow my eyes at the back of his head while he crouches down to pick up his helmet. He glances at the one we bought for me today, hesitating for half a second before he leaves it where it is.

"Xavi, if you walk out that door—"

It closes behind him, and I startle, frowning at it while I wait for him to come back.

He doesn't come back.

CHAPTER THIRTY-SIX

Xavi

I t only takes me a few minutes to pack the one bag I came here with, angrily wiping my face with my shoulder as I shove the last of my clothes inside. Clutching the two hoodies Nate gave me, I hesitate for a moment, then toss them down on the bed.

I pocket my phone, keys, and wallet, biting my trembling lip as I look at the box of photos of me and Katy. I pick it up and leave the room, refusing to let myself stop or even look at Nate's bedroom door as I pass it.

When I get downstairs, I find Carter looking over at me from the kitchen doorway, his face mostly hidden in shadows thanks to the dim lights above the island behind him. Nate and I must have woken him up because he looks half asleep, dressed in a pair of black gym shorts and nothing else.

"Does he know you're running away in the middle of the night?" he asks, using the bottle of water he's holding to point toward the stairs.

I don't know whether he knows or not, but either way...

"He doesn't give a shit," I say out loud, hating myself for how broken my voice sounds.

Carter nods, not bothering to tell me I'm wrong.

"Are you happy?" I ask, using my free hand to gesture to myself. "This is what you wanted, right? Can I leave now that I've paid my debt?"

His stoic face doesn't give anything away, but I don't miss the slight twitch of his fingers at his side. For a moment, I think he might try to stop me, but he doesn't. Shaking my head, I adjust the strap on my shoulder and unlock the front door.

"Xavi."

"Fuck you, Carter," I choke out, tossing my key on the side table before I close the door behind me.

CHAPTER THIRTY-SEVEN

Nate

I'm necking the whiskey Xavi forgot to confiscate properly when the sound of his bike roaring to life hits my ears. Turning my head, I walk over to the window and slot my fingers into the blinds, just in time to watch him drive away. At first, I think he's just going for a ride like he said he was—wearing his helmet like a good boy—but when I strain my eyes to see him better, I spot the bag on his back.

No.

Rushing to his room, I head straight for his closet and open the door, smacking the edge of my fist into it when I find all his clothes gone. I head back out to the main part of his room and rip all his drawers out, feeling my hands begin to shake when I realize he's taken everything. His textbooks, his makeup, Frankie's butterfly choker, the box of pictures I gave him for his birthday. Everything but the two hoodies I gave him...

It's all gone.

He's gone.

Kicking the desk chair across the room, I snap my head

around to find Carter leaning against the door jamb. He folds his arms over his chest, and I swallow, my eyes wide with fear and panic.

"I lost him."

Carter nods, then shrugs. "So? He's a piece of ass, Nate." He rolls his eyes at the look on my face, stepping inside to check his hair in the mirror next to the closet. "Give me a day and I'll find you another pretty hole to stick your dick int—"

I fist the hair he just fixed and push his forehead into the glass, pressing my forearm into the back of his neck when he tries to squirm away from me.

"Jesus. *What?*" he asks, wincing when I pull harder.

"Don't talk about him like that."

"Why not?"

"You told him I was in love with him, Carter!" I shout. "You know me better than anyone and now you're acting like he's nothing to me."

He frowns at me over his shoulder, looking genuinely confused, his face smushed up against the mirror. "If he's not nothing, then what is he?"

"He's *everything*, you idiot," I blurt out, blinking at my reflection as soon as the words leave my lips.

Carter's mouth twists into a slow, knowing smirk, and I release his head with a shove.

"You're not funny."

He laughs anyway, reaching up to touch his head where I hit it. "That hurt."

"It was supposed to."

"I liked it though," he says, wiggling his brows. "If Xavi doesn't take you back, we should revenge fuck against that mirr—What are you doing?"

"Chasing him."

"Don't be stupid, Nate. It's the middle of the night and you're drunk," he calls, following me when I keep walking. "What are you gonna do? Show up at his mom's house at the ass crack of dawn and drag him out of there kicking and screaming?"

I haven't thought that far ahead yet, but yeah, that's exactly what I'm gonna do.

I'm getting my boy back whether he likes it or not.

CHAPTER THIRTY-EIGHT

Xavi

I shouldn't be here.

I should have gone to my mom's like I planned. She wouldn't have bothered me. She probably wouldn't have even noticed I was there. I could have let myself inside the house without having to talk to anyone, locked myself in my room, and drowned in the misery of my own making alone.

Instead I find myself standing outside my dealer's house, struggling to keep my eyes open while I stare at the front door. I feel exhausted, defeated, fucking *destroyed*, the pieces of my stupid, shattered heart piercing my chest while I stand in the one place I told myself I'd never come back to.

It's just after five in the morning, but he doesn't usually go to sleep until the sun comes up, which is why I'm not surprised when he opens the door seconds after I knock on it. Devin takes one look at my disheveled form and grins like he's thrilled. Minus the black eye I'm assuming Carter gave him the other night, he looks exactly the same as he did the last time I saw him—tight blond curls sitting on the top of his head, icy blue eyes, and a lean body covered in tattoos and piercings.

"It's about time," he says, a lit cigarette between his fingers as he pops his hip out against the door jamb. "I've been waiting for you for a month."

"You gonna let me in?"

Smirking at how raw and scratchy my voice sounds, he reaches out and takes the collar of my hoodie, pulling me close to run his nose over my cheek. "You think you can show up here covered in Nate Grayson's hickeys and expect me to take you back?" he asks in my ear, trailing his fingernail over the marks on my neck and collarbone.

I tense and look down, yanking my hand away when he tries to burn it with his cigarette.

"Fucker," I hiss, making him laugh.

He's never hurt me like that for real, but he's a crazy bastard and he likes making me think he will.

He grins again and takes a long drag, letting the smoke glide out of his nostrils as he exhales. "Will you relax? I'm kidding. I missed you," he says with fake softness, wrapping his arms around my neck and moving his mouth over mine.

He tries to push his tongue past my lips, and I turn my face away, cringing when I feel it gliding over my cheek instead.

"I didn't come here for that, Dev. I need..." I swallow, my eyes flicking over his shoulder to the bag of pills on the glass coffee table.

"I know what you need," he teases, trailing a finger over my body and down to the outline of my cock. "What are you gonna give me for it?"

CHAPTER THIRTY-NINE

Nate

Carter all but picked me up on the driveway and dragged me to the passenger seat of his car, so I'm stuck riding shotgun, anxiously bouncing my knee the closer we get to our hometown. He drives like a lunatic, which I'm grateful for right now, but I don't miss the way he slows right down on the tight bend in the road where Xavi's brother died, worrying his lip between his teeth as if he's deep in thought.

"What?" I ask, breaking the silence between us.

"Hm?"

"What were you just thinking about?"

"Do you remember Blaine Hart?" he asks, speeding up again after he takes the next turn. "I had a crush on him when we were in high school. He was so hot. Skinny and pretty like Xavi. A little bit of a freak. I bet he'd beg me to fuck him if he could see me now. You know, if he wasn't dead."

"What is wrong with you?"

He laughs but says nothing else.

I try calling Xavi again, but he must not have charged his phone before he left because it goes straight to voicemail, just like it did the other fifty times I tried.

When we finally pull up on his mom's driveway, I'm out of the car before Carter's even parked it. I ring the bell a few times for good measure, then step back to look for any lights coming on inside. My chest hurts as I look up at his dark bedroom window. I can't stop picturing the look on his face when I told him I didn't love him.

It used to feel good, lifting him up just to tear him back down. I felt entitled to his pain, but now, it just makes me feel like I want to die. Every time I think about that vacant look in his eyes, it makes me want to rip my own heart out and give it to him.

Just as I'm considering breaking inside, the front door opens, and I come face-to-face with Grace Holloway for the first time since my sister's funeral. The funeral where I caused a huge scene outside the church and beat the shit out of her son.

"What do you think you're doing?" she asks, angrily tying a black silk robe around her tiny waist. "Do you know what time it is?"

"I need to talk to Xavi."

"Xavi?" She frowns. "He's not here, Nathaniel. He's at college. I haven't seen him in six months."

"Four," I grumble, and her frown deepens.

"Excuse me?"

"Can you just get him for me?" I ask impatiently. "Please."

"I just told you he's not here."

Knowing I'm about to lose my shit, Carter clears his throat beside me, hitting her with an awkward grin as he pulls me back by my arm. "She's not lying, Nate. His bike isn't here."

I look over my shoulder to see that he's right. Carter drove fast enough that we could have beaten him here, but I was searching the roads the entire time. I'd have seen him if we'd passed him. Unless he stopped somewhere...

The cemetery.

I make a beeline back to Carter's car.

"Good seeing you, Ms. Holloway. I'll tell my mom you said hi," Carter says, and she sneers at the both of us, slamming the door in his face.

Once we're back on the road, Carter doesn't say a word while he drives, and when we check the cemetery and Xavi's nowhere to be seen, that weird look on his face returns, and he seems to be as anxious as I am. I ignore it for now, every cell in my body filled with dread and paranoia as we pull up on Xavi's dad's empty driveway. The bike's not here either. Convincing myself it must be parked in the garage, I get out of the car and bang on the door. Bradley Hart answers, fully dressed in a charcoal suit and tie, his phone pressed to his ear as he takes in my shaken appearance.

"Gracie, I'll call you back," he says to his ex-wife, his suspicious eyes on me as he hangs up.

"Is he here?" I rush out before he can get a word in.

He shakes his head, a small crease forming between his brows while my shoulders drop in defeat.

"What did he do?" he asks, his gaze moving between me and Carter at my back.

"He didn't *do* anything," I grit out, my instincts screaming at me to protect the son who can do nothing right in his eyes. "I'm not here to hurt him. He ran away last night and I need to find him."

"Ran away from where?"

"Me," I say, trying to squeeze the tension from the back of my neck with both hands. "He ran away from me."

I didn't think it was possible to make this man speechless, but there it is, his mouth parted as he gawks at me.

"He's really not here?" I ask, and he shakes his head once more.

Fuck, baby, where are you?

I head back to the car. Just as I'm about to tell Carter we'll check the cemetery again, I look over to find him clenching his jaw, glaring at the ground as he rips the driver's side door open.

"Carter..." I warn, my nostrils flaring when I catch the look in his eyes. "Tell me where he is."

CHAPTER FORTY

Xavi

"You just gonna sit there staring at it?" Devin taunts, stroking my thigh as he leans back next to me on the couch in his living room.

I move his hand away and continue to roll the little white pill between my fingers, my head tipped back against the cushions.

I told him to go fuck himself when he wanted me to suck his dick for it, but he just laughed and said the first one was on him. Anything after this, I have to *earn*, just like before, which is the only reason I'm hesitating. I don't give a shit about myself; I just don't want to cheat on Nate. It's making me feel sick, which is pathetic because I wouldn't be cheating. We're not together. We were never together, no matter how hard I wanted us to be.

I don't love you, party boy. It's just a game.

"Come on, Xav," Devin urges, resting his arm on the back of the couch behind me while he puts his tongue in my ear. "Eat it."

My eyelids droop, and I almost do what he says, but the sound of brakes screeching outside makes me pause. I look up at the window and squint at the car parked diagonally across the driveway. My heart leaps up to my throat when Nate jumps out of the passenger side.

"Who the—*Fuck*," Devin bites out, making me startle. "You little prick, you said he wouldn't come here."

"I..."

I didn't think he would.

I need to move, *do something*, but fear has me frozen in place while Devin runs across the room. He tries to lock the front door, but it swings open before he can get to it and hits him in the face, making him grunt and fall back a few steps.

Nate comes right for me and yanks me off the couch, livid as he takes in all the drugs laid out on the coffee table.

"Nate—"

"What did you take?" he growls, holding my jaw to force my face up to his.

My eyes are wide with shock while we stare at each other, his watery gaze searching mine. I don't answer his question, but he must see the answer for himself because he relaxes a little, letting out a breath as he curls his arm around my waist.

"Baby, what are you doing?" he whispers, his lips on my temple as he cups the back of my head.

Swallowing, I shake my head and shove down all the words I want to say to him. I'm not telling him how much it hurts, how I'd rather feel nothing than this crippling pain tearing at my insides.

I turn my face away, and he tightens his arm around me, following my line of sight as I meet Devin's gaze across the room. He smirks at us, his back pinned to Carter's chest with his arms held behind him, probably to stop him from pulling out the knife we know he carries sometimes.

Carter's eyes meet mine over Devin's head, and I glare at him, gritting my teeth when he glares right back. "Don't give me that look," he says harshly. "You're the idiot here, not me."

Devin giggles like he's loving this, but he can't hide the small flash of fear in his eyes when he catches the murderous look in

Nate's. Nate's head tilts as he studies Devin's bare torso, his tattooed flesh on full display.

"See something you like, Grayson?" he teases, arching his back to show off his body. Nate's eyes crinkle when he says his name, and Devin laughs. "You have no idea who I am, do you?" he asks, clicking his tongue at me. "Naughty little boy, keeping your ex-boyfriend a secret from your new one."

Nate lets go of me to step closer to him, and I instinctively get in his way, pressing my back into his chest to keep him away from Devin.

"He was never my boyfriend," I mutter, and Devin scoffs, shaking his head at me.

"No, you just let me fuck you everyday exclusively for two years," he says dryly, wincing when Carter grabs a fistful of his curls and yanks his head back at an awkward angle.

"Shut your mouth."

"Or what?" Devin asks, looking up at Carter. "You gonna give me another black eye?"

Carter sneers at him, and Nate digs his nails into my waist from behind, grabbing me harder the more angry and confused he gets.

I need to get him out of this house.

Just as I turn around to face him, Devin says, "I knew your baby sister, too, you know? Our boyfriend there let me fuck her virgin pussy for a couple bags of coke."

Nate and I move to rush him at the exact same time, but Carter's faster than us, spinning Devin around and shoving his fist into the middle of his face. He lands on his back on the floor in front of us, and Carter plants his feet on either side of his waist, crouching over him and tugging the knife from his pocket before Devin can get to it.

"Don't listen to him, Nate," Carter rasps. "Every word that comes out of his mouth is a lie."

"You two are the liars." Devin breathes a shaky laugh, his gaze sliding up over Nate's form. "You wanna know why they look so guilty right now? Ask them what I did to your sister before she died. Ask them why Xavi tried to kill himself four months ago."

Nate's eyes cut to mine, and I pale.

"What is he talking about?"

"Nate..." I shake my head, terrified.

His chest bumps mine as he moves closer, his hand coming back to my jaw. "Tell me."

CHAPTER FORTY-ONE
2 YEARS AGO

Xavi

She's dead. My best friend is dead.
She's gone.

My vision blurs as I stare at the bed we were lying on together not twenty-four hours ago, passing a bottle back and forth and talking about random shit that's never gonna happen now, stupid hopes and dreams that are never gonna come true. Wearing and doing whatever the hell we want while I follow her on tour, getting away from our parents, living our own lives and finally being happy...

I let out a sound I've never made before and pick up the first thing I see, pulling my arm back and throwing it at the wall above my headboard. The glass bottle shatters with a loud crack, but it's not good enough. Grabbing my computer off the desk, I launch that too, trashing everything in sight until my bedroom is in pieces. When there's nothing left to break, I turn around and look at myself in the mirror, breathing hard as I glare at the worthless piece of shit staring back at me.

I hate him.

I kick out at him with a cry. The mirror falls back into the wall, and my fists are slamming into it before I can stop myself, my knuckles splitting open, the cracks in my own reflection filling with blood.

"Xavi."

She's gone.

"Xavi!" Carter growls, picking me up by waist and dragging me away from myself.

"Get off me!" I scream, kicking my legs out and scraping my nails over his hands.

He lets me go with a shove, and I spin on him to shove his ass back. He doesn't move, doesn't even flinch, which only pisses me off more. I punch him in the chest, and he watches me do it, letting me take all my anger and self-loathing out on him, until I drop to the floor, too exhausted to stay standing. I sit on my ass and stare at his feet, feeling his eyes burning into the top of my head.

I didn't want to call him. We're not friends. We don't even like each other, but he's the only person in the world who might help me. I can't get revenge by myself. I can't even get myself off the floor.

"Xavi, what happened?"

"I don't know," I choke out, rocking back and forth with my hands in my hair. "I don't fucking *know*, Carter. He promised he'd leave her alone."

"Who did?"

"My dealer. Devin." I pull my phone out and pass it up to him, letting him see the series of pictures of Katy he sent me the other day.

The first are just a few shots of her getting into my car outside her house, hanging out with me at the mall, but then they get worse. I don't know how he did it, but he managed to get pictures of her naked in some random person's bed, passed out on her back with her body on full display. Carter tears his eyes away when he gets to the close-ups, dropping the phone into my lap once he's seen enough.

"Does...did Katy know about this?"

"No. I didn't wanna scare her."

"What was he blackmailing you for? Money?"

I nod, swallowing the bile creeping up my throat. "I wouldn't let him fuck me the other night and he said I had to pay for all the drugs he's given me over the last few months. I told him to get fucked, and I thought that would be it, but then he sent me these pictures..." I pause, fighting the urge to dry heave. "He said he'd hurt her, Carter. I didn't have the cash and I panicked, so I told him I'd work it off."

"Work it off how?"

"I gave him what he wanted," I whisper, too ashamed of myself to look up at him. "He got me high and...I lost count of how many times I let him do it. That's where I was today. That's where I was when she..." I gag, leaning forward on my hands.

Carter gets behind me and snatches the fallen trash can next to my nightstand, holding it under my face as I throw up all the alcohol in my stomach. When I'm done, I feel his warm hand on my back and flinch away from him, turning my face down. I don't deserve his comfort. If anything, he should be doing me a favor and beating the shit out of me. If I could do it myself, I would.

"Xavi, look at me."

I shake my head and wipe my mouth with my sleeve. Carter crouches in front of me and lifts my face up. If I wasn't broken already, the look on his face would do it. I've never seen Carter upset. I've never even seen him angry. But right now, he looks devastated, his eyes filled with pure rage and unshed tears.

"Carter, will you help me?"

He nods, sniffing as he pulls his phone out of his back pocket. "I'm calling Nate."

"No!" I rush out, swiping the phone to stop him. "Please don't."

"Why not?"

"Because h-he'll hate me."

"He already hates you, Xavi..."

"Not like this." I shake my head, the tears pouring over my face. "Please, Carter."

He studies me for what feels like ages, deep in thought with his brows pulled down low. "If he ever finds out we kept this from him..."

"He'll kill us both," I finish, nodding my head before I drop it into my palms.

Carter helps me up to my feet, and I swipe the wetness from my cheeks, turning to face him when he doesn't move.

"Are you coming?"

"WHICH ONE IS IT?" Carter asks from the driver's seat of his car, glancing out at the dark street.

"That one." I tip my chin at the house, my nostrils flaring when I see Devin lazing back on the couch through the living room window.

He never closes those damn blinds. Not even when I was bent over the back of that couch with his dick shoved up my ass just a few hours ago.

Curling my lip at the memory, I snort some coke off my fingertip and swallow some more liquid courage, looking left when Carter's hand wraps around the bottle I'm tipping back. Instead of telling me I've had enough, he takes a drink for himself and twists the cap back on, then wedges it between my hip and the edge of the leather seat. "Let's go."

We climb out of the car, and I fall in line beside him while we walk toward the house. Devin doesn't lock his doors either, so we walk right in without knocking. He looks over at me with a knowing smile on his face, his eyes flicking to Carter for a second before they come right back.

"You look like hell," he comments, smirking as he tilts his head at me. "Rough day?"

"You sick fuck," I choke out. "Grab him."

Carter rips his ass off the couch and wraps his big arm around his neck from behind, tightening his grip when Devin tries to get away.

"What are you doing?!" Devin snaps, struggling against Carter's hold on him.

"What did you give her?" I growl, pulling open the coffee table drawer and tearing my way through all the bags of drugs he keeps in here.

When I find them, I'm gonna shove them down his throat until he's foaming at the mouth.

"Who?"

"Katy!" I scream her name, slamming the drawer shut before I stand up fully.

"Wait, you think *I* killed her?" He laughs, shaking his head at me when he sees I'm serious. "You're insane. I didn't do shit."

"You're lying."

"If I wanted to kill her, I wouldn't have handed her a few pills she may or may not have OD'd on," he states flatly, grinning right at me as he adds, "I would've hit the blind bitch with my car."

I hit him in the face, and his head knocks back into Carter's mouth, making his lip split open as his arm falls away from Devin's neck. Ignoring the pain in my hand, I try to grab Devin by his shirt, but he catches my wrists and twists them, spinning us around and pinning me down on the couch. He lets go when I stop fighting, spitting the blood in his mouth into my face. I lift my chin, glaring at him when I feel the sharp prick of a knife at my throat. I refuse to look away from his eyes.

"Do it."

"Xavi..." Carter warns, taking a careful step closer in my peripheral.

"Do it!" I shove Devin's chest, hoping it startles him, hoping it pisses him off enough to cut me.

It doesn't. He just stares at me with something that looks a lot like surprise, then amusement, then fake-pity. Knowing he's not about to kill me, my chest caves and I thump my head back against the cushion. Raising a brow at how pathetic I must look, Devin glances over at Carter with a look that says, *Is he for real?*

"Get off him."

Devin takes an exaggerated step back, lifting his hands up in mock surrender. Carter takes his place in front of me and studies my bloody face, his gaze moving down as he picks up my limp hand.

"You all right?"

I nod even though I'm not, wiping the mess from my face with my good hand.

"It looks broken."

"I don't care, Carter," I whisper, too tired to speak any louder. "Just get the pictures."

He stands and turns to look at Devin, grabbing him by the throat again and choking him so hard he can't breathe. Bashing his head back against the wall, he tosses the knife away like it's nothing and digs around in Devin's pocket, pulling his phone out and turning the screen toward Devin's face. Once he's got it unlocked, he scrolls until he finds the pictures of Katy, his lip curling as he deletes them all from the device.

Devin starts to turn blue, and Carter finally lets him go, tossing him his phone before he slides down the wall to his knees.

"You're lucky, Xav," he gasps, coughing as he doubles over. "Real fucking lucky."

I ignore him and force myself up off the couch, shaking my head when Carter tries to help me.

"You still owe me five grand, you little cunt."

Carter takes out a wad of cash and tosses the bills on the floor in front of him.

"I'll pay you back," I say once we get outside.

"With what?"

"I don't know," I mutter, stumbling back to his car and climbing inside next to him.

"Xavi," he says in a voice I'm not used to, waiting for me to drag my eyes up to his. "That guy's not your friend. You know that, right?"

"Yeah."

But he's all I've got left.

TWO YEARS LATER, I find myself in almost the exact same situation, straddling my bike on the edge of the cliff, smoking a joint in the middle of a storm while I read the message Devin sends me.

DEVIN

Last chance...

The pictures that follow are all of Nate, some around campus, on the court, working out at the gym. There's even one of him in a shower cubicle, his head tipped back with his soapy fingers spread out on his stomach. Just like he did with Katy, Devin's taken a few close-ups of his naked body, mostly of his abs, the V in his groin, and his half-hard dick.

Jesus.

Fear grabs me by the throat, and I'm scared to death. I know what Devin's implying, but I don't think he'd really do it. He's not brave or stupid enough to kill him. He'll hurt him instead. Run him over with his car. Drug him and beat the shit out of him in a dark alley. Break his leg or his arm so he'll never be able to play basketball again...

I think I'm gonna puke.

I don't stop to think before I've got the phone pressed to my ear. Carter takes forever to answer, but when he does, he sounds wide awake and highly amused, the sounds of the party he's at echoing in the background. "What do you want?" he teases.

"I need your help."

"Again?" I think he laughs, but I can barely hear him over the ringing in my ears. "You can't be serious."

"Please," I rasp, flinching at the next flash of lightning in the sky. "He—It's Nate."

He pauses, then asks, "Where are you right now?"

I shake my heavy head, feeling dizzy as I look around at my surroundings. "I..."

"Never mind. Fuckin' drama queen. I'll be there soon."

After he hangs up, I pocket the phone and wait, but I don't hold my breath. *Soon* could mean five minutes or five hours. He won't rush because he doesn't really give a shit about me. I don't blame him. I don't give a shit about me either.

The rain starts, pours, then pours some more. I'm soaked from head to toe within seconds. I don't know how much more time passes while I smoke my joint, shielding it inside my hoodie to try to keep it dry. Once it's gone, I toss the roach and tip my head back, taking one last look at the dark sky before I pull the blindfold into place.

Another text comes through, and I squeeze my eyes shut behind the fabric. Lifting it up an inch, I quickly delete all the messages he's sent me and block his number. My phone will probably break when it hits the bottom, but I can't risk anyone finding it down there and seeing what's on it.

I can't risk Nate finding out what I've done.

Shoving the blindfold back over my eyes, I hold on to the handlebars and creep a little closer toward the edge. "Sorry, Katy," I whisper.

But then I hesitate, swallowing as I flex my fingers.

Just twist it, Xavi.

Just fucking do it already.

Just fucking—

"Xavi!" someone shouts, grabbing my hood as they turn my ignition off. "What the fuck are you doing?" Carter hisses, ripping the blindfold off my head. He flips the kickstand down and lifts me off the seat, shoving my chest as he pushes me away from the edge. "Get in the car."

When I don't move, he shoves me again, making me stumble over my own feet. My ass hits the wet dirt, and I bury my face into my folded arms, curling myself up into a ball as the rain soaks my back.

"Are you done?" Carter asks. "Is that it? You don't wanna be here anymore?"

I shake my head, unsure whether it's a confession or a denial. Seemingly over my bullshit, Carter picks me up and digs his fingers into my arm, damn near dislocating it as he pulls me toward the car still running on the side of the road.

"What about my bike?"

"You think I'm stupid?" He laughs bitterly, kicking my ankles when I plant my feet. "Move your bratty little ass before I throw you over there myself."

"Fuck you, Carter."

"No, fuck you," he bites back, dragging me along by the scruff of my neck. "I didn't come out here in the middle of the night to watch you kill yourself."

"What do you care?"

"I don't!" he yells, shoving me into the passenger seat of his car. "But I know someone who does, and he'll kill *me* if I let you die out here."

I flinch when he slams the door in my face. He walks around to the driver's side and climbs inside, raking a hand through his hair before he drops his head back on the seat.

"Show me."

"I can't. I deleted them."

"Why?"

I don't answer that.

Seeing me shivering, my teeth chattering, he cranks the heat all the way up. "Did he send you pictures?"

"Yeah."

"Of Nate?"

I nod, swallowing the bile creeping up my throat. "Yeah."

He sneers, slamming his palm into the steering wheel before he puts the car into gear.

"Motherfucker."

WHEN WE GET DONE with Devin, Carter refuses to drop me off at my mom's. He takes me to his parents' house instead, not saying a word to me as he unlocks the front door. We walk upstairs quietly, not wanting to wake his parents, and he takes me into his huge bedroom, tilting his head at the door on my left. "Bathroom's there. Go take a shower before you freeze to death."

I stay where I am and scan the space. The bed is on a black wooden dais on one side of the room, there's a black leather corner couch on the other side, and a fully stocked mini bar in the corner next to the sliding patio doors.

"Why am I here?"

"Because I don't trust you right now," Carter says, once again tilting his head at the bathroom door.

I take a shower first, and then he forces me to sit on the counter while I wait for him to shower. I try not to look, but it's kind of hard when his dick is right there in front of me. Carter's hot, over six feet tall and ripped like Nate, a chiseled body that would feel so big and hard between my thighs.

He raises a brow at me, and I blush, looking down as I pick the skin around my nails. I'm hard beneath the towel wrapped around my waist.

Once I'm dressed in a pair of his sweats and a white t-shirt, I sit on the couch and cross my legs. He looks tired as he makes himself a drink at the bar, rolling his eyes when he catches me looking. Grabbing another glass, he pours me one and sits down next to me. I take the drink and swallow it in one go, barely feeling the burn of the whiskey sliding down my throat.

"Can I have another one?"

He hesitates, then sighs, walking back over to the bar and setting the rest of the bottle on the coffee table in front of me. I pour myself another drink, and he sits back down, his long legs spread out in front of him as he twists his glass on his lap.

"What happened with Devin?"

"I don't really remember," I answer, accidently knocking my knee against his as I bounce it subconsciously. "We were hanging out the other night and I must have passed out in his bed. He woke me up in the middle of the night, told me to get out and not come back until I had the money I owed him."

"What set him off?"

"Nate, I think," I admit, swallowing another mouthful of whiskey. "I dream about him sometimes. I'm pretty sure I said his name in my sleep."

Carter frowns at that. "Are you and Devin together? Is he jealous?"

"No, he's just fucking crazy," I mutter, chewing the inside of my cheek as I pick at the broken skin around my thumbnail. "How's Nate doing?"

"How do you think?"

Pulling in a breath, I hesitate for a long moment, then ask, "Does he talk about me?"

Carter slowly shakes his head, rolling his lips into a sad sort of smile. "No."

Nodding, I look away to hide my face, the silent tears rolling from my eyes while I finish my drink.

"Xav, what's going on?"

I try not to make a sound, but a sob escapes me before I can stop it. "Nothing, I just... Nobody..." I trail off, feeling his arm curling around my waist from behind, pulling me back to his chest. "I feel so alone, Carter."

"I know," he says softly, kissing my hair at the top of my head. "I know."

Letting out a shaky breath, I turn around to curl up into him and lay my head on his shoulder, his body warming mine from the inside out.

When I find the courage to look up at him, our eyes meet, and I wet my dry lips, hitting him with a lopsided grin when I feel his hard dick digging into my hip. He fights it, but then he hits me back with a knowing grin of his own.

I don't know why my mouth is so drawn to his all of a sudden, but it is, and I don't have the energy to fight it. I just go with it, craning my neck to get closer. He does nothing for a few seconds, but then he grabs my chin and pulls my mouth up to his. I moan softly at the contact, lifting myself up to plant my knees on the couch either side of him. Sitting on his lap, I tear his shirt off my body and rub my ass over the length of his cock, swallowing his groan while he kisses me hungrily. I tilt my hips up for him, and he takes the hint, his fingers hooking over the waistband of his sweats I'm wearing.

"Shit," he rasps, rearing back to look at my big dick in his hand. "You wanna top?"

I laugh and shake my head, pulling his mouth back to mine.

WHEN I WAKE UP, I feel around for my phone on the bed, confused when my hand hits the back of a leather couch. Opening my sticky eyes, I lift my head and glance at the window, frowning when I realize this isn't my room. This isn't even my house.

Pushing myself up to sit, I rack my brain for the memories, my pulse throbbing when I find Carter sitting on the arm of the couch by my feet.

"Aw, fuck," I groan, dropping my face to dig my fingertips into my eye sockets.

Regret slams into me, and I shake my head a few times, feeling more and more disgusted with myself as the events of last night come back to me. I tried to kill myself, he saved my ass—again—and then I crawled on top of him and let him fuck me. No, I didn't *let* him. I *begged* him for it, and then I poured my heart out like a pussy and cried myself to sleep in his arms. I don't remember exactly what I said to him, but I know it was bad.

"Fuck."

"Yeah, you said that already," Carter deadpans, dropping two pills into my hand. "Take these."

"What are they?"

"Aspirin," he says flatly.

Setting them down, I search my things on the coffee table for something stronger, grabbing two prescription painkillers and swallowing them dry. Carter eyes me but doesn't say anything.

Feeling awkward as hell, I spot my bike helmet and keys on the table in front of me. My clothes look like they've been washed and dried, folded in a pile next to the rest of my stuff. He must have done my laundry and gone to get my bike while I was asleep. No idea why, but I'm not about to ask him.

"Thanks," I say, and he nods. "What time is it?"

"Almost two."

Realizing I've probably overstayed my welcome, I grab my clothes and stand, trying not to cringe at the pain in my ass and the reminder of where his dick was last night. Of course he notices, a half smile on his lips as he shakes his head at me.

"You don't have to go. I just thought you'd wanna wear your own shit instead of mine."

Frowning again, I clutch the hem of his shirt. He's right. It feels nice, but I don't want it on my body because it's not his best friend's.

Jesus Christ, I'm so fucked up.

After I get dressed in my own t-shirt and jeans, I brush my teeth with a spare toothbrush and make my way back out into Carter's room. He asks if I want some breakfast, and I shake my head. I probably should because I haven't eaten in days, but the thought of food makes me nauseous, so I grab the almost empty bottle we were sharing last night and finish that for breakfast instead.

I walk out onto the balcony and smoke a cigarette, gazing out at the pool in the backyard while I torture myself thinking about every bad decision and mistake I've ever made. The pills and whiskey in my system help numb it a little, but it's always there in the back of my mind. The self-hatred and the guilt. I feel it chipping away at me every day, breaking down the person Katy knew and turning me into this empty shell of the person I once was.

"Why do you do this to yourself?"

I startle at the sound of Carter's voice, turning my head to find him standing behind me.

"Because it makes me feel better," I grumble, lifting the bottle up to my mouth.

"You think you deserve to feel better?"

My eyes fall shut, and I swallow, damn near choking on the whiskey stuck in my throat.

"You miss her."

It's not a question, but I still nod, sniffing as I wipe the drops of liquid from my mouth.

"Did you love her?"

"You know I did."

"Yeah, but that's not what I'm talking about." He moves closer, but he doesn't touch me. "Were you in love with her, Xav?"

"No," I admit. "But sometimes I wish I was. At least then I wouldn't be in love with someone who's never gonna stop hating me."

I shouldn't have said that, but it's out there now, the words hanging in the small space between us.

When I risk a glance at him, I catch him studying his feet with his lower lip pulled between his teeth. If I didn't know better, I'd think that look on his face was guilt.

"Carter?"

"Yeah?"

"Will you..." I clear my throat. "Will you take me?"

"YOU GOOD, BABY BOY?"

"No." I roll my head side to side, my stomach twisting with dread at the thought of whatever fresh hell is waiting for me behind those doors. "I can't think of anything fuckin' worse, man."

"Then why did I just drive you here?"

"Because you were right," I mutter, climbing out of the passenger seat to grab my bag from the back, squinting at the facility over the roof of his car.

I don't deserve to feel better.

CHAPTER FORTY-TWO
PRESENT

Nate

I'm practically vibrating with rage, moving my eyes from Xavi to Carter and then back to Xavi again.

"How did he get the pictures of my sister, Xav?"

"I already told you I fucked her," Devin answers for him, laughing at me with his eyes.

He's still on the floor where Carter put him, propped up on his hands with his legs crossed leisurely at his ankles. Carter's standing above him, shoving his ass back down every time he tries to get up, and Xavi's standing in front of me, his blue eyes filled with remorse and terror and a hundred other emotions while he waits for me to lose my shit.

He shakes his head wordlessly, his jaw clenched tight.

"Then how?"

"I don't know," he whispers. "But I know he's lying. She never would have let him touch her."

"Who said anything about *letting* me?" Devin taunts.

Seeing red, I move Xavi out of the way and grab the mouthy little cunt by his shirt, hauling him up and smashing my forehead into his. When I let him go, his back hits the coffee table and shatters it, his body lying in a pool of broken glass.

"*Nate.*"

Something wet drips into the inner corner of my eye, then Xavi's in front of me again, his hands on my face as Carter stands behind him, the two of them blocking my path to Devin.

"Nate, will you listen to me?" Xavi tightens his grip, forcing my eyes down to his. "He didn't touch her. I promise. She would have told me if he did."

"Then why is he saying that?" I breathe through my teeth, holding on to his wrists to ground myself. "What if he drugged her, Xav? What if—"

He shakes his head again, stopping me from finishing. "No," he says firmly. "He's fucking with you. That's what he does, Nate. He's a liar."

Devin eyes us with a half smirk, half sneer, bouncing his gaze between me and Xavi.

He's jealous.

Kissing the top of Xavi's head, I move around him and Carter and stop in front of Devin, cocking my head at the thick piece of glass he's clutching in his hand, making himself bleed. He seems like the type who won't think twice about using it on me, so I step on his wrist, making him cry out as I crouch down and pull his upper body up by his shirt.

"He's mine," I tell him, not even bothering to lower my voice. "He's always been mine. Even when you thought he was yours, it was always me he was thinking about. Every fucking time."

His lip curls, and he tries to spit at me, so I grab the little cockroach by his jaw and force his mouth shut.

"If I ever hear your name from my boy's lips again, I'll make you wish you'd never met him."

He yanks his face back and glares up at me. "Get out."

Smirking, I apply some more pressure on his wrist before I stand to my full height, making him scream as his bones crack

LIKE YOU HATE ME

under my weight. Xavi cringes, not saying a word as I take his hand, grab his shit off the couch, and lead him outside. Carter walks out with us with his hands shoved into his pockets, working his jaw when I stop and shove Xavi's helmet at his chest.

"Take his bike back to the house."

"Nate," he tries, huffing through his nose when I turn my back on him. "That's *my* car, you know?"

Ignoring him, I take Xavi to the passenger side and open the door for him. "Get in."

He doesn't, twisting his lips as he glances from Carter to me. "I'm not going back with you."

"Yes, you are." I grab his upper arm, pushing him toward the seat.

"Get off me," he demands, planting his feet when I try to shove him inside. "What are you doing?!"

"Taking you home."

"Where's *home*, Nate?" he bites out, throwing back the same question I asked him not so long ago.

Holding his wrists with both hands, I move closer until my chest is flush against his, placing his warm hands on both sides of my neck. "It's wherever I am, Xav."

His brows jump, but then he lifts his chin, eyeing me suspiciously. "You're not pissed at me?"

"Baby, I've never wanted to hit you more."

"Why?"

"Because you went to him," I growl, jerking my head at Devin's door. "Why would you come back here? What would have happened if Carter hadn't told me where to find you? Would you have gotten high with him and let him fuck you?"

He shakes his head, then swallows. "I don't know..."

"You don't know." I laugh, pushing him toward the seat again. "Get in the car."

"Nate, stop it," he snaps, then sighs, pulling his wrists out of my grip to take the keys I'm holding. "I'll go with you," he says quietly, cupping my face to touch the blood dripping over my head with his thumb. "Just let me drive, okay?"

Reluctantly letting him go, I wait while he walks around to the driver's side, ready to chase him if he even thinks about running away from me. Once he's safely inside the car, I glare at my so-called best friend and climb in next to Xavi. Carter finally shoves the helmet on and drives off on Xavi's bike, and Xavi follows him.

"What did Devin do to you?" I ask, dreading the answer but needing to hear it all the same.

"Nate..."

"Tell me."

He stays quiet for so long that I'm sure he's not about to answer me, but then he says, "He didn't do anything to me. I did it to myself."

"What do you mean?"

"My dad stopped giving me money after Katy died, a few days after my eighteenth birthday."

"What? Why?"

He cocks his head at me, and I frown, my brows jumping when it hits me that *I'm* the reason why.

The night I found him passed out in the cemetery, I took him to the hospital, gave the nurses the bag of pills he had on him, and called his dad to go get him. I don't know what happened to him after that because I went right back to pretending he didn't exist. Or trying to pretend, at least.

"He and my mom still bought me things, but I wasn't allowed any money of my own."

"So you couldn't buy drugs."

"Not with cash."

Jesus.

"I was desperate and he knew it," Xavi goes on, wisely choosing not to say Devin's name. "But he never forced me to do anything with him. I...I wanted to be there because I needed him."

My blood boils in my veins, my fists curling with the urge to beat the shit out of something.

"Take me back to his house."

"What? No."

"Turn the car around, Xav."

"*No.*"

"Xavi—"

Cursing me, he hits the brakes and pulls up on the side of the road, grabbing my sleeve to pull me back when I try to get out of the car.

"Where are you going?!"

"I'm gonna burn his fucking house to the grou—"

"Stop. Look at me." He leans over the inner console and traps my jaw between his fingers, giving me no choice but to look directly into his eyes. "I'm telling you he's not worth it."

"You are though."

The puff of air he lets out grazes my lips, and he closes his eyes, letting go of my face to move his hand down to my chest. We stay just like that for a few minutes, with me listening to him breathe, allowing the steady rhythm to calm me down, and him waiting for my racing heart to slow.

Once he's satisfied I'm not about to kill anyone, he moves back to his seat and puts the car into gear, nodding at Carter through the windshield before he pulls back onto the road.

"Xavi."

"What, Nate?"

"Promise me you'll never go back there."

"I promise."

WHEN WE GET BACK to the house, Xavi grabs his stuff from the back seat and exchanges keys with Carter. They share a look, and I flare my nostrils, stepping up behind Xavi to pull him away, my hand on his back while I walk him inside. Carter tries to touch my arm, but I shove him off.

"Nate."

Pausing on the stairs, I turn around, cocking my head when I see the guilt in Carter's eyes. He looks like he's about to say something, then hesitates, shaking his head when I continue walking away.

"Sober up and get some sleep," he calls after me. "Coach is gonna kick your ass if you miss practice."

I'm not missing practice, but I don't tell him that.

When Xavi and I get upstairs, I open my bedroom door and gesture for him to go inside first. He doesn't, anxiously running his hand over the back of his neck as if he's unsure.

"Carter's right, you know? Maybe I sh—"

"Don't talk to me about Carter."

"Nate, listen, it wasn't his fault. It was min—"

"Why would you call him?" I ask, stepping closer until his back hits the door jamb. "You barely even knew him back then. Why would you trust *him*? You tried to kill yourself and y—" I struggle to speak around the lump in my throat. "Why didn't you call me?"

He frowns at that. "You wouldn't have come."

I open my mouth, then close it again, shaking my head at how clueless he is.

"I should go sleep in my own room."

"No," I say, grabbing his hoodie to shove him inside. "You're sleeping with me."

He turns as if he's about to protest, but I cut him off before he can, guiding him back toward the bed.

"I'm not asking, Xavi."

He blinks up at me with tired eyes. "What are you doing, Nate? Why did you even come to Devin's?"

"Stop saying their names," I grit out.

"Tell me why."

"I was chasing you, you idiot."

He swallows, his eyes searching mine for intent. "Why? You had the chance to stop me and you let me go."

"I didn't let you go," I argue, wrapping my arms around his body to hold him close. "You said you were done. You didn't say you'd leave me."

"Nate..." He shakes his head, his lip trembling. "Please, don't do this to me again. I can't..."

"Is that why you went to him? Because I hurt you so bad you wanted to feel nothing again?"

He nods and hides his face in my chest, gripping my shirt like I'm the only thing keeping him upright.

"I'm sorry, baby," I whisper, running my fingers through his hair. "I didn't mean it."

I walk him up to the bed, pull the blankets back, and make him lie down. He scoots over to his side, and I push his legs open to settle there, kissing the tears running over his face and neck.

"Nate." He says my name like a warning and a plea at the same time, his hands on my shoulders to push me away from him. "Nate, stop."

"Why? What's wrong?"

"If you're playing with me..."

"I'm not. I..." I pause. "I want you to be mine. For real this time. We can be for real."

He cries as he stares up at me, pinching his lips as if he's trying to stop himself from saying something. He doesn't need to say it. I already know what's going through his head right now. I pushed him too far last night. I broke him just like I told him I would, and now he doesn't trust me.

"Xavi, please," I say, wiping his tears away with my knuckle. "What do you want? I'll do anything."

"Say you love me."

My hand pauses on his cheek, and I cock my head at him in exasperation, fighting my natural instinct to show the disgust on my face. "Anything but that."

He lets out a quiet scoff and throws his leg over my head, sitting up on the edge of the bed. I grab his arm to stop him from leaving, and he tries to take a swing at me. "Get off m—"

"Jesus Christ. I love you, okay?" I damn near shout, pushing him down on his back and crawling on top of him. "I hate myself for it but I fucking love you."

"That's sweet."

"I didn't realize before you left last night but I...I'm not letting you go. I can't do it. The thought of you walking away from me for good, finding some other guy and being with him instead of me..." My fingers curl as I picture it, and I cage his head in with my forearms. "I'll never be able to stop chasing you, Xav. I won't sit still or sleep or think about anything else until you're mine again."

By the time I'm done, he's pressing his lips together to hide a huge grin. "You're a little crazy, you know that?"

"You make me crazy," I admit, dropping my lips to his while I tug on the button of his jeans.

"What are you doing?"

"Making you mine again."

He lifts his ass up, and I push his pants and underwear down to his ankles, my mouth never leaving his while I chuck them aside. Our teeth clash in our haste to undress, his knuckles brushing my abs as he pulls my shirt up. Moving back for just a second, I help him get it off, removing the rest of our clothes before I reclaim his mouth, stealing all the breath from his lungs.

"Say it again."

"I love you," I groan into his mouth, hooking his legs around my waist. "But if you tell anyone everything I just said to you, I'll beat your ass."

He laughs and lets me kiss every part of his body I can get my lips on, his hips grinding repeatedly as I slowly make my way down to his dick. I suck on the head, lifting my eyes up to watch him shake and moan for me.

"God, Nate...Nate, shit—"

I push his knees up to his shoulders and spit on his hole, eating him out for a while before I add a finger. He whines, moving my head to get my mouth back to where he wants it. Grinning up at him, I suck his cock and finger his ass at the same time, making myself gag every time I try to get it all in.

"Nate, I'm gonna come."

Not yet, he's not.

I slap his inner thigh, and he curses as he drops back on the bed. I stop sucking him and lick him from his groin to his neck, grabbing the lube from my nightstand to coat my dick and his ass.

"You know what I want?" I ask, and he nods, his breath hitching when I push the head of my cock inside him. "You gonna give it to me?"

"No."

My lips twitch as I slide the rest of it in, gripping his ass cheek as I run my tongue over his lip. "I'm not letting you come until you do."

"We'll see."

A laugh bubbles out of me as I kiss him, my tongue swirling around his before I suck on it. Shifting my hips, I fuck him a little deeper until I'm hitting his prostate, making him cry out and curl his fist around my necklace. I look down, and he freezes, bouncing his eyes between mine as he waits for my next move. Barely hesitating, I take the chain off and open the clasp before I drop the ring into my palm. Taking his right hand, I slide it onto his middle finger where he used to wear it.

"Nate, what...?"

"It's yours, baby," I say, running my finger over my number. "I'm yours."

"Fuck," he whispers, his nose flaring as he fights the urge to cry again.

He wraps his arms around me, our mouths moving together in time with my dick in his ass. I fuck him for a long time, pulling out every now and again to rub my slippery cock between his ass cheeks, teasing him and making him beg me to put it back in.

"Please," he whines, grabbing my ass and lifting his hips off the bed. "Please..."

"Please what?"

"Keep fucking me. I want it to hurt every time I move. I want you to know I can feel you inside me while I'm watching you play tomorrow night."

That sets me off, and I shove my dick back inside him, making him scream while I stretch him and ruin his tight little hole. He sinks his nails into my neck and drags them outward, leaving a burning path along my upper back and shoulders. Slowing my pace, I raise a brow, and he smirks, cursing when I resume fucking him into the mattress.

"You gonna give it to me?"

"No," he gasps. "You can suffer until I'm ready."

I grin, trapping his dick between our abs while I roll my hips, giving him the friction he's desperate for. We come loudly, his arms and legs locked around my body as he sucks a hickey into my neck. I moan, knowing he wants everyone to see it along with the scratches on my back tomorrow night.

"Fuck. *Fuck*, you little shit."

He chuckles, his eyes closing before his body goes limp. I

gently run my fingers over his flushed neck and chest, kissing the side of his face before I move down to his jaw line. He damn near passes out in under thirty seconds, but I don't let him, grabbing him under his arms and shuffling us to the edge of the bed. He refuses to move himself, so I pick him up and carry him to the shower. After I clean us up and get us dressed, I grab him some water and something to eat, then climb into bed behind him, pulling him flush against me.

"Are you asleep?"

"No," he mutters. "I'm just trying to figure out who you are and what you've done with Nate."

I know he's joking, but my heart still twists with guilt and shame over the way I treated him. "I'm sorry."

"No, you're not." He sighs. "Not really. And you don't have to be. I deserved it. I knew what you'd do to me and I let it happen."

"Why?"

"You know why."

"But you're still not gonna say it?"

He shakes his head, his hand twitching against my side as he plays with the ring on his finger.

Pulling the blanket up to his chin, I wrap my leg over his to keep him warm, closing my eyes while I wait for sleep to drag me under with him. I can't sleep though. Not until I tell him one more thing.

"I would have come," I finally say, my lips brushing the damp hair at the nape of his neck.

Silence follows, but I know he heard me because he's stopped breathing.

"I know you probably don't believe me, but it's the truth. I would have come for you, Xav."

WHEN WE WAKE up a few hours later, Xavi lies back on my chest and checks his phone now that it's charged, huffing as he looks at the screen.

"I think I outed you to your parents."

"Yeah, I figured," he says, lifting it up to show me the several messages from his dad telling him to call him back immediately.

Instead of calling him, Xavi texts him and his mom to let them know he's okay, then tosses his phone back on the nightstand.

"Are you mad?"

"Not really." He shrugs, rolling to face me fully. "They were gonna find out sooner or later. At least my dad didn't catch me fucking the pool boy while his golfing buddies were standing ten feet away."

I frown. "How did you know about that?"

"Carter's got—"

"A big mouth," I finish for him, dropping my head back on the pillow.

He nods and rests his head on my shoulder, his brows pulled down low as he stares at his hand on my chest. He keeps playing with the ring, using his thumb to twirl it around in circles.

I wish I knew what he was thinking. I know he's doing his best not to give in to me fully, probably afraid I'm gonna pull the rug out from under him when he least expects it and break his heart all over again, but I don't miss the smile tugging at his lips when he thinks I can't see it.

He peeks up at me, and I kiss him just because I can. "I have to go."

"I know."

"I'll be back in a couple hours," I say, reluctantly getting out of bed to grab some clean clothes from my closet. "Don't go anywhere."

"I won't. I'm too tired to move," he mumbles into my pillow, wrapping his arm around it and hugging it to his chest. "Try not to kill Carter."

"Stop talking about Carter."

"Why?"

"Because I'm pissed at him."

"Because I begged him not to call you?"

"That, and because you begged him to fuck you."

"Right," he says with another hidden smile in his voice. "Well, if it makes you feel better, it didn't mean as much as you think it does. I only wanted it because I was horny and he was hot."

I pull the blanket back and slap the back of his thigh hard enough to make him yelp. He laughs when I spin him around, pushing him down on his back to straddle him. "You better be right here waiting for me when I get back."

"Why?"

"So I can fuck that bratty attitude out of you."

"Yes, sir," he jokes, trapping his bottom lip between his teeth.

I tug it out with my thumb and replace it with my mouth, forcing him to open up for me, making sure there's no doubt in his mind that he belongs to me and me alone. Then I leave him with his face in my pillow and his swollen lips stretched into a huge smile—one he couldn't hide from me if he tried.

CHAPTER FORTY-THREE

Xavi

XAVI

Did you take my keys?

NATE

Yes.

Annoyed, I toss the bag I've been searching on the floor and sit down on his bed, texting him again.

XAVI

You could give me a little more than that.

NATE

Yes, baby.

XAVI

You're not cute.

NATE

Did you really only just notice they're gone? I took them while I was at practice yesterday as well.

XAVI

How am I supposed to get to the game?

NATE

Frankie's bringing you. You're sitting with her.

XAVI

Frankie sits in the front row.

NATE

I know.

No more hiding from me, Xav. I need to see you.

XAVI

Okay.

Are you worried I'm gonna leave?

NATE

Not when I have your keys.

WHEN FRANKIE and I get to the game, she grabs us a couple sodas and leads me down to the front row of the stadium. She shoulders her way past a group of guys twice her size, and I just follow the path she's creating, letting her hold on to my sleeve as she drags me through the amped-up crowd.

"He's looking for you," Frankie shouts at me over the noise. She tips her chin down at the court, and I follow her line of sight, finding Nate glancing up at the stands while he's supposed to be warming up with the rest of his team.

As we get closer, I spot the mark on his neck and press my lips together, secretly loving the fact that he didn't cover it with a Band-Aid like I suggested this morning. It's only a little one, but it doesn't matter. There's no mistaking what it is.

Frankie raises a brow at me, and I playfully jab my elbow into her side before we take our seats.

"Shut up."

When Nate's eyes find mine, he stops jogging and visibly relaxes, his hand moving up to his head to mimic something I can't make out.

I need to see you.

Realizing what he wants, I drop my hood down and scrub my fingers through my hair. He smiles a little before he looks down, bounces the ball, and carries on doing his thing. Carter winks at me from beside him, and of course Nate notices. He shoves his ass, and I pinch the bridge of my nose.

Play nice, I mouth to Nate, and he smirks and tosses the ball at Carter, barely missing his face before Carter catches it.

After the band and the cheerleaders get done, Nate steps up for the center toss and wins it, making sure the ball lands in Carter's hands before he runs down the court. I blow out a relieved breath and try to relax, but I'm nervous for him. This is his first game back since he was suspended, and if he wants to go pro next season, he needs to prove himself tonight. He needs to show everybody in here that he can be the best *and* keep his hands to himself. It doesn't matter how many points he can score; the NBA's not gonna want him if he makes a habit out of losing his shit on the court.

"Are you worried?" Frankie asks, side-eyeing me before she puts a hand on my knee to steady it.

"No. He's got this."

And he does. I haven't seen him play this well in a long time. I don't know what it is, but it's like his attitude has done a one-eighty overnight. He usually looks so numb and withdrawn down there, almost as if he's on autopilot, but tonight, he looks like he's actually enjoying himself. Just a little bit.

He looks at me every time he scores, seeking my approval, and I light up every time he does it.

I'm still unsure if I'm an idiot for hoping this is real, but I can't help it. I've been hopelessly in love with him since I was fifteen, and unfortunately for me, nothing he does to me can take that away.

The crowd goes nuts when Nate adds another three points to the board, and I cover my lips with my knuckles, catching his gaze again. I've noticed a few people keep turning around to see what he's looking at, but I don't worry too much about it. There's no way they're gonna know it's me stealing his attention out of thousands of other people. Or that it was me who put that mark on his neck.

By the time the game ends, the Hawks win by forty-three points, and half of the stadium is losing it, the sound of them chanting Nate's name filling my ears while I stand up too. Coach looks like he's about to burst into tears while he celebrates with his boys—Nate included—and I'm right there with him. I couldn't hide the elation on my face if I wanted to. I'm so proud of him.

Coach says something to Nate, and Nate tips his head at me, his lips moving too fast for me to read. Coach turns to look right at me, and I quickly look away before I follow Frankie back through the crowd. When we finally make it outside, I check my phone.

NATE

Wait for me. I'll take you to see Katy.

CHAPTER FORTY-FOUR

Nate

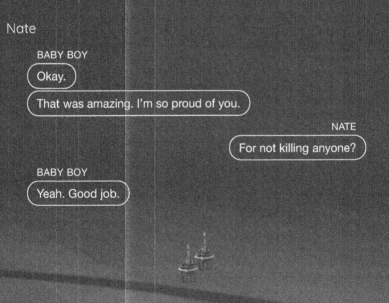

BABY BOY
Okay.

That was amazing. I'm so proud of you.

NATE
For not killing anyone?

BABY BOY
Yeah. Good job.

"Did you really just come out to Coach with all those cameras in your face?" Carter mutters as he comes up behind me, clicking his tongue when I say nothing. "What, you're still not talking to me?"

Rinsing the shampoo from my hair, I check to make sure he

closed the shower door before I push him against it, putting my hand on his chest to keep his wet, naked body away from mine.

"You lied to me. For two years."

"Yeah, and I'll probably do it again," he throws back, his face falling when I just stare at him blankly. "Fuck, Nate. I'm sorry. I didn't know what else to do, okay?"

"I get that—

"Yeah?" he asks hopefully.

"Yeah, but you didn't have to fuck him," I bite out, cursing under my breath when I hear one of the guys whistling a few showers down, reminding me we're not alone. "You didn't have to keep going back for him. *I* should have been the one—" I shake my head, lowering my voice before I speak again. "It's never gonna be you and him, C." I search his eyes. "Tell me you know that."

His brows dip, his mouth curling up at the edges like he's amused. "I know that."

"Don't play with me."

"I'm not," he says, and I relax a little, letting my hand fall away from his body.

"I love him."

"I know you do."

Nodding, I inhale a breath and let it out slowly, chewing the inside of my cheek while I think back to the reason he came in here.

I shouldn't have said anything to Coach without talking to Xavi about it first. We haven't even talked about what we're gonna say to our parents yet. I just got caught up in the moment and opened my mouth without thinking.

"You think he's gonna be pissed at me?"

"For telling Coach? Nah." Carter shakes his head, bumping me out of the way to steal my shower gel. "Trust me, that boy'll walk outta the closet with no shame if it's you standing next to him. He'd do anything for you, Nate. You know that."

WHEN I GET to the parking lot, I find Xavi and Frankie sitting on the hood of her truck together, smiling as they talk about something I can't hear. Making my way over to them, I bring Xavi to the edge by his thighs and stand between them, lifting his chin up to kiss his parted mouth.

"Nate," he whispers, subtly shaking his head before he looks around to check no one saw.

"Baby, I don't care if anyone sees me kiss you."

"Since when?" He leans back on his hands to look at me. "What did you say to Co—"

"Nathaniel!"

"Aw, fuck," Xavi and I say together, turning our heads to see my father walking over to us with the rest of our parents at his side. Our dads look furious, my mom looks mortified, and Xavi's mom looks like she'd rather be anywhere but here.

"Your performance tonight was incredible, Nathaniel," Xavi's dad says after a long, awkward silence, glaring at his son while he talks to me. "You should be proud of yourself."

Xavi drops his gaze to his feet and inches away from me, gently pushing my hand off his leg when I try to stop him. My mom notices the gesture and looks from me to Frankie, eyeing her short skirt and army boots with clear disdain. Frankie hops down off the hood, gives me and Xavi an understanding look, and leaves.

"Why don't we all go to your house so we can talk in private?" my mom asks, clearing her throat as she looks around at all the people still lingering.

"Mom, we're going to see Katy," I tell her, clenching my teeth when she winces at the sound of my sister's name. "Whatever shit you have to say to us, you can say it right here."

"Have some respect, will you?" my father barks. "Your mother's done nothing wrong."

"Have I done something wrong, Dad?"

"We know you're together," he hisses, flicking a hand between me and Xavi.

"Do you have a problem with that?"

"Yes," my mom blurts out. "We do."

I nod and try to keep the hurt off my face, not missing the way Xavi flinches behind me.

"What is the matter with you, Xavier?" His dad sneers. "First, it was Katy, and now you're dragging Nate down with you. You're gonna ruin his life, just like you ruin everything else you touch."

"Watch your fucking mouth."

"Nathaniel!" my dad shouts, moving closer and lowering his voice. "I told you your...*preferences* need to stay out of the press. You can't play basketball and be in a relationship with a boy."

"Why not? Carter's queer and they love him."

"Yes, well, Carter's..." my mom trails off.

"He's what?"

"He's a menace," she huffs. "People expect that kind of behavior from him. You're supposed to be..."

"Normal?"

"Yes."

Sighing, I reach back and take Xavi's hand, running my thumb over his knuckles to soothe him.

"I can't help who I love, Mom," I say, pulling him up to stand by my side.

"Love?" Xavi's mom echoes, pulling her head back in surprise. "I thought you hated him."

Running my fingers over my pounding head, I don't bother trying to explain it to her because I couldn't if I tried. I don't know how I got here, but I do know I'm not going back.

I *can't* go back.

"I won't hide him," I say, eyeing Xavi before I look back at our parents. "Not unless he wants me to."

"You don't have a choice!" my dad bites out.

"Please, Nate," my mom begs, putting her hand on my father's arm as if she has the power to calm him down. "Just until you make it to the NBA."

"No." I shake my head, tightening my grip on Xavi's hand. "If the NBA tells me it's him or them, I'm choosing him."

"That's a mistake," Xavi's dad says bluntly.

"No, it's not." Bringing Xavi in front of me, I turn him to face me, his back to them while I take his face in both hands, looking my boy dead in the eye while I say, "The mistake would be listening to you guys and losing the one person I can't live without."

Xavi grins at that, his fingers curling around my wrists as his body melts into mine.

"Nate," my mother warns, probably anxious about the photographers moving closer to us.

"Baby, let me kiss you."

Xavi nods without hesitation, and I press my lips to his, threading my hands through his hair while the flashes from the cameras surround us on all sides. A couple reporters start throwing rapid questions at me, but I don't bother answering them, letting my actions speak for themselves while I take Xavi's waist and guide him through the growing crowd. When we get to my car, I open his door, and he turns to face me, his hands sliding around my neck as he leans us back against the passenger side.

"I love you," he finally says. "I've always loved you."

"I know," I tease, brushing my lips against his. "I just wanted to hear you say it to *me*."

CHAPTER FORTY-FIVE

Xavi

When we get back from the cemetery, it's late and the afterparty is still going on, the house full of people celebrating the biggest win of the season so far. Nate and I head inside and make our way to the kitchen, finding Carter, Easton, and Frankie doing shots with the rest of the team at the kitchen island. A few people glance our way as we pass them, their eyes lingering on Nate's hand in mine, but most of them look more curious than anything else.

"Please tell me one of those is for us," Frankie says, gesturing to the two bags of Chinese food Nate's holding.

He sets one down in front of her and kisses the top of her head. Groaning her thanks, the girl rummages through the bag like she hasn't eaten in weeks. Easton shakes his head at her and takes the box of food she gives him, eyeing us and all the people watching while Nate pulls me closer, sandwiching me between him and the island. With my hips against the counter and my ass on his thighs, I lean back into his chest and place my hands on his arms across my body.

"Eat," he demands, so I eat, smiling when his breath ghosts over my ear, his soft lips moving across the scar on my jaw.

"Ugh." Frankie scoffs, scrunching her nose at us in disgust. "I'm so jealous."

We laugh, and Easton pats her head, smirking when she bats his hand away. He grabs me a soda from the fridge, then offers Nate a beer, which Nate refuses.

"We heard about what happened after the game," Easton says, grabbing another soda for Nate. "You think your parents will come around?"

I tense and chew the inside of my cheek, relaxing a little when Nate tightens his arms around me.

"I don't care whether they do or not," he says, inching his hand beneath my hoodie to run his thumb over my hip bone.

I'm sure he does care, but he's too proud to admit they hurt him tonight.

"They will once they realize nobody gives a shit," Carter says, speaking around a mouthful of food.

I hope he's right, but I won't hold my breath.

"Eat," Nate reminds me, and I roll my eyes, tipping my head back to look at him.

"Why are you rushing me?"

"Because I want you all to myself," he answers, guiding my hand behind my back to let me feel how hard he is.

Discreetly adjusting my own hard-on, I finish my food and throw my trash away, not missing the smirks headed my way by Carter and the others.

When Nate and I get up to his room, he locks the door and pushes me down on the bed, falling down on me to take my mouth with his. We strip all our clothes off while we kiss, and I groan at the feel of his big, hard body against mine.

"When we're done, I want you to move all your stuff in here," he says, nipping my lip ring as he spreads my legs and fingers me open with lube.

"What?" I rasp, my eyes glazing over as I run my greedy hands over his abs and chest.

"I want you to live with me." He lifts my chin up, forcing me to look into his eyes. "Not just in this house but *with* me. I want you to make it yours."

"What about after you graduate?" I ask. "Once you're drafted, you could end up on the other side of the country. What happens to us then?"

"Nothing." He eases his fingers out, making me moan when he rubs the head of his dick over my hole. "You're coming with me."

"I have school."

"Fuck school." He pushes it in, slowly filling me up until he's balls deep inside me. "You can get a business degree anywhere. I need you with me, Xav. I'm not leaving you here."

"What makes you think I wanna go?"

He smirks and rolls his hips, making me cry out when he hits my prostate. "Baby, you'd follow me through hell and back if I asked you to."

Nodding, I pull his face down to mine. "Kiss me."

"You still want it rough?" he asks, coaxing my mouth open with his tongue.

"No," I breathe out. "Fuck me like you love me."

EPILOGUE

Nate

"No," I say, glaring at the ridiculously hot guy covered in ink standing on the other side of the tattoo shop. "Find somebody else."

"Why?" Xavi asks, smirking when I turn my glare on him. "Please? He's really good."

"I don't care how good he is," I grit out. "I'm not gonna sit here and watch him touch you."

"It's going on my wrist, Nate, not my ass." He rolls his eyes, grabbing my hand to pull me down next to him. "Will you relax? You're making me nervous."

Dropping my ass down on the couch, I do as I'm told and keep my damn mouth shut.

Xavi's never been to an NBA game before, so I surprised him with Lakers tickets and brought him to LA to watch the game last night. We're flying home later tonight, but he begged me to bring him here first to see if this guy could fit us in. Apparently, he's the best artist on the West Coast or some shit, so I agreed. Now I'm wishing I'd just dragged him to the airport.

"You worried it's gonna hurt?" I ask, glancing over when I catch him playing with his ring.

He nods, then shakes his head, his gaze dropping to the list he's holding. "I'm worried it's gonna be over."

"Baby."

He looks up at me, his blue eyes filled with sadness and grief as he swallows. "I don't want her to think I've forgotten about her, Nate."

"She would never," I say firmly, tugging his chin to pull his soft lips to mine. "She knows you'll always love her, Xav. She knows you're the only person in the world who would have done all this for her," I add, tapping the piece of paper on his lap.

Nodding, he smiles and looks at the last two things to cross off.

It's been six weeks since I told him I loved him, and we've spent that time doing as much as we possibly can together before the season ends and I start prepping for the NBA draft. I've been putting it off since my sophomore year, feeling too guilty to go for it, but after several conversations that mostly led to fights, Xavi finally convinced me to stop being such a pussy and go after my dream, just like Katy would have wanted me to. When I found the courage to call my mom to tell her, she burst into tears and asked if Xavi and I wanted to come home for dinner. I almost told her no, but agreed when Xavi gritted his teeth at me and smacked me upside the head. His parents were there too, which made it weird and awkward as fuck, but it's getting easier. If I didn't know better, I'd think they seem genuinely happy for us. But I do know better. They're only accepting us because they'll look bad if they don't. I don't care though. As long as they treat Xavi the way he deserves, I'm happy.

"Nate, look," Xavi says quietly, tilting his head at one of the large canvases on the wall. It's a picture of the owner of the shop, Xander Reid, and Niko Reid, a famous rock singer who died about ten years ago. "He's Niko Reid's little brother."

"That's probably why this shop is famous, Xav," I mumble. "Not because he's *good*."

"Shut up," he whispers. "I showed you his work. You're just jealous."

"You're damn right."

"Nate and Xavi," Xander calls, tipping his chin at us. "You're up."

Xavi stands, and I follow him to the counter, my jaw set tight as I take in Xander's appearance up close. He's a purple-haired punk with more piercings than Xavi and a grin that makes me want to punch him, and I'm pretty sure the fucker knows it.

"You have the design?" he asks, doing a double take at me, his brows lowering as he studies my face. "Have we met before?"

"No."

Xavi snorts at my attitude and sets Katy's list down on the counter, pointing to the bottom of the page. Watching Xander's face, I wait for him to make fun of Katy's handwriting or ask if it was written by a child. He says nothing as he reaches out to take the paper. Xavi hesitates, pulling it back, and Xander looks between us.

"I'll be careful with it," he promises.

Xavi hands it over, and we wait while Xander creates the stencils. Once he's done, he hands the list back to Xavi and leads us to one of the black leather chairs in the far corner.

"Who's first?"

Xavi nervously pushes me in front of him, and I sit, glancing at the ring on Xander's left hand while he preps the skin on my wrist.

"You're married?"

"Yep."

"Are they covered in ink and piercings too?"

"She's a *she* if that's what you're asking." He smirks, not taking his eyes off his task as he applies the stencil. "And no, she's not."

He shows us the little devil tattoo on his wrist. "She's got one of these and a tongue ring."

"You're straight?" Xavi blurts out, flushing and lowering his voice. "Sorry."

Xander chuckles, and I relax back into the seat, the buzz of the gun filling my ears while he permanently marks my skin.

It hurts more than I thought it would, but I don't tell Xavi that, keeping my face as straight as possible to avoid spooking him.

When it's his turn, he removes his hands from his pockets and sits down, nervously shifting his ass around to get comfortable. The first time the needle drags over his wrist, his eyes damn near bug out of his head, his teeth clenched as he looks up at me.

"I hate you."

"Liar," I murmur, and he blows out a breath.

Once it's finished, he leaps off the chair like it burned him and protectively clutches his wrist to his chest, glaring at the amused grin on Xander's face.

"Fuckin' sadist," Xavi mutters.

Xander laughs and wraps us both up, talking us through the aftercare before he runs my card at the front desk. Just as we're about to leave, a blonde girl wearing a pale pink sundress and carrying a small child on her hip walks inside the shop. I gawk at her without meaning to, but she doesn't spare me or anyone else a glance, her entire face lighting up as she catches Xander's eyes.

"Xan, she's walking!" she says excitedly, setting the little girl down on her feet. "Look."

Xander crouches down in front of her and holds his hands out, grinning when the kid takes a couple steps and walks right into his arms. He laughs and picks her up, throwing her in the air and catching her again. The girl, who I'm assuming is his wife, smiles, clasping her hands in front of her while she watches the moment with pride. She's gorgeous, and I know Xavi notices, squinting at me before he shoves my chest. I smirk and wrap my arm around his neck, pulling him into my side to kiss his head.

"Should we have one of those?" I ask, gesturing to Xander and his daughter.

Xavi looks up at me in horror. "Now?"

"No." I laugh. "One day though..." I hedge, and he wrinkles his nose in thought. "What?"

"I don't really like kids," he says a little too loudly.

"You'll like your own," Xander's wife assures him, looking at me twice before she parts her lips. "Hi," she says after a moment's pause.

"Hi," I say back.

"You're Nate Grayson."

"Who?" Xander frowns, his hackles raising as he looks between me and his girl.

"You know. He plays in the NCAA. He's about to win his fourth championship in four years."

"Oh yeah." Xander grins, bumping my fist while he wraps his arm around her waist. "Nice to meet you, man. This is Jordyn. She thinks you're hot as f—"

"*Xan*," Jordyn cuts him off, reaching out to cover her daughter's ears. "You are such an asshole!" she whisper-yells, making me chuckle.

Xavi rolls his eyes and forces a smile for the picture she asks us to take with them. I sign a basketball for their kids, and then Xavi and I head out, hand in hand while we make our way down the busy street, looking for somewhere to grab dinner.

"What do you wanna eat?"

He shrugs, giving me the silent treatment. He's in a mood, trying to walk ahead of me and pull his hand out of mine, so I tighten my grip and spin him to face me, stopping in the middle of the sidewalk and forcing everyone to walk around us.

"What?"

"What?" he bites back, his nostrils flaring when I raise a brow at him. "You know your parents would be a lot happier if you found a girl like that to fall for," he says, tipping his chin at the tattoo shop. "She's cute and funny and she *loves* basketball—"

"Xavi, shut up." I move my arms around his waist, pulling his little body into mine. "I don't give a shit what makes them happy. *You* make *me* happy. Most of the time," I joke, and he runs his tongue over his bottom lip, fighting a grin.

"Do you think she's prettier than me?"

"Baby, nobody's prettier than you," I tease, leaning over him to brush his mouth with mine.

His grin slips free, and he kisses me right here in the middle of the street, causing a few people to turn their heads as they pass us.

"I want pancakes," he says into my mouth, nipping my lip before he backs away from me.

"For dinner..."

"I want pancakes," he says again, so I keep walking until I find him some damn pancakes.

WHEN WE GET HOME from the airport, we drop our bags on our bedroom floor and collapse onto the bed, propped up on our elbows while Xavi unfolds Katy's list on his pillow. He grabs his marker pen from the nightstand and uncaps it, chewing the inside of his cheek as he crosses out number nine.

Get a tattoo.

"I like that we got something for all three of us." He smiles softly, holding our arms out to study the matching ink on the insides of our wrists. "She probably thinks we're fuckin' saps though."

I scoot closer to take his hand, gently running my thumb

around the small, wonky heart at the end. "Nah. She's loving this."

He nods and turns his face to catch my eyes, pinching his lips from side to side as he hesitates.

"Cross it out, Xav."

Still smiling, he draws a line through the three words Katy wrote at the bottom of her list.

Nate and Xavi <3

THE END

ACKNOWLEDGMENTS

To my husband, our boys, and our beautiful family and friends, for your never-ending love and encouragement. It means the world to me.

To my wonderful friend and one of my favourite authors, Becca Steele (yes, you're the Becca this book is dedicated to), for inviting me to be a part of the Anti-Valentine anthology where Nate and Xavi made their first appearance. This story and these characters wouldn't exist without you. Also for convincing me that everything would be okay when I thought the sky was falling. You were right, and I can't wait to awkwardly hug you someday.

To Corina Ciobanu, my amazing PA and alpha reader, for everything you do and for putting up with my stubborn ass. You're a freaking superstar.

To my beta readers, Mari, Xander, Amy, and Season, for your early feedback on this book and for loving these characters as much as I do.

To Zainab M, the best editor and friend, for your enthusiasm, hilarious commentary, and for smashing it yet again. I'm so lucky to have you in my corner.

To Cassie Chapman, Kate Lucas-Morrison, and Leila Reid at Opulent Designs for this stunning cover, the interior formatting, and the hundreds of graphics I begged you to make for me. You guys are the best.

To Michelle Lancaster and Mick Maio for this stunning shot on the cover. It's been a year and I still can't stop staring at it.

To Katie and all the bloggers at Gay Romance Reviews, and to everyone on my ARC and Street teams for reading, reviewing, promoting, and shouting about this book to anyone who'll listen. I read every post, comment, and review and I cannot thank you enough for your support.

To Megan Hope, Andi Jaxon, and all the incredible friends I've made in this community. There are too many of you to name, but I hope you know who you are and that I appreciate the hell out of you. You keep me sane (most of the time) and I could not do this without you all.

And to you, my readers, thank you for wanting (and begging for) the rest of this story. Thank you for reading it. Whether you've been here forever or this is your first book by me, I'm so grateful to each and every one of you.

All my love,
Bethany <3

ALSO BY BETHANY WINTERS

The Kingston Brothers

Kings of Westbrook High

Reckless at Westbrook High

Joker Night

Nightmare

Standalones

Little Devil

Dirty Love

ABOUT THE AUTHOR

Bethany lives in South Wales with her husband and their two boys. She loves iced coffee, books, big hoodies, and Machine Gun Kelly, although her husband is still pretty mad about that last one. When she's not writing, she's either daydreaming about all the crazy characters inside her head, reading, getting coffee, or raiding bookstores for pretty paperbacks to hoard.

Join Bethany Winters' Book Baddies to be the first to know about anything and everything Bethany related.

Sign up for her newsletter to receive (irregular) updates on what she's reading and writing about, early teasers, new releases, bonus scenes, giveaways, and more:

https://bethanywinters.co.uk/subscribe